MW00479202

COMPELLED
TO ACT

COMPELLED TO ACT

To Rhoda
Alter
with
affection

NORMAN SINEL

stonesthrowe press

stonesthrowe press
3721 Harrison St. N.W.,
Washington D.C. 20015
www.stonesthrowepress.com

First Stonesthrowe Press edition May 2022

Library of Congress Control Number: 2022905726

Designed by Meghan Day Healey of Story Horse, LLC

ISBN 978-0-9993113-2-5

10 9 8 7 6 5 4 3 2 1

For Ellen

COMPELLED
TO ACT

Chapter 1

I set up breakfast on the flagstone patio that surrounded our shade maple: freshly squeezed orange juice, toast in a silver caddy, coffee in a French plunger pot, preserves in a fine antique dish, and a rose in a bud vase. Van loved it when I lacked subtlety.

She came outside wearing a don't fuck with me outfit—tight jeans and high black boots. Her sleeves were rolled up to show her muscles. She stretched to her full height and then settled into a chair.

I poured us coffee.

"If you're trying to get me to forget about my father's deal, it won't work. We need to put a bomb under his desk."

I leaned forward. "Maybe it won't be so bad."

She put her coffee down. "It will be bad. We have to stop it."

I moved my chair closer to her. "It's too late."

I had thrown gasoline on the fire.

"It's not. If he doesn't listen to reason, we'll take action; not talk, real action."

"What does that mean?"

I passed her the toast and preserves. She took her time responding. "I don't know. My gut tells me this joint operating deal is part
of a bigger plan to destroy our democracy. I'm not sure he's an innocent. He's hiding something. I can tell."

She reached out and took my hand. "We need a small army to
derail this thing, whatever it is, and if my father is a player and has
to pay a price, so be it."

I waited for her to burst out laughing. She didn't.

"I've been thinking about this ever since he mentioned it at dinner last week. He's turning over the paper to the puppet masters.
This is way more than you think it is."

"You're blowing this way out of proportion. It's just a joint operating agreement among the big papers. It will save lots of money," I said.

"I'm not. You're just hiding under a rock, as usual."

Van had been like this years ago when we took over the science
lab to stop our university from using monkeys for research. She had
wanted public apologies from the chairmen of the drug company
funders and the university president, and she had wanted repara-
tions to the countries that gave up their monkeys. She still hasn't
forgiven me for getting our group to declare victory when we got the
university to stop the experiments.

She took a sip of coffee.

I moved my chair out of the sun and back to the table.

"You haven't been this fired up since you blew the lid off that Ivy
League prostitution ring."

She was pensive for a moment. "You're right. That professor
pimping out those twenty-year-old beauties was way up there on the
evil scale. This is bigger. This is a fight for the soul of our country. I
can feel it. I'm going down in history as the woman who saved our
democracy."

"Can I be a part of it?"

Her face tightened.

"I'm dead serious—not the history part. You can be part of it if you have the guts to fight."

"I'm in, as long as we don't do anything."

She leaned over and kissed me. "Thanks for the breakfast. I love you."

"Love you, too. By the way, if we're going to recruit people, we should pick colors and design a logo so I can order baseball caps and shirts for the team."

"Don't fuck with me, Will. Time to go to work. I'll be ready in fifteen. This outfit was just for you." She wasn't smiling.

Chapter 2

For the fourth time in less than two weeks, I had to choose between clogged arteries and mercury poisoning.

"Will, you seem preoccupied."

"I am, Jim. Fish or meat? The usual weighty question at lunch with you and the other rulers of the universe. Maybe next time you could pick a restaurant with a menu that isn't designed to kill us."

"Is that an edge in your voice, son?"

I'd probably learn something about myself if I took the time to figure out what kept me from calling him Dad.

"Has my daughter been giving you trouble?"

"No."

"Did you know she's going after our largest advertiser, claiming it has convinced the White House to kill a WHO resolution in favor of breastfeeding so that the sales of infant formula in the underdeveloped world won't falter? Get her off that story or she might find herself on the street."

"If you fired her, Jim, she'd team up with the other big shareholders and vote you out."

He smiled.

"Fine with me. This business is no fun anymore."

I couldn't keep my tone neutral.

"You could run the paper the old *fun* way, with integrity, and see if it survives. You don't have to be the propaganda arm of the corporate-government axis."

I surprised myself with my anger.

"Feeling superior, Will?" he said in a tone that wasn't friendly. "The paper paid a small fortune for your magazine. You're financially secure; others aren't."

I wasn't in the mood for his bullshit.

"You can do better than the 'mouths to feed' argument, Jim. These people were counting on you not to abandon the search for the truth."

That got to him.

"Save your self-righteous talk for drinking fine cognac before a fire in your oversized house. Just get Vanessa off that story."

The arrival of the rest of the group saved me from responding. Four of us were supposed to discuss the boundaries of the agreement with other major papers: the head of finance, the head of advertising, Jim, and me. But there was a fifth, Mike, who identified himself as the leader of a multi-industry consortium. He didn't list the industries.

Mike described the plan. The deal to combine our operations with other papers was further along than I had thought. Other than an odd lapel pin—a celadon-colored rosette with a tiny bright red dot in the center—he fit in perfectly with the thirty-five to fifty-five-year-old DC or NYC steak crowd. He was just another dark gray pinstripe suit with a white shirt and a tastefully conservative dark tie.

"Do we get to know who you work for and your role in this deal, Mike?" My question hung in the air.

"My role will become clear at some point, Will. My group operates on a strictly *need to know* basis."

This guy was a total asshole.

"Can I at least get an answer to what door your lapel pin opens?"

He smiled for the first time since we sat down. "All doors."

I was done. I let the rest of them focus on the business details. I would focus on the editorial issues. Our paper was going to be the control point for the operations of a dozen major newspapers in the United States, Great Britain, and Europe. I asked him what "control" point meant.

"Your role and the role of your paper will become clear soon. Be happy you're at the center of the wheel. The power you will wield will be heady. We've watched you, and we believe you are up to the task. And Jim has vouched for you. So that seals it."

He said this in almost a deferential whisper as he nodded his head ever so slightly toward Jim. I assumed it was a joke.

"Sounds pretty cloak-and-dagger for a simple joint operating agreement. What am I missing?"

Jim stepped in. It wasn't a joke.

"You're not missing anything. This is going to be very good for the paper and for you."

I was witnessing the end of the planning and not the beginning.

Lunch ended, and a car pulled up outside the restaurant to take Mike to his plane. I decided to walk back to the office to give myself time to process what was happening. The look from Jim as he closed his taxi door was easy to read: *don't make trouble; get on board.*

Chapter 3

My fantasy about Van's response to my command that she drop her infant formula story—a frying pan closing in on my head—was interrupted by a knock on my door.

"Time for your first editorial board information meeting."

I wanted to get back to my fantasy to see if I survived.

"I'll pass."

The chair of the editorial board walked to the front of my desk.

"We need someone from management, and it's your turn, so suck it up."

"What's it about?"

"Read your emails."

I leaned back in my chair. I didn't like this imperious prick.

"Just tell me what I'm in for?"

He was smart enough to realize he was close to the line.

"An earful about healthcare from an ad hoc group put together by Eric Sadler."

I gave him a blank look.

"You haven't heard of Sadler?"

My dislike of this man was growing. "Obviously not."

"He's a well-known lobbyist; a gun for hire. This afternoon will be about the benefits of holistic medicine. We limited the size of the group to six. So, in addition to Sadler, I assume we'll have a doctor or two, a mental health specialist, a granola nutritionist, and maybe someone practiced in Eastern medicines."

"Sounds interesting."

"It won't be," the editor shot back. "They'll start off okay, but by the time they're done, you'll be bored out of your mind. That's how it always is."

This guy and people like him will be the first to go when I'm running the paper, I thought.

"The reason everyone hates newspapers is that they're run by people like you, who have seen it all. Your cynicism has destroyed the press, and it's destroying our democracy."

He smiled.

"That's true, Will, and soon you'll be like me. So, let's see whether this afternoon will be different."

The conference room had a nice view of the western sky. I was looking forward to watching the clouds. Our guests had already arrived. They were pouring themselves coffee and filling little plates with cookies and fruit.

It was an eclectic group. I assumed the guy with the ponytail was Sadler. He had the presence of a leader. The members of the editorial board were already in their seats. There were assigned seats with name cards in front of small white writing pads with the paper's logo on the top and cheap pens placed diagonally on each pad. We were on one side of the conference table, and they were on the other. I was surprised we weren't elevated at least five feet above the *petitioners*. The structure was designed to avoid any real interaction.

Our side was all white men. That had to be fixed right away; it couldn't be good for developing sound editorial policy. Van and I would talk to Jim about that at dinner along with our effort to get the paper out of the joint operating agreement.

"Good afternoon, gentlemen," said the man with the ponytail.

It was hard to miss his emphasis on the word *gentlemen.*

"We appreciate the opportunity to present our perspective on the healthcare crises that will soon overwhelm the federal and state budgets and continue to drive millions of people into poverty."

I was tired of hearing about universal single-payer systems and healthcare for the poor, followed by some strained transition into the standard complaints about evil banks, the growing gap between the "one percent" and the rest of the country, tax breaks for the rich, blah blah. Those subjects had been dissected over and over again with our friends at dinner parties. The subjects were fatiguing. The country lacked the soul to provide for its people, and the entrenched power structure was indifferent to the needs of the people. Everyone with any sense knew that, but the tilting at windmills continued unabated. I didn't have the energy to listen. I had no right to have judged the senior editor for his lack of enthusiasm, since I was equally at fault.

"Have I lost you already? People don't usually drift off in the first five minutes, Will. After that, I'm fair game."

"Sorry."

He nodded.

"So, the crises can be averted if we treat sick people with intelligence, focus on prevention, and make our population healthy in mind, body, and spirit, and, of course, help people die with dignity before they've used up all of their, and the country's, resources in the last few months of their lives. We must shed ourselves of our US-centric view of medicine. Our new drugs and machines aren't necessarily better than the old ones; they just cost more and provide more profits to corporate America. Our obsession with youth and longevity is not good for society. That's our agenda. My colleagues will take it from here."

Eric's team was naive. Insurance companies won't pay for people who are sick, and they won't pay for people not to get sick. The group's belief that doctors and patients could be educated to be content with old drugs instead of the new ones advertised in the media and pushed on doctors was out of touch with the power of the drug industry.

The meeting lasted for an hour, and after the health group left, the members of the editorial board discussed the issues for fewer than ten minutes. There would be no editorials about holistic medicine, the evils of the insurance industry, or the failures of the medical educational establishment.

I went back to my office to gather my papers so I could finish my work at home. I was about to head out when my phone rang.

"This is Will."

"Hi. It's Eric. Eric Sadler. I want to apologize for singling you out at the meeting."

"No problem. You caught me in a brief mind wander. In fact, the presentations were quite good. But we both know too many people are making too much money from the current healthcare system. It won't change."

There was a pause.

"That's kind of cynical. Anyway, I'm sorry that I was rude. Let me buy you a drink."

A little weird, I thought.

"Sure, I'll bring my wife, Vanessa. She's working on a healthcare story. I'm sure she would like to meet you. I'll check her schedule and we can set a time."

"Great."

He definitely had known who I was before walking into the meeting, and he probably knew Van's background, too.

He has an agenda, I thought.

Chapter 4

I like Eric."

"I thought you would. Maybe we should recruit him for your revolutionary army."

"Don't make fun of me, Will."

We watched Eric wend his way around the tables filled with millennials. In our upper thirties, we were at the edge of being too old for the bar we were in. We had no tattoos, piercings, or stripes in our hair. Eric, who was in his fifties, fit in better with his ponytail.

"Sorry, beer makes me pee. So, let's continue with the interrogation."

We were in triangular formation at the corner of the bar. He filled his glass from the new pitcher that was just put down in front of us, which created the space in time he wanted to give extra weight to his last comment.

I was relieved that Van chose to respond.

"We're not on a newspaper assignment, if that's what you think."

"Okay, not newspaper, then what kind of an assignment are you on? Are you working for the Feds? I don't have the energy for *we're watching you* crap. It's open kimono or I'm out the door."

Van took a long drink from her glass, put it down, and swiveled on her stool so she was facing him.

"We're not here to spy on you. We can continue to talk about the corruption in the world, or you can walk out the door, afraid to get to know us. It's your choice."

"Give the guy a break, Van. He's a lobbyist and we're newspaper people. You'd be cautious, too."

She fired back.

"No, I wouldn't. I'd jump right in—headfirst, or feetfirst, however it's done. Never did know which it is. Which is it Eric—head or feet?"

"Good head, he's a head, give good head. Has to be headfirst," Eric said with a big smile.

"See, Will, I haven't frightened him."

"No, you haven't frightened me, but you're both a little weird."

Van smiled and swiveled halfway around and back on her stool like a kid at an old-fashioned drugstore counter.

"We're not weird. We're looking for a few people who are concerned our government, controlled by corporate interests, is on a mission to destroy the existing world order and who are prepared to take action."

"If that's it, I am interested."

Van stopped swiveling on her stool.

"Great. It's settled. I'm starving."

"I'm hungry, too, and I'm okay with talking about our rogue government and our corrupt corporate structure while we eat."

Van smiled at Eric and said, "Actually, I've had too much beer to have a serious conversation. Let's order some food and talk about movies."

"You're shifting gears."

"I am."

Our conversation was lively. It was a good start to a possible new friendship.

Chapter 5

At home, we clinked our crystal glasses. The sound filled the otherwise quiet room.

Van was pensive.

"Is this the remains of the port we drank last week when my dad questioned my breastmilk story? He sounded so desperate."

"Yes. I thought we should finish the bottle while we're happy with finding Eric and before I try to convince you to drop that story. I need to tell your father that I tried. He's under instructions from some powerful people to kill the story."

She moved farther away from me on the couch.

"You know I'm not going to drop the story, right?"

"Of course."

She came back to me and leaned her head on my shoulder. "Now that that's settled, what's your take on Eric?"

"I like him. He's definitely a candidate. But I don't know what your revolutionary army is going to do. He is a gun for hire, so who knows if he'll be playing some double agent game with us. I'm afraid you're going to take us down a road that will end in front of a brick wall with us blindfolded, smoking our last cigarette, and listening to 'ready . . . aim . . . fire.'"

She smiled.

"I was wondering when the real you would surface—my rational, risk-averse husband."

I went to our cabinet and got another bottle.

She raised her eyebrows.

"Opening a bottle just for the two of us this late at night?"

I shrugged. "We'll finish it the next time your father visits. You know, even though I just said I like Eric, he may be too much of a free spirit for me—for us. I didn't like his 'give good head' comment, which you seemed to appreciate."

"Will. You're acting like some bourgeois banker."

I took a sip of port.

She shifted her position on the couch. She now sat cross-legged in the corner to face me. I thought it was her signal to talk seriously. And I figured it wasn't a signal to talk about my concern that Eric had been coming on to her.

"Let's talk. What's happened to push you over the line? It must be more than the WHO story. Do you really want to blow things up?"

She thought I was mocking her and leaned a little further away from me.

"I don't know, Will. I woke up the other day and everything seemed different. Everything we thought of as progress toward a more equitable society has been reversed by this callous government. It's wearing me down. I don't want to sit on my hands and wallow in tears at the downfall of the world. I want to try to do something, and you're going to help, whether that frightens you or not."

I held back a smile.

"So, we're going to be superheroes."

She gave me the finger.

"This is serious. We need to be prepared to put ourselves on the line. I'm not talking about carrying some sign at a march. I mean, we need to pick a target and do something. No more just sitting and talking."

That scared me.

"I think you have a better idea about what you want to do than you're letting on. If we're in it together, you can't play all secret with me."

"Are we in it together? I'm not sure you're up to it. It won't be a conventional war."

"War?"

She paused and took a sip from her glass.

"I'm not going to sit back and poke at the enemy from my desk. And the deal my father is pushing has something to do with the danger I feel."

I moved closer to her and said in almost a whisper: "Van, I'm with you through thick and thin, but I still don't have a clue what *do something* means or how the newspaper deal fits in to some larger world-order destroying evil. It's just wrong all by itself."

"*Do something* means we'll have to fight a very powerful cabal. As I've been researching the drug industry, I've found references to a secret multi-industry project to alter the political and economic shape of our world that's either in the planning stage or the execution stage. I'm sure the newspaper deal is part of it. I just haven't been able to put the pieces together, so I need an army to help figure it out and then take whatever action is needed. I want us to live in a decent country that's not controlled by a few people with no sense of compassion or fairness. We'll have to tear things down before we can build them back up on a stronger foundation."

She was very deep into a dystopian fantasy which felt sophomoric.

"That's the French Revolution and the Russian Revolution. We wouldn't have survived either one of them. We can make more of a difference by doubling our charitable giving. We could form a co-op of anonymous givers. We could help things change for the good and no one would know who was doing it."

That didn't get the attention I thought it deserved.

"You're really frightened, aren't you?"

"I am. I don't think you understand the consequences of revolution."

She gave me a big smile. "Revolution?"

At least she hadn't lost her humor.

"Don't play dumb."

"I won't play dumb if you apologize for the 'little rich girl doesn't know there's a big bad world out there.'"

"It's true. You've walked through life on a tightwire with a safety net that has never been more than a few inches below you. And now I have one, too. But I didn't grow up with one, and that makes a big difference in how I see the world. I don't like risk. There won't be a safety net where you want us to go."

She snuggled closer to me and said, "I promise you'll have a say in how much risk we take." She was silent for a minute, then she said, "You know, we have to plan something to get to know Eric better. He may be more establishment than his ponytail suggests, or he may have no center. I don't want a nihilist in our army."

"I agree. If we still like him after we see him again then I'll take the credit for the find. Then it will be your turn to find someone.

That's my final before-bed thought. It's been a fun night and I'm exhausted and a little buzzed."

She put her arms around me, "I'll find someone. Bed sounds good. I'm buzzed, too."

Chapter 6

Sorry I'm late. It's been a hell of a week. Our night with Eric seems like a lifetime ago and it was only three days ago. I'm beat."

I was halfway through my first beer.

"It's okay to be late, if you're in pursuit of the truth."

"I am. I'm going to knock the cover off this breastfeeding thing. Dad called again today to tell me to drop it. No way. This is front-page stuff."

I had to sprinkle some reality on her enthusiasm, which wasn't terribly kind.

"You know the story isn't going to see the light of day. Right?"

"Of course. That doesn't mean I won't push it as far as it will go."

"Good."

I ordered two more beers and settled in to tell her about my day.

"My afternoon was spent discussing editorial policy with Jim and the guy with the lapel pin, Mike, from some no-name secret agency. He's not in any of our databases."

Van smiled.

"Lapel Pin is probably a management consultant. What's strange about a discussion of editorial policy? That's what you guys do: talk and talk and accomplish nothing."

She was enjoying making fun of me.

"This was different."

I paused to drink my beer.

"They talked about Eric."

I enjoyed dropping that little bomb.

"What?"

I put my finger to my lips to signal we were in low-voice territory.

"I kid you not. They discussed how dangerous Eric was to their plan."

Van could hardly contain herself. "Cut the shit."

"It's true."

"I don't get it. I thought the deal was about operations and ads. So, there'll be lots of drug ads and ads for hospitals and health insurance companies and whatever, and our editorials will support the industry, so what? The paper has always supported industry over the government and the people. How does Eric threaten that?"

"We're not talking editorials. We're talking hard news. They're afraid Eric will expose Lapel Pin's group that, with your father's blessing, I might add, intends to control the news. It sounded a little like Lapel Pin thought Eric was in some other undercover group and dangerous on many fronts. It was so weird."

"Hard news. Eric a threat. Give me a break."

"I'm serious. Lapel Pin asked Jim if he 'had killed his daughter's WHO story yet.' Jim said not yet, but he would."

I waited for her to get her voice back.

"Fuck. What were you doing when they were talking about me? Silence is complicity."

"I was listening and trying to find out who Lapel Pin was, what role your father was playing, and what they knew about Eric. As far as I could tell, Jim is turning the paper over to the drug and chemical companies and to some dark part of the government. All health-related and environmental content will be vetted by a panel of experts—which is being put together by the industry, big-money guys, and Lapel Pin, who I think is in the White House."

"You're making this up."

"Nope."

"And they're afraid that Eric will somehow blow open their scheme?"

"Yup."

She was stunned.

"It's time to form our secret army, and Eric should definitely be a charter member. If they're afraid of him, then he'll be our asset. We can ask him why Lapel Pin is afraid of him. Maybe that will give us some clue about my father."

I raised my glass to her. "We can't tell Eric about Lapel Pin. The deal and everything about it are secret. But we should absolutely get him to join us. We need to find more recruits."

She smiled.

"I've found someone. She monitors grants for one of the big foundations. She's a card-carrying socialist. We'll learn a lot from her perspective."

"I'll be pissed if you've already talked to her without discussing it with me first."

She tipped her beer toward me and said, "Don't be pissed."

We sat in silence for a few minutes.

"I know she will be as right for us as Eric."

She waited a few seconds before she spoke again.

"I have an idea," she said. "Let's invite Eric and his significant other, if he has one, and Jean and her husband to dinner. We can test out our idea on them."

I assumed she wasn't serious.

"How do we do that: *Hey, would you like to become part of a revolutionary army and help us blow up some buildings and disrupt the course of history?*"

"No, dummy. I'm sure we can figure out who they are over a nice dinner and then we'll know what to do."

She was serious.

"I doubt it, especially with two more people in the room, whom neither of us have met. Let's just ask Eric and Jean."

"Get real, Will. You think we could tell Jean to leave her husband home on a Saturday night or not ask Eric if he has someone he would like to invite? I'm talking about a dinner party at our house on a Saturday night, not burgers and beer at a bar after work."

I was too tired to argue.

"Okay, dinner for six. If it bombs, it'll be your fault."

She leaned over and kissed me.

What did I just agree to? This was moving way too fast. In the abstract, I liked the idea of meeting with people who can help sort out what's going on in the country: are we in short-term disarray with a dictator-fool in the White House or on a steep slide toward the collapse of our democracy and the decay of our society? If we say too much, we could be in deep trouble. With the right 'army' as Van wants to call it, we might catalyze a revolt, whatever that means in the twenty-first century. I wondered how far I'd be willing to go to put my life, or at least my lifestyle, at risk for the larger good. This might involve more than sitting behind a desk and writing opinion pieces. This could involve action; it could be dangerous. I needed to slow Van down.

"You're off in some other world, Will. What's up?"

"Just trying to figure out how dangerous talking about forming a revolutionary army with people we really don't know will be, especially since we, or at least I, have no clue what we're going to do. Maybe we need to know exactly what it is we want to do before we add others into the mix. Our careers could be ended with just one indiscretion by any one of them. We're moving too fast."

"Scared of a little revolution? There's no tiptoeing into the fight with the rulers of the universe."

"Okay, Van, now you're officially making me crazy. Let's go home."

Chapter 7

We were stuck in the kitchen cooking on a warm, sunny Saturday.

"It's a shitload of work to make dinner for six, and I'm pissed at Jean's husband."

"Why?" I asked.

"I guess you weren't listening, as usual?"

This is how Van would often start a minor fight.

"I always pay attention. You never said anything about Jean's husband."

I said this with just the slightest edge of *fuck-off*, which wasn't lost on her. She ignored it, and I was glad because I really didn't feel like fighting.

"When I invited her, she said they don't usually go to dinner parties because Matthew, her husband who is an artist, doesn't like to be around people who are part of the establishment."

I stopped chopping vegetables.

"Are you serious? Let's call off dinner."

Van gave me a pained look.

"We can't. I told her I didn't care whether Matthew came. She said she was looking forward to dinner. I'd be surprised if he comes, but we'll set the table for six."

"I told you we should meet with just Eric and Jean." I don't know what possessed me to dish out blame.

Her shoulders slumped.

"You're right. I'm sorry. I thought we should get out of our comfort zone and let the unseen forces of the universe take control. I wanted the creation of our army to be fluid."

She lost me with her *unseen forces of the universe.*

"Whatever. We need to be careful. If we reveal too much, these people could wreak havoc with our lives. The upper class would not take kindly to two of its gold-star members disrupting the given order."

My comment wrapped up the conversation. We finished prepping for the evening in silence and had time for a shower before the doorbell called us to action.

Van opened the door to a woman dressed in classic sixties style with long red hair, very white skin, and green eyes. With her was an outdoorsy type who was in his fifties, easily fifteen years her senior.

"Come in, Jean, I guess your husband decided to join us. I'm glad. This is Will."

If I were Van, I wouldn't have been able to hold back some sarcasm like, *so good of you to come to our bourgeois dinner party.*

"Nice to meet you, Will," Jean said with an earnest look on her very strong and somewhat angular face.

"I dragged Matthew here. If he misbehaves, I hope you won't hold it against me."

I pictured the evening deteriorating into small talk—the ritual bourgeois dinner—and it would have been his fault.

"We wouldn't dream of holding you accountable for your husband's behavior. I certainly don't take responsibility for Will," Van said with an uncharacteristic upturn at the end of the statement.

I nodded my agreement.

"Well, Matthew, you'll be a welcome addition. I'm usually the curmudgeon in this household."

Matthew looked at me with no hint of aggressiveness or anything else negative.

"Jean has painted me further into a corner than usual. I'm pleased to meet you both and I'm pleased to be here. I don't often get to see the inside of such a grand house. If I offend you or any of the guests, feel free to show me the door."

Van knew my patience for his brand of put-down was very thin. She took control and moved us out of the hallway and told them drinks were in the kitchen before I could say anything in response to his "little rich kid" comment.

I tried to make some light conversation on our way to the kitchen.

"I heard you are an artist. What's your work like?"

He stopped and turned to me. His face was closer to mine than I was comfortable with.

"You can go to my website and see it."

Before I could respond, he added, "I hear that you and Vanessa work at her father's paper." With emphasis on *father*.

"If being here makes you uncomfortable, you really don't need to stay. There would be no hard feelings. I'm sure Jean can get home after dinner on her own."

"Sorry."

We were standing around the big island in the center of our kitchen. I took two beers out of the refrigerator.

"I'm in management and Van is a reporter," I said as I walked out of the kitchen to greet Eric as he arrived.

I found Jean looking at our family pictures in silver frames on the closed top of our grand piano. I couldn't hide the scowl on my face. She smiled and said, "Once you get to know him, you'll like him. I promise."

I turned and walked to the hallway where Van was already in conversation with Eric and his plus one.

"It's good to see you again, Eric."

He opened his arms to give me a hug. I wasn't particularly fond of that form of male greeting. Refusing the hug would have been more awkward than accepting it, though, so I let myself be hugged and patted on the back.

"This is Alexa. I hope she'll give you a peak into the life of a radical who has been arrested for throwing rocks at the World Bank—or was it the IMF?"

"The Bank," she said without a smile.

Alexa could have been a model on the pages of *Bazaar.* I guessed she was on one or the other side of thirty: tall and thin with very light brown skin: a mixture of at least two ethnicities. Her hair was short and curly.

Eric went on with his introduction.

"She's more than a simple radical. This beautiful woman is a serious microbiologist, and she writes a very impressive political blog— *The Cat's Eye.*"

"Great name. Where's it from?"

She turned to face me.

"It's the name of the glass reflectors installed on roads to keep drivers from shifting lanes when they fall asleep at the wheel. They were invented in England in the thirties. Under an assumed identity, I tap out warnings when something happens that is off the track. Not too grandiose, right?"

I wondered if she was okay with Eric revealing her secret. If she used an assumed name for her blog, she might not be happy that we now knew it was her. If she was upset, she didn't show it.

"An important service to humanity," I said.

"Thanks, Will. I'll assume the compliment is genuine."

I felt a little dumb for being so pompous.

"It was."

Now it was Van's turn to engage. I was surprised she hadn't moved us into the living room, letting the four of us continue to cluster in the hallway.

"I'd love to hear about your bomb-throwing."

"It was rocks." She told the story of how a group of her friends decided to demonstrate at a World Bank board meeting and things escalated until there were rocks and police and jail.

"Eric hopes my reputation will rub off on him so people will overlook his membership in the establishment. I doubt there's any issue that would get him to throw a rock through a window. I make him feel young and extreme. That's fine with me. He's a good dance partner for now."

That was a lot to say about her boyfriend on a first meeting.

"Are you okay with giving Eric his left-wing credentials?" Van asked Alexa.

The tone of Van's voice took me by surprise.

"Are you dumping on me?"

The conversation was odd for people who were meeting for the first time.

"No. I'm envious of your risk-taking. I don't know if I have the guts to really cut loose. Maybe you can help me."

I had no idea what Van was doing.

"No offense, Vanessa, but given how you dress, your family background, where you live, and the things you do in this town, it would be hard for you to shake the establishment persona. You're definitely part of the ruling class, and it seems to suit you."

I couldn't tell if this was some form of female bonding or if the two of them were squaring off. Either way, I couldn't let them keep at it.

"You guys are being weird. Let's go join the others."

"Sorry. My mouth gets me in a lot of trouble. Doesn't it, Eric, dear?"

The situation was diffused.

"No need to apologize. You're not the first person to be put off by these surroundings, and you won't be the last," Van told her.

And with that, Van left me to introduce Eric and Alexa to Jean and Matthew.

Chapter 8

Our plan to talk revolution had to be put aside. There was no way we could trust Eric's young radical not to make fun of us on her blog. And it wouldn't go unnoticed. It was probably on the watch lists of the FBI, Homeland Security, the CIA, and a handful of other agencies.

It was time for introductions, which had been sidetracked by Van and Alexa's exchange.

"Eric and Alexa, let me introduce you to Jean and her husband, Matthew."

"Hi, Jean, good to see you again, Matthew. You guys haven't met Alexa, the new love of my life."

I wasn't pleased they let me make an introduction that was unnecessary.

Jean smiled and said, "I hope we like Alexa. Neither of us liked your old girlfriend."

"I guess you guys know each other," I said with an edge of sarcasm.

"We do. Eric and I serve on a committee that monitors the health-care industry. We have fun throwing darts into the wilderness."

Eric smiled. "Don't be a cynic, Jean. We've attracted media attention that has helped my consulting career. It's because of that committee that I met Will."

He turned to me and nodded and then turned back to Jean.

"I'm surprised you got Matthew to come to a dinner party. I'm glad you did. I want you both and Will and Van to get to know and appreciate Alexa, as I do."

There was too much inside baseball for me. "I'm sure I'll get to know the famous Alexa as the night goes on. Now I have to help Van," I said a little too crisply.

"Before you go, if this is a drinking party, Alexa and I will drink red. If it's a smoking party, that would be fine, too."

"There are glasses and a bottle of red on the coffee table."

I was glad we had pocket doors to separate the kitchen from the dining room. That had been one of our few design disagreements. Van didn't want the doors, and I had wanted to be able to close off the kitchen from the rest of the main floor. We compromised with pocket doors. And now their usefulness had been proven. I closed them so that Van and I could talk without being seen or overheard.

"What's up?" Van said, turning toward me as I struggled to pull the doors closed.

"Jean and Matthew and Eric are friends?"

She shrugged,"So?"

"And Alexa can't be trusted. She'll broadcast our ideas to the world under the heading: Establishment Knee-Jerk Liberals Living in a Grand Georgetown Mansion Make Believe They Care. We have to be very careful about what we talk about with this crowd."

She put down her kitchen tools.

"You're right. Let's at least try to make it an interesting evening."

"We should be so lucky. Alexa will be like a loose cannonball rolling on the deck of a ship in a storm. Is that what you mean by *interesting?*"

Van stroked my cheek. "Quite poetic, my dear. We should be able to handle this."

She opened the doors and surveyed the group and said, "So, have you guys solved world hunger? Did you bring about peace in the Middle East, stopped the spread of nuclear warheads, and beaten the NRA into ploughshares? We've left you alone long enough to let you get something useful done."

Alexa picked up on the invitation.

"You did leave us alone for a long time. Watching Will trying to get the doors closed, I assumed creating that barrier wasn't your usual dinner party protocol. I guess you were trying to figure out whether you could discuss whatever it is that's on your agenda in front of me, the young rebel, and in front of some of your other guests who may not be what they seem to be. Life is a bit risky, isn't it?"

I could see Van stand a little straighter and square her shoulders. They were face to face just a few feet away from each other.

"You're right. We do want to know if you can be trusted. And we sure as hell want to know what you mean: *may not be what they seem to be.*"

Alexa stood her ground in the face of Van's hostile tone.

"You will have to figure out who each of us really is. I can't speak for the others or reveal their secrets. But, if I make an oath of silence, which I am making now, you can trust me. I don't break my word. So, maybe we can get on with the dinner and you or Eric can tell me why I'm here. This is not some social event. I've been there and this isn't it."

I wanted her out of my house. Van's take was different. She liked risk and assumed everything would work out.

"We did bring you all—at least Eric and Jean—together with a purpose in mind. Maybe after we've had more to drink and have eaten some food, we can discuss our grand scheme."

We were committed. I leaned in close to Van and whispered loud enough for all to hear, "Don't reveal too much."

She whispered, "Okay."

The routine got everyone laughing except for Alexa, whose face was stone cold.

"Will and I need trustworthy colleagues to carry out a plan to save the world. We thought there were two recruits tonight, but maybe there'll be four. And as Will says, we can't let the cat out of the bag too soon or we may go up in smoke."

The laughter stopped. Jean took a position behind a chair.

"Bullshit, Vanessa. Not revealing your grand scheme until you get to *know and trust us* is insulting."

To my surprise Matthew spoke.

"That's okay, Jean. I'm prepared to drink fine wine, eat good food, and watch all of this unfold. It might be interesting, even if it's sophomoric."

Alexa took the floor again.

"Sophomoric," she said in an aggressive tone, "that's putting it mildly—this is a total waste of time." She turned to Eric. "Let's get pizza and go to a movie. I don't need these people to feed me."

This was not a typical beginning of a dinner party at our house with people we really didn't know. It was bizarre. It was Eric's turn, and he didn't disappoint.

"We've seen all of the good movies in town, and we had pizza last night, so let's see where this goes."

My head wanted them all gone, so it must have been some primitive host instinct to give shelter to the traveler that caused me to go against my strong desire to throw them out into the cold.

"Stay. It'll be a good dinner—home cooked by Van and me. And in keeping with our solidarity with the workers, it will be simple food, simple red table wine, and revolutionary ideas. That's what we're serving up tonight."

Alexa's face tightened. "Jesus, how fucking pretentious can you be?"

Eric stepped in, again.

"Give the poor guy a break. You have to be nice, or I won't be able to take you anywhere."

She wasn't having any of his patriarchal behavior.

"Fuck off, Eric. If they want to toss my ass out into the street, so be it; you can follow or not. Makes no difference to me."

Jean stepped in, "Alright, you guys. Dinner is on the table. Let's enjoy ourselves."

Van watched it all unfold without a comment. When they were done, Van took charge of arranging the table: she sat Alexa and Matthew on either side of her, and Eric and Jean on either side of me. I was relieved not to have Alexa or Matthew at my side.

Our table was made of very thick wide oak planks that were scarred by at least five centuries of use—nobility banging tankards and carving meat directly on it, and, I've always assumed, dead bodies laid out on it. I liked this ancient black oak. If these guys knew how much the table and chairs and the sideboard cost to buy and ship from England, they would shit. I smiled and saw Van give me a quizzical look, but this was my private musing.

My mood was getting heavier thinking about what abuse we would take if they had any idea what we spent on pleasing our aesthetic taste. I put my thoughts aside and tried to engage in the talk around the table. It helped that the food was good. Our guests softened somewhat. It felt almost like a normal dinner party until we had finished the main course and had started on our third bottle of wine. Eric clinked his wine glass with his fork and asked for attention.

"Vanessa, this is a wonderful dinner. I don't think it qualifies as simple, as you put it. It's splendid. And now that we're all getting along, it's time to tell us why you brought us together. I'm getting looks from my beautiful Alexa that are saying *Eric, find out what this is all about now or you're going to have one pissed-off girl-friend*. So, you can understand my incentive to draw you out."

Van raised her glass to toast Eric and, without asking me if it was okay, said, "I wouldn't want to come between a woman and her lover. If I can get a commitment from all of you that this stays in this room—no blogs or loose lips—I'll discuss our plan—which is not fully formed."

They all nodded assent, even Alexa.

I got up and got another bottle of wine for the table on the assumption that we might move to our fourth. Van waited for me to sit before she started. From the look she gave me, I could tell she wasn't pleased. I sat down and said, "Sorry."

"I, we, want to start a new version of the old SDS and its underground off-shoots. We're not students so I want to call it the XDS—we're all part of or close to the boundaries of Generation X, and 'Weathermen Two' didn't sound right to me. Our democracy is at risk. We need help to make and execute a plan to expose and stop the rot."

The faces around the table were inscrutable. I had no idea what Van was talking about. We had had plenty of conversations about the evils of corporate America, how it was more dangerous than our dysfunctional government that was sucking the energy out of the country; but this was different. She seemed to have something in mind that she hadn't shared with me.

Alexa broke the silence.

"Do we get to elect a secretary and a treasurer?"

"There are lots of ways to rebel. Some noisy, some quiet, some accomplish stuff, and some don't, so give me a break."

"Sorry, Vanessa. I couldn't pass it up."

Van took the apology as an okay to keep going.

"The people at the top are heartless. And it's going to get worse."

There were nods of ascent.

"You can't have a just society based on unregulated capitalism and power-hungry corruption at the top layer. The country's soul was at stake during the fight for civil rights, women's rights, gay rights, and the end of the Vietnam War. It's at stake now. It's just more difficult to pinpoint the enemy—the head of the snake."

Eric got up from his seat and leaned on the back of his chair.

"You and all of my friends want to bring fairness and justice to our land. Talk is cheap."

Van didn't take offense. "It is. All day long, I'm on the street digging up facts, interviewing people, playing hunches only to have the assholes at the paper—my father's paper—not you, dear—kill the stories because they aren't satisfied with the sources. I used to think it was just some timid editor, but it's a bigger problem: the paper is integral to the success of this layer of corruption. It's not there to protect and educate the people. It's part of the propaganda machine."

She sounded like a college kid who'd had her eyes opened to the real world for the first time. I was about to try to fix it, but Alexa got there first.

"So, your father's newspaper doesn't want to offend the administration or its advertisers. You can't really think we could do anything about that. We'd be better off standing in the park and shouting out slogans: 'Stop the War!' 'Down with Imperialism! Up with the Ten Commandments!' 'Off with Your Bra!' It feels like we're in a freshman dorm trying to decide who we're going to hook up with and when."

The two of them weren't finished with each other.

"You promised to behave," Van said with enough humor in her voice to keep the peace, which was just a little easier since we were all a little buzzed.

"I am behaving. You want to have a little group of revolutionary friends so that you can feel like you're alive and different from the other members of your elite class. Instead of a book club, you'll talk democracy and politics and meet in this castle of yours and eat simple meals off your priceless dining room furniture. You could feed a lot of people for a very long time for what this old oak must have cost you."

She paused. No one seemed uncomfortable. They all wanted to see how the little drama would end.

Van said, "Fuck the furniture. I want to turn this world on its head."

Alexa couldn't contain herself.

"Jesus, Van, King Arthur probably raped countless servants on this table, and you say, 'Fuck the furniture, let's start a revolution.' We're killing people right and left with our guns, our drones, and our chemical poisons. We're giving whole populations diabetes with our processed foods and sugared drinks. We're putting all the young black men in jail; soon, we'll put all the Hispanic men in jail, as well. We kill abortion doctors; beat up gay men; foreclose on houses and let bankers walk away rich and free. We have burdened a whole generation with college debt they will never be able to pay. We have designed the system to enslave 99.5 percent of the American population and 99.9999 percent of the world's population, and you want to have some secret club with a catchy name and a secret handshake to fix the world. Give me a fucking break."

She turned to Eric.

"Let's get out of here."

Her anger shocked us all. Neither Jean nor Matthew said a word. We stayed in silence for what seemed like an eternity.

Jean stepped into the awkward vacuum.

"Vanessa, it's late, and Alexa seems hell bent on turning this into a free for all. You're not naïve, so I'm assuming you have a plan we can sink our teeth into. Let's call it a night. At this point, I'm not prepared to accept or reject revolution. If you don't mind us leaving you with the dishes, we're off. It was a great dinner."

Matthew got up and gave a bow to Van. "Lovely dinner. Thank you."

Van got up from her chair and gave them kisses on each cheek. Eric gave Jean a slight nod, which I read to mean that he agreed that he was going to think about it as well, and then he turned to Van and to me to thank us for the evening.

And then it was all quiet and we went into the kitchen.

"I thought we were playing around the edges Van, and now it seems you have some grand plan."

"Well, it's still formulating. But the other night when I went out for drinks with my dad, remember how angry I was when I got home?"

"I remember. You just went to your computer and worked until it was time for bed. I wasn't happy."

"Well, he sent me over the line. We were at the bar at our club, and he went after my breastfeeding WHO story, again."

"Why would that put you over the line? You know he needs to kill it."

"He was way too aggressive. I kept pushing him. Who was pressuring him? How was he being pressured? Why? The story just couldn't be doing that much damage to the company or the complicit White House to make them go to such efforts to pull me off the story. It just didn't make sense."

This was going to be a serious conversation, so I suggested we go into the living room and sip some cognac while she finished the story.

"So, finally, he told me there was more to the issue than the baby formula business. He said the same company is behind the increase in ADHD diagnosis and drug sales, and that after the newspaper deal is done, you would be in so deep that you would understand why caution was the proper course."

"What? Me?"

"You. Then he just clammed up. He asked if I wanted to share a dozen oysters and we didn't talk about it again. I respected his need to shut down; but my mind was racing. There's something big happening and I guess you are going to be a key player. My hunch is that this drug company has something going on that is way bigger than selling baby formula and ADHD drugs. We have to find out what it is and what to do about it."

Chapter 9

I was up first and made breakfast. There was a sun-filled corner of the kitchen where we liked to sit and linger over our morning coffee. Van filled her bowl with the cereal I had put out for her and joined me at the table.

I tried not to sound too down.

"This has been an awful week, and today and tomorrow are filled with more awful meetings. Let's be just the two of us this weekend. No plans, okay?"

She nodded.

"I'm feeling the same. I still haven't recovered from last Saturday night. Eric's girl toy really rattled me."

Other than some talk about the evening on Sunday morning—deciding we liked Eric and Jean, had no clue about Matthew, and didn't like Alexa—we hadn't yet focused on the disaster. I avoided the discussion for fear I would have to say that Van did sound like a college kid, even though her reasons for being pushed over the line were real. I think Van was avoiding a discussion for the same reason. And while we agreed we didn't like Alexa; I was surprised Van had called her Eric's "girl toy." She had acted badly, but she wasn't some girl toy.

"What's that about?"

"I forgot her name."

"Bullshit. She threatens you."

"Fuck-off, Will.

"That was harsh. So, we're in sync on a quiet weekend?"

The tension released from her face and shoulders. She said, "Yes. Some steaks and just us. We need to decide if we can destroy that company and, perhaps, others like it on our own."

"Let's figure it out this weekend. For the next two days, I'm totally under water with the deal."

"Do you want to talk about it? I promise you can trust me."

"Are you prepared to give me absolute control over your use of the information for any purpose—future stories, shareholder votes, and anything else that I decide is covered? I need an iron clad commitment of confidentiality before we can talk about this."

She hesitated for a second and then squared her shoulders and offered her hand. I couldn't tell if she was serious.

"I'm not playing with you. My commitment is real. Tell me what's happening."

I was grateful. I needed to share my burden.

"It's total content control by industry and the government."

"Didn't you tell me all of this last week?"

"Last week I was speculating. Now I know. Remember last Sunday when I noticed the health-related articles on the front pages of a bunch of local papers, even though there was no health-related news that was worthy of any front page. You laughed, remember?

Well, two people in a meeting yesterday talked about the articles they placed in Sunday papers around the country. This is not a joke."

She gave me a big smile. "Yeah, right, the big-city boys and the small-town idealists are handing over their front pages to the ad guys and their clients."

"It's true. Dark money is in total control of the information stream."

She was trying to hold back a laugh.

"That's a lot to draw from some boasts by guys who want to carve up the advertising market."

"It's not about advertising. We're talking a super editor with an agenda. Oligarchy will seem benign by the time these guys put the pieces of their plan in place."

Her smile was fading.

"You're serious."

"Dead serious."

It was time for another cup of coffee.

She put her hand on mine.

"These are the same guys who are pressuring my father to kill the WHO story, right?"

"Probably."

"We need to act."

"What does that mean?" I asked.

"I don't know. We need a group committed to derailing whatever is going on. Not some social club, as Alexa has called it. We've got to work on Eric and Jean without their partners. You should meet with Eric, and I'll meet with Jean. Let's get it done by the end of next week. I don't think we can figure out what to do and then do it all on our own."

"Maybe," was all I could commit to.

We finished our coffee in silence.

Chapter 10

Van put down the knife she was using to slice tomatoes, wiped her hands on a dish towel, and motioned me to stop my slicing, as well. She pulled out the two stools that fit neatly under the counter. When we were sitting and facing each other, she poured two glasses of a crisp, white wine, and we drank in silence for a few minutes. We had had a great weekend—just the two of us—and now it was already Wednesday.

"Tell me about your pizza fest last night with Eric? You didn't seem happy when you got home."

"I didn't like the way the evening ended."

I told her Eric would commit to our venture, if we could define it, but he didn't think we'd be able to narrow our focus enough to establish a clear path to success.

"Then he accused me of coming on to Alexa."

Van laughed and leaned into me.

"So, he was upset that you were coming on to his trophy? For the record, I thought you were, too, even though you said you didn't like her. I guess you just couldn't help yourself."

Her response was not what I expected.

"I wasn't."

"You were, and we'll deal with that later. Let's focus on revolution. You know we'll be going down a path that will take us away from this cozy oasis. Maybe forever."

One minute we're joking about me and Alexa, and the next, she's telling me we're walking off a cliff.

"Why are you trying to make me crazy?"

"Because it's fun, and because this isn't a game. Eric knows that. That's why he's asking us to get focused and for you to stay away from his young mistress, or whatever he calls her. He's in solid."

Van stood and put her arms around me. I untangled us.

"What about Jean?"

She sat back on her stool.

"She wants definition, too. And she agrees that we start with the drug industry."

If Van wanted to be serious, I was prepared to engage.

"There are so many groups focused on that industry; how are we going to make a difference?"

"I've been thinking about that. If we go after the baby formula scandal, especially after my story hits the paper, we'll just blend in with the dozens of groups that will pick up the cause. Instead, we're going to pick one of that company's drugs that has escaped attack. And since we have access to the paper's assets—its stories in progress and those that never see the light of day—we should be in front of the curve."

I got up and paced around the kitchen.

"We're not going to steal stories from the paper. The 'ends justify the means' conversations we're going to find ourselves in every step of the way will drive me up a wall and may even drive a wedge between us if our baselines are really different."

I was surprised Van would even think about stealing stories. We'd had countless conversations about colleagues who have crossed ethical lines, and we have always agreed that we would never cross those ethical boundaries.

She picked up her glass and led me into our library. She was tired of the kitchen stools. I was relieved. I wanted to sit in a comfortable chair and be quiet for a few minutes. Finally, she broke the silence.

"We're going to have to decide the ethics as we go along."

That didn't help. I put my glass down on a leather coaster from a set of eight a dinner guest brought us a year ago: the best house gift I can remember. I think of her, a documentary producer, whenever I put my glass down on a horse's head engraved in leather. It distracted me for a minute. I could hear Van in the background asking if I was still in the conversation.

"I'm here. There's no need to make up the ethics as we go along, Van. We both know right from wrong."

"Ethics and revolution don't make good bedfellows," she said as she picked up one of the coasters and ran her fingers over the raised image of a stallion.

I decided it would be best to wait for an actual issue before I forced her into a serious ethics discussion.

"Changing the subject, I've already told Jean we're going to get this thing started. She wants in and she said Mathew is leaning toward joining, as well. If he does commit, he will be responsible for the technology. We'll need to keep the authorities from finding out who we are. This is exciting."

"I'd call it scary and dangerous; not exciting."

Chapter 11

Eric and I sat in the same booth that we had been in a week before. Two would-be revolutionaries drinking beer and eating pizza. He leaned back into the angle between the bench and the wall, topped off our beers, and sat in silence for what seemed to be a very long time. He drank at least a quarter of his glass and then spoke. It was as if a graduate student in a film program directed the scene.

"I need to know what you guys have up your sleeve."

"I'm not sure that I'm sober enough for a serious conversation," was all I could say in response. I had reached my limit and the coffee hadn't quite worked yet.

I signaled the waiter for two more espressos and tried the corner lean. It wasn't comfortable so I moved to the aisle side of the booth so we could look straight at each other diagonally with just the right distance between us.

"Van has a journalist's hunch that there's a deep multilayered conspiracy that may be led by a drug company she's been following. She believes the strands of the conspiracy go deep enough to threaten our democracy. We need help to track it all down and to destroy it before it destroys us. We want you and Jean to join us."

"Has Jean signed on to this? She was on the fence yesterday."

"Not yet."

The waiter brought our coffees.

"Which company? What does it sell? Opioids?"

"No. It makes the drugs kids take to quiet their ADHD."

Eric stirred some sugar into his tiny espresso cup. It seemed like the ritual took forever. He seemed lost in some private thought.

"That doesn't sound like something that requires a revolution."

"I agree. On the surface, it seems like it's just corporate greed. But the corruption behind creating that *sickness* is overwhelming. More important, she suspects they are the leaders of other schemes considerably more dangerous. That's what we're really interested in and what we need help with. We need to figure out what card to pull from the bottom of that tower. It would be great if we can do it without bloodshed and without going to prison."

Eric smiled. "Very dramatic."

"Are you making fun of me?"

"No. As I said when we sat down, I'm intrigued. You guys have set your sights pretty high, if you want to bring down one of the largest drug-chemical conglomerates."

"We're hoping that as card-carrying members of the establishment, no one will suspect us."

Eric let some silence surround us. "What got you to this point, Will?"

Van and I had decided beforehand that I should not discuss the paper deal as the tipping point. In the wrong hands, that could cause big problems for us. If I could have discussed it, that would have tied a nice bow on the conversation. Instead, I had to stay abstract.

"It just kind of happened. I woke up one morning and the news of the day together with what I had been learning about this company put me over the line; Van was already there. Now it's important to figure out what to do. I think Van is okay with bombs and stuff. I'm not. So, we need to have an open conversation with committed people to set a course."

What was on the table wasn't much and wasn't all of it, but it was the truth.

"Alright. I'm in. And Jean will be, too. To make it work, Jean and I think Alexa and Matthew should be invited to join."

I shook my head no.

"It will be a better group, Will. They see the world from different perspectives. The six of us will make a good team."

"You want me to ask Alexa and Matthew out for pizza and go through this with them? She'd pour her beer on my head and leave, and he would get up from the table and ask if my driver could take him home. No. No way."

He laughed.

"No. We don't need more one-on-ones. The six of us should go somewhere for a weekend to define this thing. I'll get Alexa to sign on, and Jean will take care of Matthew. They'll be on board if we can come up with a solid plan."

I sat back and tried to get one last sip of cold coffee out of my tiny cup. I couldn't imagine spending a weekend with Matthew, and I doubted that Alexa would last more than an hour before she would bolt. I wondered if he knew that Van had a family compound in Virginia horse country that would be an ideal place for a weekend retreat. The house was big and comfortable, the pool was surrounded by trees and very private, and the walks in the woods—500 acres of woods—were quite calming.

"Is this a condition of your going forward?"

He nodded.

I was trapped. "Okay, I'll propose it to Van. Her family has a country house in Virginia that would be a good place for a retreat."

He reached over the table to shake on it.

Chapter 12

Absolutely not. I can't believe you'd even think about taking them to the cottage in Virginia."

"Unless we give it a try, our two most promising recruits will be out of the picture. Our friends can't be part of this. They're far from revolutionaries and we may need them to vouch for us as card-carrying members of the establishment and not revolutionaries. We lucked into Eric and Jean. I think we have to try to build our group or army or whatever it becomes around them. So, if the price is a weekend in Virginia, so be it."

We were having coffee on our patio. I was about to put more words into the air, but she signaled for silence. We just sat for a while. I waited for her to break the silence.

"Okay. We'll do it. We'll give them three weekends to choose from—one email invitation and no negotiating. If they can't do any of the weekends, we move forward without them."

Van's family was not pretentious, except for what they called their very large Virginia estate. Like the wealthy families with compounds in upstate New York and Maine, they called their stone house with six bedrooms a "cottage," even though it came with a name when they bought it—Pine Hall, Frog Hall, Brookside Hall, or something like that. All the properties in Virginia horse country had names. I looked up the word *cottage* in the Oxford Dictionary. Of the six listed definitions, only one was relevant—a single-family holiday residence. The rest suggested rural and small. Van's cottage was rural, and it was a holiday residence, but it was anything but small.

"Van, darling, I assume you know you can't call it a cottage when we invite these people out for a weekend. You get that, don't you?"

She gave me a nasty look.

"Just saying."

That little phrase got her to lighten up.

"Shall I call it our family weekend house? Do you think that'll make it any better?"

"No, it wouldn't be any better. I can just hear Matthew in a very innocent voice: *This is so cozy. I guess you could put a roof over the heads of half of the homeless in DC with your two houses.* If he tries that shit, I'll boot his ass into the pond and let the turtles eat him. Alexa won't say anything. She'll just roll her eyes and leave."

It was quite an image: Poor Matthew gulping for air as he bobbed up and down being eaten by snapping turtles the size of manhole covers and Alexa turning to walk back down the driveway to call a town car.

I poured us more coffee.

"I like your image." She was smiling and totally into it. "There'll be an undercurrent of *you little rich kids bore me* and then there'll be an undercurrent of *you're so sophomoric* and another of *you're so naive* and dozens more. This will definitely turn out to be a disaster. If we're going to ask my folks if we can take over the place for a weekend, I'd rather invite our friends. We haven't had them out there in a while and we could have some real fun. Let's do that and just meet with Eric and Jean and their sleep mates in some restaurant here in town."

I was up and pacing. I didn't want to spend a weekend in the country with these people, either, but it had to be done. Everything was going to be a struggle, and everything would be judged. *You have such a big pool and such a nice hot tub. It must cost a small fortune to keep it heated year-round.* And that would be benign compared with the other zingers I assumed would be tossed our way.

"You're right. We should just say no to a weekend with them and get our friends out there for a good, fun weekend. I'll call Eric's bluff and tell him that he and Jean are welcome to work with us, and Matthew and Alexa are, too, if that's their desire, but no weekend retreat."

Van motioned for another silence. Taking time-outs to gather her thoughts was new behavior. I stopped pacing, slouched into my chair, and picked up my coffee. I was in no rush to get to work, and I wasn't going to rush her. She just sat there staring into the corner of our garden.

Finally, she pushed her chair back, stood, and leaned on the table for effect before saying, "Be not afraid, my faithful squire. We'll sally forth on a new adventure and slay us a dragon. The adventure begins at our country cottage." Then she dumped the strawberries out of the bowl they were in, wiped the inside clean, and put it on her head.

It was brilliant. The great Don Q had nothing on us, except we weren't old and demented.

"Do we keep a diary of our exploits?"

"No," she said, "that's a direct route to prison."

I put my arms around her.

She smiled and kissed me. It was like we were high school kids behind a tree on the football field. She took my hand, and we went into the house. Work could wait.

Chapter 13

The weekend was set. The six of us were going to hike, swim, and be together from Friday to Sunday.

"Do we really need to bring all this food? Can't we go out one night?"

She stopped searching the shelves for jars of preserves.

"No. They need to be locked in our castle, so we can keep them under our spell."

I was in a bad mood.

"Joke. Get it?"

"It's not funny."

"I know it's not funny. I'm just as concerned as you are. But we might as well try to have some fun. So, get out of your bad mood."

"Let's cancel? We can say I'm sick."

Van shook her head and returned to searching our shelves for stuff to put in the food box. When she finished, she gave me a list of things to get at our overpriced local market. Her chore was to go to the butcher shop and the wine store. The weekend was going to cost us our careers and a small fortune, as well. Unlike Van, I looked at prices.

We got on the road around noon so we could have some quiet time before they all arrived. There was no traffic, and we made it in slightly under an hour. The house had been opened and cleaned by the caretaker. Everything was in order.

Van slid the bottles of wine into the wine rack. She was nervous. "I hope they call when they get close. I don't want them just driving up the driveway. Did you ask them to call?"

We were both rattled.

"It didn't occur to me. I hope they don't get here for a while. What are we going to do once they get here?"

"Let's leave the unpacking of the kitchen stuff for a group activity. That will give us something to do if we need to occupy them. For now, my dear husband, let's just sit outside and enjoying the calm and have some lunch."

I settled us on the patio with two beers, a baguette, some cheese, an avocado, and a good-sized tomato. We were going to eat well for the rest of the weekend, so Van was happy I set out some simple food for our lunch.

She broke off the end of the bread, took a sip of beer, and said, "I'm having trouble visualizing the six of us together out here. I can't get a fix on what to expect."

She was a visualizer. She often surprised me with the accuracy of her predictions.

"Just visualize a total disaster and you will be right on target."

She was on my wavelength. "What the fuck are we going to do with these people?"

She sliced up the remaining half of the tomato, which seemed to settle her down.

"This afternoon and tonight should be okay," she said. "We'll give them a tour, let them settle into their rooms, and then we'll meet down here to unpack the groceries and have drinks. They can help us make dinner. The evening will work out fine, except for the crap that Alexa and Matthew will throw our way."

I was with her on the drinks and dinner part.

"I don't think it will be that simple. They're going to want us to tell them what we want to do with the group. If we play around the edges, they'll probably all go up to their rooms to pack."

She let the inside of a big slice of tomato drip down her chin and onto her white T-shirt to make me laugh. She said, "We'll lock our bedroom door. No one is going to kill us while we sleep. If they pack up and leave, we'll have a nice weekend on our own. I want to eat, get drunk, maybe get stoned, and be with you. I'm treating this as a fun weekend with crazy people. If we move the project forward, that's fine; and, if not, that's fine, too."

She was blowing hot and cold: one minute we need to start the revolution before it's too late, and the next, we're going to party and have fun. She wasn't making it easy on me.

Lunch was over. We showered and made it back out to the patio just minutes before a dark blue minivan came into view on our long tree-lined driveway.

"By the time these guys stop in front of our fieldstone entryway, they're going to be full of uncharitable thoughts."

She nodded and said, "I know, but we can't let their reactions to my parents' cottage sidetrack us or them. It's just a nice weekend in the country with new friends; that should be our focus."

"You promised not to call this place a cottage."

She just smiled and we went to the front of the house to meet our guests who had all come in the same car.

Eric was the spokesperson. He said driving into the country and getting long-distance views of the blue ridge mountains had been great. They all smiled their agreement, which put me at ease, until Alexa shattered the peace.

"Do I get to stay in the main house? This is Virginia, right?"

Even Eric was caught off guard.

"Knock it off," he said.

I could imagine what the conversation had been like in the car. They were in horse country: big estates, miles of wood and stone fencing, long vistas, and cows and horses grazing in the fields. Alexa would not have been a free person here. Meeting to talk about revolution in this bastion of the confederacy must have been cause for some good laughs among the four of them. The disconnect between our daily lives and our fantasy mission would be amusing even to people who were nice, and at this point, I was pretty sure these people—all of them—were not very nice.

Van took charge. She paid no attention to Alexa's broadside.

"Welcome to our humble place in the country. Everyone gets to stay in the main house. There is only one ground rule: we can say anything we want to this weekend, and that includes making fun of Will and me or anyone else in the group—thick skins for all. That's the motto of the weekend."

Everyone smiled, the ice now floating down the river in big chunks. The weekend had begun.

Chapter 14

I waited outside in the late afternoon sun as Van showed everyone around the house. I set out some food, opened the wine, and filled a cooler with beer. If they were all still in a touring around mood, I would show them the stables and the pool house. Van's parents leased out the land and the stables so the place would feel like a working horse farm, and they would have access to horses.

Van could jump over logs and little streams to chase a fox with the best of them. On occasion, she still rode with the local Hunt. If she decided to ride this weekend, she would definitely get some snide comments from the group.

I had to stop playing out their responses in my head. Worrying about what they thought of us was not productive, and it wasn't going to help make this an okay weekend. If they decided not to help us, we would figure out how to go forward without them. The best thing for me to do was get buzzed and stay that way until Sunday afternoon— as long as I could stay on the functional side of the buzz. That was my plan. I finished my beer and had achieved the beginning of my buzz when Van, followed by Jean and Matthew, came out to join me.

"Nice place. If you don't book us up for the next two days with your deep secret revolutionary agenda, I'd like to have some time to enjoy this grand estate."

Matthew seemed to be incapable of saying something nice without an edge.

"You're totally free to do whatever you like this weekend. The weather's going to be great. You get to decide what you want out of the next two days. But if you keep pissing me off with comments like 'deep secret revolution' and 'grand estate' I might put a poisonous snake in your room."

He was dumbfounded. I was happy.

Jean looked at me and smiled. "He deserved that."

"Just a joke. What would you guys like to drink?"

The four of us settled around the big round table shaded with two large umbrellas. Van had a beer and I had coffee. My buzz needed caffeine. Jean and Matthew drank white wine. We passed the time without incident as we waited for Eric and Alexa to join us. Van was finishing her beer, and most of the bottle of wine was gone by the time they finally joined us. Now we were six around the table, and the sun was moving from late afternoon to early evening. It would set behind the mountains in less than an hour. The light was getting soft, and a noticeable breeze was coming in. I loved this time of day.

After a few minutes of pleasantries, Eric asked what the architecture of the weekend would be. Van was prepared.

"I thought we would swim, take walks, just hang out, ride horses if that appeals to anyone, and set a time to talk about our plan."

"That sounds great, but what I really want to know is whether we are planning to eat at restaurants, or can we drink and smoke with no thought of driving?"

That was an easy question.

"Will and I brought all the food we need, which you all can help us unpack soon. So, if it's your pleasure to hide the car keys for two days, that'll work just fine."

We would talk about our plan when and if we trusted each other enough to talk about it. That was Van's real answer, and Eric seemed pleased.

"Good, then I'll have a beer and if no one minds, I'll light up a joint. I'm old-fashioned; I don't like to vape or eat my THC."

I looked at Van. She knew what I was going to say.

"We're in Virginia. I doubt the sheriff will come into our driveway, but you have to pay attention to which way the wind blows here in the South."

Eric laughed.

"Do you actually think the authorities will come down your very long, tree-lined driveway? Are we living a Buffalo Springfield song? Lighten up, Will."

Alexa smiled at me.

"Leave poor Will alone, Eric. He hasn't said you *can't* light up, and I could use something to take the edge off after the drive. We don't have to leave this place for two days, so let's just relax."

I wanted to take out a notebook and keep a list of surprises. Alexa acting civilized and on my side was the first.

Eric passed a pre-rolled joint from a DC medical marijuana dispensary. He advised us all that it was of the one-to-two-hit variety. We acted accordingly.

Within ten minutes, we were all stoned—a great state to be in to watch the trees sway in the early evening wind and the bats swooping in to eat their six trillion bugs. It was also the perfect state to enjoy periods of silence as we drank beers and wine and ate the guacamole and salsa Van had brought out from the kitchen. Getting high got us through the first potentially awkward part of the weekend. By the time we gathered in our kitchen to put away the food and work on dinner, it felt like we were on a weekend in the country with friends.

It was my job to sound out Alexa. Van was to deal with Matthew.

"Alexa, we've chopped enough stuff for the salad. Would you help me set the table? It will give us some time to be alone."

"Alone? Why?"

"I just wanted to see how you felt about discussing our plan."

"Oh. I thought maybe you wanted to seduce me."

"What?"

"Don't you find me attractive, Will?"

"I do, you are breathtaking. Let's sneak upstairs. We won't be missed for a good half hour."

She wasn't sure of her next move.

"Just kidding. We really do have to get this table set. Dinner is almost ready."

I handed her six of our finest country plates, and we set to making the table ready for dinner. I didn't quite know how to deal with her. Since our first meeting, she had been hostile to both Van and me, and now there was this playful woman I found myself warming up to. Maybe whatever protective veneer she had displayed up until now was just that: a thick shield to give her time to decide if she liked us. Maybe we were going to be friends and she was going to be part of the group.

"I've changed my mind about you, Will. You're decent and genuine. I believe you have some pretty good values buried underneath your establishment exterior. I might even end up liking you; but I'm still on the 'no' side of your club. Can we keep our relationship, if we develop one, and my decision about the club separate? Can we do that?"

Her gaze was intense. There was something about her that made me feel special. It was weird.

"If you promise to respect our need for secrecy then, as far as I'm concerned, you can decide to be in or out. Either way, we may want to get to know each other better."

We finished setting the table and went back into the kitchen where the others were sipping wine, passing another joint, and watching the food cook. Alexa went over to Eric and gave him a rather intimate kiss and then held her hand out for the joint. I let it pass me by. Van was going down the path to wasted. One of us had to be in control.

"The table is set. Any other chores for me before we sit down?"

I was hoping that Van would get my hint that people should eat instead of getting totally wrecked. She didn't. Jean stepped between us and put her hand on my shoulder.

"Dinner isn't quite ready. Why don't you come over to this end of the kitchen and help me watch the sauce cook?"

She took my hand and led me to the far side of the kitchen. It was just the two of us. Matthew and Van were slicing tomatoes and comparing methods and knives. Eric and Alexa were in that space that couples get into where no one else exists: a rude space in a public setting.

"Will, can you come up to the surface and talk with me?"

Jean said it without any rebuke in her voice.

"Sorry."

"I'd like a 'get to know each other' conversation before the serious stuff starts. Are you up for that, Will?"

"I am. And I doubt we'll ever get to talk about serious stuff. Everyone seems ready to spend the weekend unwinding, which is fine with me."

She moved closer to me. We stared at the pot on the stove. She was stoned, I wasn't.

"Just hanging out is a good thing. It was a great idea to plan a 'no plans' weekend. I needed a break, and Matthew did, too. We've been flat out for months with very little to show for it. The thugs who control the Republican party have made Congress dysfunctional, which makes my work miserable. And Matthew is stuck in some mathematical puzzle that he needs to solve for a work to be installed in a private museum in Maryland. He hardly has time to sleep, let alone have fun. He was going to cancel last minute like he usually does, but I convinced him this weekend would be rejuvenating. I promised him that when we got started on our revolutionary talk, he could go up to bed, watch a movie, or just sit out under the stars."

I got up to stir the sauce.

"Good. If we do talk revolution, he can be on his own. I'm glad you're here."

We talked for a few minutes more: the little facts that people share as they begin to get to know each other. After a few minutes of silence and staring at the saucepan, we slid off the countertop, turned off the burner, and walked to the corner of the kitchen where the others were sitting and waiting for the oven buzzer to signal that dinner was ready. Van gave me a look that meant something, but I had no clue what.

We arranged ourselves around the table and spent three hours eating and drinking. As dinner parties go, this was a good one. Not at all like the fiasco at our house in the city.

We talked about the identity politics and cancel culture that was eliminating real discourse and bringing us a step closer to fascism. We talked about the economics of runaway capitalism and the end of a livable climate. Revolution was just under the surface. We all agreed that a path to the destruction of our civilized society had been paved and we were walking down it. We talked about the inevitability of cyber-war and the role of social media in the manipulation of ideas and the destruction of reality. And we discussed the speed of the developments in artificial intelligence. I said that those of us who could afford it would download our brains into hard drives and live forever. Alexa believed that AI would lead to a Terminator-dominated world and the others fell in between the two of us. We talked about whether the country would be better off if it split into smaller units with a series of joint defense agreements and trade agreements—an EU-type structure but with more autonomy in each of the new countries. We all wanted the South and the Midwest to secede. I was very excited about this solution to the fundamental problems facing the country. We talked about patriotism and what it meant and why it wasn't a good thing. And we even tackled the sins of our country: genocide, slavery, colonialism, greed. We all felt somewhat cheated by the mythology taught us in our formal schooling.

The conversations were interesting, better than most; we functioned well as a group of six. We ended the dinner with a great blueberry pie, moved into the living room for a quiet down period, and then couple by couple, we went off to our respective bedrooms.

The cleanup would wait for the morning—not our usual practice but a necessary one.

Chapter 15

Eric and I were the early risers. I made coffee, we toasted the seven-grain bread Van bought each week at the farmers' market a few blocks from our house, and we opened the special blackberry preserves Van had packed for the weekend.

If we lingered over coffee, there was a chance the others would join us for the cleanup detail. Once the kitchen was put back in order, we could make a real country breakfast for the group.

"Good morning," Jean said as she settled between us and stirred some sugar into her coffee. "Great night. Even Matthew was inspired by the conversation."

He wasn't much of a talker, but what he had said was right on target. He was well read and extremely well grounded in world politics.

"I thought it was a great night also," I said.

Eric poured himself a fresh cup of coffee and settled in to watch the bread toast.

Jean waited for Eric to get his toast and then she said, "It looked like Alexa was engaged. Did I misread her, Eric?"

He put his coffee down on the counter. "You didn't misread her; she is intrigued. But we all need to know more about what this revolution is before we become part of it. If it gets us all in trouble, only Will and Van and Alexa have substantial financial safety nets. The rest of us get to fall on our faces."

Eric's comments threw me off balance. We were all similarly educated and had real jobs. No one was going to fall on his or her face.

"Are you serious, Eric?"

"More or less," he said with a shrug.

Jean stepped in.

"He's bullshitting you, Will. I've seen him like this before. When he's not sure of what he wants to do, he tries to distract. There's no 'safety net' issue here, and they'll both be on board."

"Caught me in the act, Jean. Assuming we discuss it seriously and it makes sense, I'll join the group, and I assume Alexa will, too."

"I'm sure we'll discuss it at some point, but now it's clean-up time," I said.

It took the three of us about a half hour to put the kitchen back to its pre-dinner state and another short time to straighten up the rest of the house and the patio. As soon as the three of us settled in to feel the sun on us, the remaining members of the group appeared.

"Great timing, you guys. Did you think you could waltz down here to kiss us all a big thank-you and assume we'd make you breakfast? No way. We cleaned up. Now you get to cook—eggs, bacon, and French toast. And one of you has to make a big batch of Bloody Mary's."

Everyone laughed and took my comment and their assignments with grace.

The drinks, which were Van's handiwork, came out within a few minutes. A grand breakfast followed. Everyone moved into a mellow zone. Twosomes formed and reformed over the hour or so we sat and ate. I spent time talking with Matthew, who, as he had the night before, impressed me with his dead-on insights. Once he got past his need to define his boundaries, sometimes quite abrasively, he revealed himself to be a solid, decent person. Jean was right when she said he was an acquired taste. Van was also connecting to the group in quiet one-on-ones. I decided it was time to move the project forward. I clicked my fork on my empty Bloody Mary glass.

"When should we talk about revolution?"

Van gave me a sharp look. She obviously thought it was her place to set the agenda.

"Will, I'm not sure I want to put us on a schedule. I want it to evolve. I'd rather discuss what everyone wants to do on this beautiful day."

"It's your show, Van, you get to make the rules."

My harsh tone did not go unnoticed.

"Shame on you, Will."

Alexa was extremely attuned to the nuances of relationships.

The others piled on.

"Bad Will."

"Sore sport Will."

"Okay, I apologize. I want to enjoy the day, too. I was just trying to get us to decide when we would discuss our future: after dinner won't work because we'll be wrecked; at dinner doesn't work because we'll be working on getting wrecked; and now is not a good time. Maybe teatime—that would fit this manicured countryside setting."

I was digging a hole for myself.

Eric came to my rescue.

"I agree with Will. I'll enjoy myself more during the day if we've picked a time to talk about revolution. We can vote it up or down at teatime, and until then, and after then, we can just have fun. Does that suit you, Van?"

She nodded assent. "Teatime: four o'clock. Until then, there are lots of things you can do. Will will guide you. I'm going riding. There's food for lunch in the refrigerator, and the town is a fifteen-minute drive from here. See you all later."

Without another word, she went to change into her riding gear.

Matthew signed up for sitting in the shade with his computer and a sketchbook. The rest of us decided to walk. We could walk the trails on our property for at least two hours, and if we wanted an extended hike, the riding trails across other properties could take us for dozens of miles before we would have to cross a road. I loved walking in the Virginia woods: the mix of pine, spruce, and cypress, the hardwoods, and the ground covers all vibrated with different shades of green. They were set off by dozens of copper beech in small groves at the back of the property; their gray-white trunks were scarred with initials from the owners who came before Van's family. Against a blue sky, their dark purple leaves were quite beautiful.

"Hiking shoes, long pants, and a bottle of water for each of us on this walk. I'll carry the snake kit and the hunting knife in case we encounter a copperhead or a bobcat."

I was already dressed for hiking, so I moved a chair into the shade of one of the big ash trees that flanked the patio and waited for the others to get ready.

Jean was first. She sat in a chair next to mine.

"This has been great so far. You and Van are very gracious hosts, and this place is way more comfortable than I thought it would be.

Matthew and I are going to owe you big. He's a good cook, but I'm not sure we can match your feasts or ambiance. No sixteenth-seventeenth-century tables and sideboards at our place."

"We don't need anyone to match our dinners except in good conversation and warm feelings. We have some nice things, but they are just things. We love our friends, and we hope that the two of you will become friends."

I couldn't believe how uptight I sounded.

"I hope so too."

That was all we had time for before Eric and Alexa came out to the patio.

"We're all laced-up and ready," Alexa said, and then they both burst out laughing.

The way she said it made me laugh, too, even though there wasn't anything particularly funny about the phrase. I was relaxing into the day.

I led us out into the woods on a pathway that was well groomed at the beginning and would get a little tangled as we went on. We could walk two by two for a while and then the path would force us into single file. I paired up with Jean to start. I was sure that by the time we had finished our walk, I would have had some private time with each of them. That was how walks in these woods with friends usually sorted out. It happened naturally.

Eric and Alexa were at least ten paces behind us and were falling further behind. I could hear their cheerful banter, but their voices were getting more distant with each step. Then I lost them completely. I turned back to see if they needed help and saw them just coming out of a kiss. They were fine.

Jean turned to look at the same time. She turned back to me. "This is a great walk, Will. Do you do it whenever you're here?"

"No. Sometimes we drive into the mountains for hikes and sometimes we just stay at the house and read. I don't ride, so Van does that on her own. On occasion, the people we're with want to go into town to check out the shops. That bores me, but I do it if our guests aren't prepared to go into town on their own. This walk is one of my favorite things here."

She smiled. "I think I'd do this every day if I lived here. My mind is always spinning with so much clutter. This would be my meditation pathway. Do you meditate?"

"I'm not that disciplined. It felt good when I did it for more than a week in a row, but then travel, work, or just staring out the window would get in the way."

"You should make more of a commitment to it; it works. I do twenty minutes twice a day and it has centered me. The stuff that used to make me crazy, like Matthew living in his own world, just doesn't bother me anymore. And my work, which can be terribly stressful, sits in its own box. I can close the lid on it whenever it suits me. Like now, for example. I'm totally here with you."

We walked in silence for a little way. Soon, I knew the pathway would narrow to single file.

"So, how did you and Matthew meet?"

That was lame.

"Is that your way of getting to know me better?"

"Maybe. I guess 'How did you and Matthew meet?' is as good a question as any to learn someone's history."

She told me she met Matthew at a gallery opening in Georgetown. She was with her boyfriend, and he was alone. They found themselves in a corner of the gallery studying the same very tight pen and ink drawing. Their shoulders touched. She said they both felt the electricity. That's the story she told. Personal stories with no witnesses can be tailored to fit the mood. And this one fit.

"You don't really expect me to believe that?"

"I do. That's my story. And that's who I am. I'm a hopeless romantic. Where are you on the romantic scale?"

"I'm not a romantic. I analyze and assess risks before I act. Which, of course, doesn't mean that I get it right. This revolution thing is out of character for me. And I don't know whether I'm glad you're a spontaneous romantic, if that's what you are, or whether I would be happier if you were a plodding rationalist like me."

She stopped and turned toward me. "Don't fool yourself. I live with a plodding rationalist, and you're not him."

The path narrowed and we were single file. Eric and Alexa were nowhere to be seen or heard. I hoped they had the good sense to keep their pants on; there was poison ivy everywhere off the pathway.

"Let's slow down so Eric and Alexa can catch up," I said.

We walked in silence under the dappled late morning light for a little while. I was sorry the pathway required us to walk single file. I wanted to share more stories with Jean.

Eric and Alexa caught up with us just as the pathway widened. Alexa moved ahead to walk with me, and Jean held back to walk with Eric. I was pleased with the way the morning was unfolding.

"What were you and Jean talking about? We could catch words here and there but not enough to tell what you guys were up to. We heard 'love' and something about 'passionate' and 'not rational.' Were you guys planning to declare yourselves?"

"Not yet."

She smiled and we walked along in silence for a few minutes.

"So, Will, what's going to happen this weekend? Are we going to plan something radical?"

"There are enough guns for all of us in the gun room, Alexa. So, after tea we can drive into town and rid it of the horsey set."

"I'm serious. I need to get my head around where I'm going well before I get there. I'm really not very spontaneous."

"It's not teatime, Alexa. That was the deal."

She gave me a fake pout.

"Okay, then tell me something about you and Van that might give me some insight into where you're going with this toy club of yours."

"Toy club? Maybe you shouldn't be allowed to be at the meeting."

"Sorry, I couldn't resist."

We walked another few minutes without talking.

"Van and I managed our college newspaper. Fell in love and got married. She found her way to her father's newspaper. I published a rarefied news magazine that was bought by her father, who then insisted I become his understudy. It's all very American who-you-know nepotism. We lead typical high-pressured DC lives. We take pleasure in our house in the city, even if it is a little too grown-up for us, since we usually feel like we're in graduate school, and we love coming out here."

"A little defensive, Will. I'm not interested in your physical surroundings, your playthings, or your portfolios—I have my own set of those—I'm interested in who you are: what do you see as important and how do you think a civilized society should function? I want to know whether your compassion is real or just the talk of the upper classes that were trained in New England. Who you are? That's what I want to know. Your things are not relevant to me."

I didn't much like her tone. Fortunately, Eric and Jean were just a short distance behind us, so I had time to gather my thoughts as they approached and stepped around us to take the lead. This would be the time for me to walk with Eric and let Alexa and Jean walk together. I let the opportunity pass. I gave them directions since we were close to a turn in the path—to the left took us another two miles into the hills, and to the right was a loop back to the house. We all agreed on the loop back—the hungers and thirsts of lunch beckoned, and it was about three miles back, which gave us all at least another hour to talk.

After Eric and Jean were out of earshot, Alexa said, "I'm waiting for your answers, Will."

"You'll get the answers over time by watching me in action."

She stopped and turned to face me. "That's evasive. As I said, I need to have things laid out in advance. Learning something real about you will give me a sense of what's going to go on later this afternoon and perhaps the future also. It will make me feel much more at ease. So, who are you?"

We were still standing and facing each other. I told myself to be calm and give her a little glimpse into who I thought I was.

"I'm a lot of things. I'm kind. I don't gossip and climb over people for my career or for anything else. I talk more than I should. I like to search for the truth and expose evil and lies. It drives me crazy that the level of discourse has become uncivil, and that greed is king. I'm troubled that we've given the keys to our universities to the students, who seem to have no capacity to deal with unfamiliar or unappealing viewpoints. There is no compassion in the land. Capitalism has destroyed our democracy, assuming we had one. The world is going to keep getting worse. We need a new ethic. We need a new morality. I want to do something more than give my fair share to charity and

serve food on holidays in our local soup kitchen. I want to do something that might make a difference. I might even be prepared to put
my current lifestyle on the line. These are platitudes, but these are
the thoughts that fill my head."

To my surprise, she was listening.

"That's a good start, Will. A good start."

With that, we walked purposefully like horses that knew they
were headed back to the barn for fresh oats.

The four of us gathered on the patio to make our lunch plan. No
one wanted to go into town, so it was up to me to set the prepara-
tions in motion. I suggested that everyone take some time to freshen
up and meet back in the kitchen to help create a midday feast. Jean
went off to find Matthew. Eric and Alexa went off hand in hand,
and Van was still out somewhere in the countryside. Normally, she
wouldn't be back from a ride on a day like today until mid to late
afternoon, so I decided we should have lunch without her.

I washed up, changed out of my hiking boots, and went to the
kitchen to start preparing lunch for five. Van and I had assumed we
would all have a big lunch at the house, so we had brought lots of
interesting salads and meats, great tomatoes, and very fine cheeses. I
figured this was a lunchtime wine-drinking group. I opened a white
and a red. Alexa and Eric were the first ones down.

"You look surprised. Did you think Eric and I were going to stay
in our cozy room while the rest of you gathered here in the kitchen
and obsessed over whether you should come up and get us?"

She was so out there.

Eric had a very big smile on his face.

"Okay. I know your game: *Make the innocent host blush.* You
win. But I want you to know, Eric, that if Alexa were my girlfriend
and we had just come back from a nice walk in the country and had

a little time before lunch, we'd be under the covers and lunch would wait."

Eric's smile vanished. What I had said was a come on to Alexa and it was rude. There was no taking it back.

"Sorry," I said. "Let's slice tomatoes and unwrap cheeses, put the salads in these bowls, and do whatever else needs to be done. I'll pour some wine."

After my stupid comment, the three of us worked in silence.

Alexa declined the wine and Eric asked for a beer. I poured some red for myself.

Jean and Matthew came down to the kitchen just as we had finished putting out the lunch.

We filled our plates and went out to the patio. We ate and drank and talked for at least two hours. My comment about Alexa still hung in the air. Eric seemed a little more distant and Alexa a little closer. Even so, the conversation was fine. Matthew told us about his most recent series of drawings and the computer programs he had constructed to add elaborate detail to them. Judging by the sketches he showed us on his iPhone, the series was going to be very special. He obviously had warmed up to the group.

We talked about the art market and its corporate ways. Eric knew a lot about the subject. He had just finished a project for a university museum that had acquired artifacts from Peru in the early twentieth century, which raised the flashpoint issue of whether they had been acquired fairly and who should own them now. He was in the middle of the very high-end art world of auctions and private deals. It was an interesting conversation.

"Did you guys save me anything for lunch? I'm starved. You can catch a fox, but you can't eat her."

Van was radiant.

"It looks like you guys have been drinking and eating for hours. Did you walk or have you been sitting here since I left?"

"Will took us for a great walk through your woods. We didn't encounter any fox, but Eric and I did see a fat copperhead slither in front of our path."

I was surprised Jean hadn't told me about the snake. Usually, when our friends see a copperhead, they freak out.

"Are you a country girl, Jean?" I asked.

Jean got out of her chair and took another beer out of the cooler.

"I'll reveal my hidden past as long as it stays here on the patio."

We all agreed.

"I was born on a commune in northern California. One of the last remnants of the sixties. It was a beautiful spot not too far from Point Reyes. It was a barter economy. There were snakes on our land, not copperheads of course, but big snakes with rattles. I'm comfortable with wildlife."

She twisted the top of her beer bottle with a grand gesture and sat back in her seat.

The rest of us stared at her for a moment and then, as if on cue, we all burst out laughing.

Van said, "Good try, Jean, but none of us believes you. We think you shrieked and jumped and ran for safety and that you probably grew up in a classic six on the Upper West Side."

That was a little aggressive.

"Why should I make believe I'm someone I'm not? I grew up on a commune in California—it was sweet while it lasted. I went off to Berkeley and the rest is history."

As far as I was concerned, the subject was closed. Van, on the other hand, was about to say something. She had grown an edge while riding that threatened to make our teatime a disaster. I needed to signal her to loosen up.

"Van, tell the group about your effort to catch the fox."

She understood she had to take it down a notch.

"Aside from getting thrown on my ass, it was uneventful. The dogs were good, and the fox was dumb. So, everyone was happy."

Matthew raised his eyes from the beer label he was examining.

"Did you stab the fox with your steely knife?"

"Are you making fun of me, Matthew? Riding is a perfectly good thing for a country gentlewoman to do on the Saturday in Virginia hunt country, especially if it's the day she plans to start a revolution."

That got us back into mellow moods. We stayed on the patio for another half hour or so and then Matthew got up and said he was off to his private corner in the living room to work. Since it was already after three o'clock, we agreed that tea would be at five thirty instead of four. Jean said she would hang out in the garden, and Eric and Alexa went up for an afternoon nap. Van and I wished them well and then set off for a short walk.

We walked for a few minutes, hand in hand, without talking. The afternoon sun would soon begin to slant behind the tallest trees and the shadows would lengthen.

"This is a good group. I spent time walking with both Alexa and Jean. Matthew stayed at the house. Alexa seems genuinely enthusiastic about our idea. I wonder what's changed her?"

The color in Van's face deepened ever so slightly.

"Have you been working on her?"

"Yes, we've had two or three lunches together."

"Was it two or three?"

"Does it matter? The point is I have convinced her to trust us and to get on board."

"Playing behind my back isn't right." I took my hand from hers and tried to figure out whether I was upset or just thought I should be.

"Get off it. You've been afraid Alexa would tell our secrets. I did us a favor. She'll be loyal all the way to prison with us." My mood changed. I wasn't interested in walking or talking. I'm not sure why it bothered me that Van met with Alexa to talk about our venture without telling me, but it did. We turned and headed back to the house.

Chapter 16

We gathered in the living room: a large room with a grand fireplace that was set off by limestone columns holding up a broad mantle. The room had seating for the six of us around a coffee table that was filled with art books piled six or eight high on almost every inch of its glass top. Two small couches and four comfortable leather chairs surrounded the table. It was intimate while still providing enough space for everyone to feel a sense of autonomy.

I brewed three pots of tea: black, green, and herbal. Van and I arranged two big trays of cookies, which got us a round of applause. We settled in and Eric started us off.

"We're here, we have our tea, we've taken a blood oath to secrecy, so, let the games begin."

Van leaned over and put her tea down on the table.

"Will and I trust you and hope you've come to trust us."

Grunts and nods around, which surprised me. I had assumed this group was made up of silent types—no nods, no visible or audible signs of agreement or disagreement.

"Okay, then I'll jump in. The country is controlled by a handful of obscenely wealthy people. The rest are spread on a spectrum from living reasonably well, to just making ends meet, to food insecure, as the government likes to call people who are hungry. There are tens and tens of millions of people with no healthcare: no dentists, no eye doctors, no internists, no specialists, and no money for medicine. The poverty in this country parallels the poverty in the underdeveloped world. Our political system has been broken for decades, and now it's moved into deep evil territory. The ruling class has no moral compass. Twenty years ago, no one would have thought it acceptable to buy a company that made drugs for a serious disease and then jack up the price a thousand times. That's acceptable business behavior now."

"We all know this, Van." Eric's tone was gentle, but the point couldn't be missed: this wasn't supposed to be a gathering to plow over the obvious.

"Indulge me. I'll get to the point, I promise. Our democracy can't be fixed with marches and demonstrations."

It was Alexa's turn to speak for the group. "We all agree, Van. So, what's up your sleeve?"

To my surprise, Van took this interruption in stride.

"I've been working on a story that deals with a drug company that has been running a campaign to convince world leaders to promote baby formula over breastfeeding so it can sell product even though it knows that pushing formula in places with unsafe water supplies will cause great harm."

Now it was Jean's turn. "Van, those of us who follow the WHO and its dealings know about this campaign. What are you driving at?"

"Actually, Jean, there are very few people outside of the DC circle who know about this issue. So, I've been working to expose them. Except there are people in very high and powerful places who have instructed my father to kill the story."

They all looked at me for confirmation. I was totally caught off guard by Van's very serious indiscretion. But I had no choice. I nodded that it was true.

Van went on.

"Getting pressure from a company and its lobbyists is not uncommon. This is different. The pressure is coming from secret places at the top of the government. This company has leverage that is more than the usual political clout. I've been studying the company and its other key products, and it's the perfect target—it is a symbol of the corruption that is destroying our democracy. We should learn everything about this company and take action to destroy it and those who have enabled it to become what it is. That's how we can begin to change the trajectory we are on—one company, one industry at a time."

Eric took center stage.

"Well done—a grand, or should I say grandiose, idea. Van, certainly something that could be interesting to work on. I recommend we vote to form the group and then move from tea to whiskey. And I suggest we close ranks with just the six of us for now and talk about next steps at our next meeting."

There were nods around the table. I was surprised that Eric wanted to close the conversation so quickly. Van had revealed the possibility of a high-level, perhaps government-run conspiracy, and he didn't let anyone pursue it. That was strange.

Jean took the floor.

"Drinking and smoking sounds very good right now; it's been a full, fun day. So, I move that we establish a ten-dollar a person entry fee, close the membership, and elect Van president and Will the treasurer and secretary. I also move that we call the group the XDS, as Van suggested."

Alexa shouted out a second.

It was ironic that they resorted to classic rules of order to form a revolutionary group designed to challenge order. For a moment, I thought I was back in my high school's student council meetings.

Everyone raised their teacups to signify their yes vote.

While I was trying to figure out why no one wanted to push for more information about the possible conspiracy that Van described, and why Eric and then Jean closed it down so fast, the XDS was formed.

The business of the weekend was done. We turned to partying. I made margaritas. I went heavy on the tequila and light on the triple sec and lime juice, and we were soon on our way to a raucous evening. Van and I had planned a simple dinner: steaks and tuna on the grill and a big salad. To keep it easy, we had planned on ice cream and berries for dessert.

By the time we were ready to make dinner, anything more complicated wouldn't have been possible. Van was supposed to be in charge. If I had left it up to her, there would have been no dinner. While a little unsteady in mind and body, by the time the big grandfather clock in the hallway started to chime out that it was eight o'clock, I decided to get the dinner show on the road. Both Alexa and Jean offered to help.

Alexa set the table and then went into the garden and cut some flowers. Van and I rarely filled our city house with flowers. As I watched Alexa put together the simple arrangement for the table, I decided I would talk to Van about changing our pattern. It would be nice to have flowers around the house.

I moved to the table and put my hand on Alexa's shoulder, which was warm to the touch. "I love how you put that together so easily."

She stood there facing the arrangement and admiring her own handiwork.

"I can't imagine living without fresh flowers in every room. And here, where they're in such abundance, it gives me a thrill."

I told her it was time for me to cook the meat and fish. She smiled and said she was going to cut some more flowers to put in the living room for after dinner.

"Are you off to cook? Let me help!" Eric called out as he extricated himself form Matthew and Van.

"I need all of the help I can get. Grilling is a big responsibility. If the meat is too well done, it's the griller's fault. If it's too rare, it's his fault, as well."

"Happy to share the inevitable blame, Will."

I refilled our glasses with cool, pale-green margarita.

"I see you and Alexa are hitting it off. It would not please me to see the two of you get much closer. Keep your distance."

"What? I have no intention of getting *closer*, as you put it. We're getting to know each other, that's all. I want to know the people I'm heading toward a cliff with. I assume you do, too."

His only response was, "Time to turn the tuna."

We spent a few minutes in awkward silence, which he broke with, "Alexa has a target painted on your back. Be warned and keep your hands off her."

He was being an asshole. I didn't like it, and I wasn't going to excuse it because he had had too much to drink and smoke.

"Your take on Alexa and me is pure fantasy. If you feel threatened, then take it up with her."

We finished the cooking in silence, filled a big platter, and announced our arrival into the dining room with great fanfare.

Everything else was already on the table.

Matthew got up to give the opening toast. There were many layers to Matthew—a painter, philosopher, spiritualist, introvert, mathematician, computer expert—and by the general demeanor displayed by Jean, a decent husband, and now a member of the civilized elite.

We had a feast. Everyone was in a great mood, except for Eric. The edge he had while we cooked was lingering. And every so often, I caught Alexa looking at him with a puzzled look. I kept my attention focused on Jean, who was on my right, and Matthew, on my left; they were good company. We finished dinner and sat around the living room for another hour of drinking. When the evening finally wound down, I was too tired to clean up. Eric had already gone off to his room. Matthew was still full of energy, and Van seemed to be, as well. They volunteered to clean up. The rest of us volunteered to go to bed.

The next morning was waffles, strawberries, and whipped cream, followed by a walk on our pathway through the woods. And then, we all departed to our houses in the city.

Chapter 17

We were in our kitchen having breakfast.

I was energized. "We're pretty lucky. A dinner party, a weekend in the country, and we have our group. I'm glad it's off the ground. I'll change the sixty dollars into silver, so we'll have precious metal to use after we destroy the banking system."

Van was as pleased with the weekend as I was.

"Amassing silver is a great idea. We'll set dues at ten dollars a person a week."

Van took a final sip of her breakfast coffee.

We drove to work mostly in silence, which was not unusual for a Monday morning. As we got close to the office, she asked what my week was going to be like.

"If I'm lucky, I'll get to sit in on another editorial board meeting. And then the week will be filled with work on the deal, which will put me in a foul mood, so be forewarned. What about yours?"

"Jean invited me to a job fair focused on health-related non-profits, which should help with the WHO article. And I'm going to have lunch with Matthew to get his take on the patterns developing in the industry. Jean may join us if she can get free."

The information was distracting enough to cause me to run a stop sign.

"You didn't invite me?"

"Pay attention." She was not very forgiving of my driving skills.

"I'm leaving you out on purpose. And I wouldn't have asked Jean, except that I thought you might be upset if I planned a lunch with just Matthew."

"Why would I be upset?" My tone gave me away.

"Stuff it. We'll get more done if the dynamic isn't always the six of us partying."

"Very modern." I still couldn't get my tone to be neutral.

"What's with you? You can't be jealous. Matthew is way too old and serious for me. I like them young and malleable, like you."

She put her hand on my shoulder.

"Don't humor me. I understand the benefit of uncoupling. But, if I were going to have lunch with Jean or Alexa, I'd tell you before making the plan."

Van took her hand from my shoulder.

"That's first-class sexist. Be careful or this could take an ugly turn."

The conversation didn't help me face my Monday, and the way she closed the car door at the front of our building made it clear that this wasn't the way she had wanted to start her Monday either.

A ringing phone greeted me as I opened the door to my office. I called Van as soon as I hung up.

"I'm sorry our morning got off to a bad start. I'm on the noon shuttle to New York. I'll leave you the car. Your dad told me to pack for the week, even though he thought we would be done in two or three days. I'll call you when I get settled in."

"I'm sorry, too. Come give me a kiss before you go. If your plane goes down, I'll be doubly sad if we didn't say a proper good-bye."

If your plane goes down was a sweet touch.

"I'm on my way."

Fortunately, the paper's policy was that only two executives could be on the same plane. The others had left on either the 11 or the 11:30, so I had the flight and the car to the hotel to myself. My hotel was in Midtown on the east side. I was scheduled to meet the group for a late lunch at a nearby Italian restaurant. Then it would be meetings with the lawyers until the basics of the deal were done. I checked into the hotel, put my bags in my room, and walked the three blocks to the restaurant.

It was just our team for lunch, and everyone but me appeared okay with being in New York.

Jim spotted me looking over the crowd to find them. He came over to get me, since our table was hidden in a corner.

"Did you and Van have a good weekend in the country? We were going to come out, but once we learned you had guests, we thought better of it.

"It's your house, Jim. Van and I thought you were going to be out of town. We would have changed our plans if we knew you had wanted to be in Virginia."

"We wouldn't ask you to cancel your plans for us. I'm sure it was a beautiful weekend in the country."

Under the surface he was saying, *it's my house and I was upset not to be able to use it.*

He continued, "I hope you're rested from the weekend. You're our point man on this deal. It's going to be a stretch. I hope you can rise to the occasion."

He held up his hand to stop my protestation.

"You can handle it professionally. It's the emotional part I'm worried about."

"Sorry, Jim, I don't get it?"

"Don't play dumb, Will. To make this work, you are going to have to get over your romantic view of the press. Big business and the super-rich have controlled the news ever since man learned how to make symbols. This deal is just part of that reality."

I had no idea his cynicism was so deep.

The lunch was what one could expect from a fine Italian restaurant in New York: homemade pasta and fresh vegetables—perfect food. We had a little over an hour and a half before we needed to be at our lawyer's offices. When the small talk was done, Jim announced to the other senior executives that I was taking over for him as the point man on the deal. I couldn't bring myself to say anything nice. I offered to turn the responsibility over to anyone else who might like it. I could see the marketing vice president was not happy the responsibility fell to me. I don't think the others cared. To them, it was just more work.

We finished our coffee and walked two blocks to our lawyers' offices. This would be considerably more intense than the deal the paper made to buy my magazine. Jim wasn't kidding when he said he hoped I was rested.

It took four days to establish the framework of the deal. It was a whirlwind of back-to-back meetings with our lawyers, our counterparts on other newspapers, bankers, and a very odd assortment of executives from different sectors in the healthcare industry. And the PR and salespeople from the ad agencies who were there just to listen. Except for the lawyers, who were a diverse lot in terms of gender, age, color, and, I assumed, sexual orientation, almost everyone else was mid-thirties to early fifties, white, male, and most likely heterosexual. And, by their comments, many of them appeared to be sexist and racist, too. This power structure was still the exclusive domain of the frat-boys. I felt a perverse need to share with Van her father's response to my observation. "Get off your high horse, Will. This is business. If women belonged here, they'd be here."

His response was mind blowing. I had never heard him be so blatantly sexist. The lack of diversity was kids' stuff compared to what the deal was about. The key newspapers from the United States and Europe were going to share editorial decision-making with the pharmaceutical industry as the initial test bed. A content committee would set the editorial policy for the members of the consortium, and executives from the industry would be members of the committee. Everyone except for me seemed to be fine with the structure.

I couldn't remain silent. I accused the group of participating in a conspiracy to commit a fraud on the public. My lawyers called a break and pulled Jim and me off to another conference room.

I couldn't contain my rage.

"Jim, you can't be serious. To go from an operating agreement to cut printing costs to a sale of our editorial independence to these thugs is criminal. The Justice Department ought to send a team in here and put all of us in jail. They should charge us with treason. That's what this is: we're destroying the very foundations of this country. What the fuck are you up to?"

Jim got up and left the room without saying a word. I was alone with the lawyers.

The senior lawyer was out of central casting—in her mid-fifties, thin, probably a marathon runner, with an impenetrable face.

"Will, I know it's been three long, hard days and nights. So, losing it in there, and here, as well, is understandable. This deal is going forward. You can embrace it and try your best to protect your journalistic birthright, or you can turn your back on it and let others decide how much power to give to the money guys. It doesn't have to turn out as badly as you think it will. Just because the industry people get to tell you what's important to them doesn't mean they get to force you to write what they want. Give them access and then publish your paper and let them like it or not. Their vote on your secret committee will mean nothing if you're smart enough. They can't sue you and call attention to their deal. They can have you killed, but I think that might be a stretch even for them."

It took me a while to decide how to respond.

"You know this deal is a fraud on the American public as well as the people of France, England, and Germany. Do you really think their seats will be at the back of the room? They will stand in front, just a little behind the screen, and I'm the screen. Don't you care?"

She asked the other lawyers to leave the room so we could have a one-on-one.

"Will, the deal is set in stone. Jim has been the driving force from the beginning. This has been years in the making. None of us knows who is calling the shots behind him. The pharma group is a pawn in this game for world domination. And that's more than I should share with you. You need to make peace with it on the surface or turn down the appointment and gather up your family and belongings and get out."

Her tone turned almost conspiratorial.

"If you want to have an impact on how this deal gets implemented, I suggest you accept being the paper's rep and figure your moves from there. If you're on the outside and someone else gets the job, all your worst nightmares will come true. Of course, they might come true with you in charge, as well."

It was just a tiny crack in her armor. She was as upset by the deal as I was. Maybe she could be an ally.

"Okay. I'll try to behave."

We returned to the big conference room where everyone was drinking coffee and eating cookies.

"Will, are you with us?"

It was Jim. I had wandered off into a fantasy in which I blew up a conference room filled with the members of the secret editorial committee. I got out alive.

"Sorry."

After another hour or so, the basic structure of the deal was in place. Now it was up to the lawyers to work on refining it so that no one could get blamed if anything went wrong and that the people in the room all came away with something they needed.

This phase was done.

In the elevator on our way out of the building, I told Jim I would take a pass on dinner. He liked to wrap things up with markers, and a final dinner was clearly a marker in his mind. This would just be another example of me not being a team player. But I was going home to be with his daughter, and there wasn't much he could say against that.

He nodded acquiescence and I was off to the hotel to pack.

Chapter 18

I'm beat. I need to clean up and change."

I was glad to be home. When I came down dressed in my jeans and a comfortable shirt, she took my hand, and we went out to the backyard where she had already opened a bottle of wine. I told her everything that went on in New York—the nature of the deal and the role her father played in it. She was not a happy camper.

We sat under our giant Ash in silence. When she was ready to talk, it was as if a dam had burst. She had so much anger about the paper, her father, the deal, and the world around us that it was like a roadrunner cartoon. She was revved up and heading for the cliff. She kept it up for a while until she finally collapsed in on herself. She put out her hand for me to hold and took a deep breath.

"This is really awful."

"Yup."

"This is why you've embraced my sophomoric idea of revolution, isn't it?"

"Yup."

We went inside and made a simple dinner for ourselves, read for an hour, and decided the day was over.

We were in quieter moods than usual the next morning. She didn't bound out of bed and head for the shower; instead, she sat on the side of the bed and stared at her feet. I put my hand on the small of her back. When she was ready, she got up and slowly walked to her bathroom.

Then it was my turn to sit on the side of the bed and let my mind adjust to its awake setting. My mind was blank.

We started our breakfast in silence, which I eventually broke.

"Maybe I should talk to my contact at Justice to see if she can get them to stop the deal and slap a few hands. That's where my heart is telling me to go."

I needed to hear that thought out loud to know how crazy it was, since the first hand to be slapped would be her father's, and it might be slapped right into prison. I wanted it to hang in the air for a while, so I got up and ground more coffee beans. Van grimaced.

"Way too loud."

"Sorry, I thought the distraction might help you consider my last comment."

She smiled.

"I knew why you were making noise. You don't go to Justice. We're not going to leave the dirty work to others. We will stop it, neutralize it, or make it work for our benefit. And we have to decide whether this is a project for the group or whether it's our private project."

"Private," I said with no hesitation. "Involving outsiders would be a terrible breach of ethics."

"Breach of ethics? More than going to Justice? Let's sit on it for now. Maybe the deal will fall of its own weight." She was dreaming.

I shrugged.

"No chance. The best we can hope for is that I can disrupt some stuff from inside."

"What kind of *stuff*?"

"Who knows? Everything they do will be bad, and I'm going to be a functioning part of it. Our group, or maybe some other group of revolutionaries, may have to blow me up. We should drive separate cars from now on. I'd prefer to die alone."

The die alone part didn't get a smile.

"I'm serious, Van. We're playing with fire. We have enough money to pull out: be done. We can live anywhere in the world. Our lead lawyer suggested we gather our belongings and flee. We can write books, read, fish, and grow vegetables. This isn't going to turn out right. Let's make a new life for ourselves. I love you enough to do that. Do you love me enough to do it?"

She thought for a short while and then said, "I do love you enough, but I don't want to run. We're going to fight for change or die trying. I really feel compelled to act."

She stood up to sip the last bit of coffee from her cup.

I got up, too, so we could be standing close to each other, and I said, "I'm serious about running away and starting a new life. I want to talk about it tonight, after work."

"Fine," she said, hesitating for a minute and then following it up with "but to move things forward, we need another meeting of our group somewhere other than our house. I'm going to call Eric and see if he'll do a dinner."

I nodded. It was time to face the day.

Chapter 19

We were in an environment not controlled by us, which created a notable shift in the dynamic. I wanted to declare there was revolution in the air, but I held back to give Eric, our host, the chance to set the mood, which he did.

"Let's toast to revolution," Eric said.

I thought his tone was a little condescending. No one else in the group seemed to pick it up. We raised our glasses and drank to our new enterprise.

Eric lived in a nicely proportioned Arts and Crafts–style house in Cleveland Park made mostly of gray granite quarried in the area that is now the National Zoo. That put into context hundreds of houses that Van and I have admired that were built before the depression with that stone. I liked the Arts and Crafts aesthetic: the Stickley furniture, the oak paneling, and the big stone fireplaces. Eric obviously liked the era, as well since he had filled his house with furniture from the period. The living room floors were polished dark oak without a single scratch—no kids, no dogs—and it was big enough for a seating area that included four Morris chairs with brown leather and a big Stickley couch with very wide solid oak arm rests situated around a square coffee table that was easily five feet across. His dining room was also furnished in the period. The table wasn't set for dinner, which I assumed meant we were going out for dinner or ordering pizza to be delivered.

"To the second official meeting of the august XDS. Let's raise our glasses again to Will and Van for bringing this eclectic group together."

I raised my glass and swallowed the shot of tequila, which was high quality and made for sipping, not for gulping. I would sip the refill. We were in the middle of an Eric ritual. Everyone had to propose a toast. I was glad it was a Friday night and that we had used a car service.

Alexa filled my empty shot glass and said it was time for my toast. Then she moved on to make sure everyone had a full glass.

"I'm told by our beautiful hostess that it's my turn to toast."

Van shot me a deep glare and all the others stared at me.

"I'm prone to say inappropriate things when I drink on an empty stomach; and this will be my second or third. I've lost track."

"Third," Van said with enough nuance in her voice to tell me that I was on her shit list.

"Whatever. I'm very glad we're together. Last week, I watched the rulers of the universe take over the free press. We need to bring them to their knees."

"That was totally cheesy, Will," Eric said. "But I'm happy to drink to it, if you promise to tell me your secret in private, later. I don't think the group is ready for your grand reveal."

He had done a good job of protecting me. I assumed he did it so he could pump me for the details later. Gathering information to trade was his business.

The others were hoping for inside gossip, but they didn't push; Eric had effectively stopped them. They raised their glasses and drank with me.

Jean took the floor.

"Eric sure saved your ass. Maybe blowing up your paper would be a good thing to do?"

"Give Will a break. He's not used to tequila shots. It's not my party, but I think we have to have food, or he'll disintegrate." I was surprised Van helped after I had called Alexa beautiful.

Eric moved over to Alexa's end of the couch. He sat on the sturdy oak arm and put his hand on her shoulder.

"Shall we feed this group or let them drink themselves into oblivion?"

"Let's feed them," she said.

And with that, they sprang into action.

We were going to eat sitting around the big coffee table—a good way to keep everything informal.

I watched them set the table for dinner. It was a routine they had down well: placemats with colorful tie-dyed napkins, ceramic dishes and bowls, heavy stainless knives and forks, and blue-hued glasses from Mexico. I assumed we would be eating a simple but hardy dinner.

And that's what it was: a fish stew and salad with locally grown vegetables. The farmers' market, which was just a couple of miles from each of our houses, if you pictured it as the hub of a wheel, was open for business twice a week. It was the place where the enlightened people who were not on a budget shopped for their favorite breads, honeys, lettuces, tomatoes, and countless other foods.

I was pretty sure I was the only one who would have preferred eating at the dining table. Everyone else seemed to be able to relax into the casual posture of post-grads sitting on the floor eating lasagna at a potluck dinner.

"Will, you don't look very comfortable," Jean said.

"I never could sit comfortably on the floor."

My comment created a silence that lasted an interminable amount of time.

"I reserve the dining room for fundraising events and dinners that are social obligations."

Alexa was next to me and helped me get into a tolerable position, while Jean was leaning on Eric and Van and Matthew were sitting very close together. Dinner was great and the conversation easy. I was totally buzzed and decided to move the ball forward before we were no longer capable of rational thought.

"I'm calling this meeting to order."

Everyone yelled "Order! Order!" and laughed and yelled some more. The group had been pretty much done in by the tequila and wine.

"Host—that's you, Eric," I said, "it's time for coffee. We need to be sobered up if we're going to have a meeting before it gets too late."

Alexa looked up at me, opened her eyes as wide as she could, and said, "Oh dear, oh dear, we're late, we're late for a very important something or other." She sighed and continued. "Why do we need to have a meeting when we're all having so much fun?"

I just shrugged and said: "You're right. We can eat and drink and let the world come to an end."

"What kind of a wife would I be if I didn't step in at this point?"

Van made eye contact with each person as she said this in a very slow and deliberate way.

"The meeting has been called to order, and since we're not running on all cylinders, any decisions we make tonight will be subject to confirmation in the morning. That will be the rule whenever we meet and are under the influence of alcohol, sex, rock and roll, or drugs. Agreed?"

There were approving nods all around. Van wasn't finished.

"Those are the rules unless, of course, two-thirds of the group are too blasted to even consider revolution in any form. Then the meeting will be suspended until such time as the two-thirds comes back down to Earth. Agreed?"

More nods.

"So, a show of hands, who would like to suspend the call to order—remember, it takes four hands to make that happen."

Alexa raised her hand. No one else did. She put her hand back down and rested it on my hand on the table in plain view.

"Alright then. The first item on the agenda is to decide if we still agree that pharma is going to be our first industry target." Van paused for effect. "There are other candidates: banking, insurance, healthcare, chemical, telecom, media, and education are the big silos, and lots of companies fall into more than one"

Eric took the floor. "I vote we shift from your favorite pharma company to Wall Street. A few thousand of them made more in bonuses last year than over 12 million hardworking people. And try this: 82 people at the top have the combined wealth of the bottom 3.5 billion people. We should bomb Wall Street into rubble."

Jean raised her glass. "I agree. Let's wreak havoc on Wall Street."

"You're not taking this seriously."

Van was more sober than I thought.

"I'm serious, Van. Wall Street is a better target than baby formula in the undeveloped countries and whatever else this company
pushes," Eric said.

It was Alexa's turn. "I agree with Van. We should stick with
pharma, which does about as much damage as the banks. Will and
I have been talking about how the major research universities are
controlled by pharma, and our target company is a big player in the
research university world. We should start with the universities who
get money from the company. They won't be protected by layers of
technical people safeguarding their secrets and their data."

Alexa got blank stares. She made believe her feelings were hurt,
and I put my arm around her to mime consolation. I liked having my
arm around her.

"Will, always there when a young girl needs a helping hand."

That was not the usual Van. The edge was sharp. Before I could
say anything, Alexa took charge.

"It was comforting to have your compassionate husband hold me
when the rest of you treated me so disrespectfully. You're the group
leader, Van. You should be encouraging us to explore ideas that hav-
en't already failed, like Occupy Wall Street. Trust me, Eric and Jean
pushed the Wall Street thing to keep us ineffectual. They'll try to
keep us from acting. You'll see. They may actually be working for
the other side and are here only to spy on us true revolutionaries."

"That's pretty cynical. Maybe they're just timid. In any event, I
agree with you. We should practice on something small, but I'm not
sure a research university is the place to start." Van handled herself
with grace.

Before Alexa could respond, Matthew spoke: "It's getting late. I'd
like to get us to a soft consensus and then help Eric and Alexa clean
up. Here's my suggestion for moving forward."

I was tired and hoped his suggestion would be worth acting on.

"Alexa is right. A university will be much easier to infiltrate than a big bank or a pharma company and it does almost as much damage. Big money manipulates the curriculum and the research paths, all of which goes unnoticed. We could learn a lot about our future tactics and strategies if we focus on a major research university. I propose that Alexa and Will come up with a specific university for our next meeting and tell us what we should consider doing. We need options: bombs and no bombs options. That's my suggestion."

Everyone bought into it.

It was a silent ride home. Van wasn't pleased that I had put my arm around Alexa. I wasn't happy that she seemed so intimate with Matthew, and I told her so.

We had issues to discuss in the morning.

Chapter 20

Let's keep the weekend to ourselves. We have some patching up to do."

I reached over and took her hand. "I agree," she said.

She took a sip of coffee and gave me a serious look.

"Are you sure that it's me you want to spend the weekend with? You seemed quite content to have that little tart by your side."

"Do you mean our new friend, Alexa? She is very intriguing."

"Don't push your luck, Will. I may be willing to overlook your cozying up to her last night, but you're mine and I don't share."

"You were doing the same thing with Matthew, and I don't want to share either, so let's be done with this. I'll start breakfast."

She turned to her paper. I went off to the kitchen. I liked cooking. I put our breakfast on a tray and brought it out with great fanfare.

"An omelet and toast for my beauty."

"Thank you."

She was remote.

"What's up?"

"I've been thinking about what you said about me and Matthew. You're right, and it wasn't fair for me to go after you and Alexa. We were both too available."

"We were just being friendly and getting to know them better. We're not going to become clichés: join the revolution and have sex with your fellow revolutionaries. Right?"

"I hope not."

"You're scaring me, Van."

"You're right. We're not in college and we're not going to become clichés. Let's enjoy the morning and pick a movie for tonight."

We kissed and settled in to talk about the next steps in our revolution.

"Let's pick an Ivy," I said. "They're all tools of corporate America and the government. Any one of them should be an easy target."

She was silent for a while.

"An Ivy; right. I wrote an article about waste at the three most prestigious research universities in the Northeast two years ago. I'll see if I can find my files."

A new pot of coffee finished brewing just as Van emerged from our library.

"Look at this stuff," she said. "The salaries of the presidents, the coaches, and key research scientists are outrageous. Greed rots the souls of those institutions and then they rot the country."

"Do you really think university salaries have an impact on values in the US?"

"I do. It's corrupting. Students see celebrity status and salaries go to the football and basketball coaches while the star players get concussions. I really think it changes the way young people see the world. And when we connect the research grants to the needs of the corporate funders, and then track the students who are instructed to find the answers the corporations have paid them to find, we get to see an even greater corruption—not just personal greed but a broken ethical system. The universities are rotten to the core."

She was making the kind of leaps that continue to get her in trouble with her editors: stating speculative theories as fact and sweeping whole groups into her circle of evil.

"I don't see the connection."

"Open your eyes, Will."

I just listened. She didn't take kindly to interruptions when she was in her preachy mode.

"If you see greed canonized and you're building up a behemoth-sized college debt, which you can pay back only if you sell your soul to some corrupt corporate giant, and some professor, who has inherited a fortune from his grandfather, tells you not to work for corporate America but to do public service, as he gets in his Range Rover to drive to the country estate he inherited, you might find yourself less than enthusiastic about the *public service* advice. And then you read about some college football coach who is reported to be a bully and a sexist, if not also a racist and a homophobe and maybe a sexual predator, negotiating a multi-year, multimillion-dollar pay package, while you struggle to afford books that are priced at more than ten times above normal retail. You might become disillusioned. That's how the universities destroy and corrupt the soul of our youth and our country."

"You're pushing it, but there may be a grain of truth in your theory. So, let's focus on one of them. We'll follow the pharma money and see where it takes us. We just need to decide which university to target."

"We shouldn't act on our own."

That confused me. "Why not?"

"We need to get everyone on board with a specific plan, otherwise they might decide they can do whatever they want and drag us into something that we don't want to be part of."

She was more tuned into the dangers of our venture than I was.

"Fine, but we have to find a place to meet. In the movies, the revolutionaries always have a bar to call their own. Let's find a place where none of us would be recognized."

She looked at me as if I were a little boy.

"Don't make fun of me, Van."

"Sorry. I really wasn't making fun of you, just your paranoia."

She was holding back a laugh. But then, with a sudden motion, she jumped up and actually said, "Eureka!"

"There's no need to ride around the city looking for the perfect bar. We can meet in our carriage house. No one even has to come to our door. We'll go in the back way from the garden, and they can go in the door on the alley. It's perfect. We'll give everyone a key. We'll get some comfortable furniture and make sure the plumbing works. And we'll get blackout shades so the lights in our little cell won't be noticeable from the street when we need to meet in deep dark secret. How cool will that be?"

She was serious.

"Brilliant idea. Let's see if we can get them all to come here next Friday night.

I've always wanted a fort in my backyard."

Chapter 21

The carriage house had enough old wicker in it for the six of us to sit.

Eric was first to speak.

"You're too much. We each get a key on a chain with an X hanging from it. Where did you find them?"

"A trinket shop on Wisconsin Avenue. I'll replace them with real silver as soon as I can."

Then all four of them looked at Van and said, "No fucking way."

"Why not? I wouldn't carry around some cheap trinket, and none of you would either."

"I think the men should have X's and the women should have O's. That could make for some very interesting games." Matthew had come a very long way from the first dinner party. Van gave him a smile.

Then Alexa said, "Why not triple X's. Maybe that's what we'll be about in the end."

Jean picked it up.

"*In the end?* Is that generational?"

We were spiraling downward.

"Okay you guys, Van still has the floor," I said.

Van nodded a thank-you.

"Yesterday, we bought furniture for this space and now that we have a place to meet, I'd like to move us into substance."

Alexa said that she couldn't wait to hear what Van considered substance; she hoped it would involve 18-karat gold necklaces for the girls and matching bracelets for the boys. She obviously had lost her patience for the material things that we had been focusing on.

"The fancy jewelry will have to wait. Will and I tried to think of a restaurant or bar that could be our meeting place. We couldn't come up with any, and then we thought of this. If you guys don't think this is right, now is the time to speak up so we can cancel the furniture order."

"It's a great spot. I vote for it."

"Thanks, Jean. Anyone else?"

Eric put his arm around Alexa and whispered in her ear. She pushed him away playfully. She said, "Okay, we're in, but I want to contribute. I'll buy us a computer and disposable prepaid cell phones to round out the conspiracy."

It was hard to tell whether she was still making fun of us.

"That would be great. Matthew is the resident techie," I said. "Maybe you can shop computers together."

"No offense, Matthew. I'll fly solo."

"No offense taken. Will was being sexist."

I didn't like the vibe. We were about to spend a pile of money to give us a place to meet, and they were dumping on us. If they saw all of this as our ego trip, it would be the end of the mission.

"This isn't some power play. If anyone has a better idea, put it on the table."

I wondered when Eric, the consensus builder, would step in. This was the moment he should smooth it all out . . . and he didn't disappoint.

"I'm stoked, Will. We can use this place for our meetings and for our private reading-room getaway. I think I speak for everyone, our poking fun at you guys aside, this is a brilliant move. Break out the bubbly, which I saw in the refrigerator, and start the meeting. You guys asked us to come over to participate in some decision that you thought required our okay. Alexa and I canceled other plans for this, so we're here and ready to function. Is everyone on board?"

Nods around. I got out two bottles of a modest French bubbly, not champagne, and poured us all a glass for our first toast in our new space.

"Here's to our venture."

We sipped our wine and settled in. Van took them through our thoughts about researching the grants from our target company to the university we had chosen for our project. She gave credit to Alexa for moving us in that direction.

Alexa couldn't hold back a sigh.

"You're kidding, right? You've called this meeting just to tell us that you want to research conflicts of interest at a university. Give me a break. You guys are still in high school."

I couldn't control myself.

"If you can't see the benefit of consensus before we launch a project, then maybe you should give us back the key and go home. Going after a university was your idea in the first place. I've had it with you."

She didn't flinch.

"I've had it with you two sophomores, as well. Enjoy your new frat house. Here's your little trinket back. I'll see you later, Eric. As for the rest of you, this is good-bye and good luck."

The room stayed silent as the sound of the front door closing echoed up the stairs. We were all a little shocked.

Eric broke the silence.

"That's her style. She'll be back."

"I don't want her back, and she doesn't get back into the group without a unanimous vote," I said.

I had begun to like her. I felt betrayed. Van's look seconded my emotions.

The rest of the meeting was subdued. Matthew agreed to take on the computer task. We all agreed the pre-paid cellphones could wait. Jean said she would start some research on the link between the drug company and the university.

We didn't open the second bottle. Alexa had sabotaged the meeting. It wasn't clear to me that we would be able to pick up the pieces.

Chapter 22

C an you believe her?"

I didn't want to pretend nothing had happened the night before.

"No, I guess we're a little tame for your young friend."

"She's less than ten years younger than we are, probably only five years, give me a break. Maybe she's right?" I approached Van and began to massage her shoulders. She leaned into my hands and rested the back of her head on my stomach and put her hands up to her shoulders to hold mine.

"I'm sure she was hoping you were going to New Haven to blow up a science lab, and you wanted everyone's buy-in. We need to expose the rotten core of our targets; bombs won't do that. We can't let some little rich girl who play acts at being a rebel while she cashes checks from her trust fund suck the wind out of our sails."

It was the pep talk I needed. I would spend the rest of the week-end researching and outlining different approaches to slice at the ties between the university and our target drug company.

"You're right. I won't let her sidetrack us."

"Right. Let's forget her and focus on what we need to do. I think you will need to do some research on-site, and you can't leave any traces. I'll get us fake IDs."

She was enjoying playing spy. And, she already had the name of a person who would provide the necessary papers. She had written an article about that part of the underworld a year ago. She protected the people who had helped her do the story. They owed her a favor.

"This is getting a little dark for me. You go to prison for using fake identities. It's no joke."

She smiled. "You're cute when you're scared. We're now part of the underworld. A fake identity is just the beginning. Wait until we buy explosives. I'll take care of everything. If the FBI tortures you, you won't be able to tell them our sources."

She didn't see the risk. She was ready to take the first step down the wrong road. I said as much. She paid no attention. And I realized we had taken the first step down the wrong road together when we let this weird group into our lives.

"We'll have to keep our new identities secret from the group. A time could come when we'll need these identities, and we won't want anyone else to know them. And tomorrow, we should move some more money into our accounts in Switzerland and Canada. I'm going to get us fake EU and Canadian passports."

She was on a roll.

"You're making me crazy."

"Sorry. I don't mean to, but we'll need the documents so we can be someone else, if that's what we need to do. While cash is king in the underworld, the real world likes credit cards. You use them to pay for lots of things, where using cash would raise questions— like train tickets and hotel rooms. We may need cards that can't be traced to us."

"Fine. Surprise me with our new names. I'm going to the library to research our target, but before I go, we should decide if it pays to furnish the carriage house. I'm not up for spending the money if this thing is going to drift off into oblivion."

She took a while to respond. "Let's not give Alexa the power to destroy our efforts. I'm sure she'll want to get back into the fold. This may sound weird, but I kind of like her. I think she may have a lot to add to the group. If it all comes apart, at least the carriage house will be furnished."

I wasn't sure she was being serious.

"She's a destructive force—self-centered, narcissistic, and full of herself. I know these are all the same. She's not a team player. She can't be trusted. If it served some hidden purpose of hers, she'd turn us all in."

I wasn't sure I could get Van to agree that any effort by Alexa to rejoin the group was a non-starter.

"Be prepared to be the only holdout. Leave yourself a little room to maneuver. I plan to vote her back in."

That was weird. She obviously saw something in Alexa I had missed.

"Thanks for the advice, but I won't need room to maneuver. She's not going to want to come back, and if she tries, my vote will be no. If her idea about tracing money into the universities proves fruitful, I'll send her a handwritten note of thanks."

Chapter 23

The main reading room in my local library was old school: four big oak tables and walls lined with bookshelves. Except for three people paging through over-sized books, the room was empty. I put my jacket over a chair that was at the end of a table, spread out my things, and settled in to let my mind drift. I needed a plan of attack.

The library's catalogue system made it easy to find histories of my target university. The task was to determine when it, and others like it, became the research arms of the chemical and pharmaceutical industries. It occurred in the late seventies after the protests of the late sixties and early seventies subsided and the budgets controlled by the science departments expanded. The cry against the military industrial complex and its ties to the universities had all but stopped and the new focus was diversity, so the insidious take over by pharma and the chemical industries went unnoticed.

I would need to trace the creation of the endowed professorships, the size of the departments, the courses offered, how they changed over the decades, and where the money came from. And I would need to match the corporate interests of members of the board of trustees to the research programs. I was outlining my next steps when my phone vibrated.

I went out onto the steps of the library and returned Van's call.

"How's it going?"

"Fine, I'm making progress. Anything you want me to pick up for dinner on my way home?"

"Nope. We're having dinner with Jean and Matthew. At their house."

I let a little silence build and then said, "I thought we agreed to keep this weekend just us. Can you call back and cancel?"

"I can't. Given Alexa's performance last night, I felt I had to say yes."

I had no desire to make small talk with Jean and Matthew, and I certainly had no desire to talk about the big questions of life and society with them either. I felt pretty much talked out.

I finished my outline and put the books I had been using on the library cart for shelving. I decided to take the long way back to our house. I hoped a walk would clear my head. I wasn't going to rush home now that Van had screwed up our evening. I sat on a bench by the river, drank coffee, and watched the people walk by. The students from the nearby college were in various forms of casual undress, and the rest were either shoppers on a mission or tourists just walking, talking, and looking. Watching people was calming. There was no reason I should resent a quiet dinner with Jean and Matthew. Van was right. There was no way she could have said no to the invitation. I would have done the same thing if the call had come to me, although I would have checked with her before saying yes. When I felt centered I headed home.

Van was sitting out on the little patio in the front of our house. Our house was set back from the sidewalk at least twenty-five feet, a luxury in Georgetown. The patio was private and shaded nicely by big trees. She was making a statement by sitting there and waiting for me.

"It's been almost two hours since we talked. You weren't answering your phone and I was getting worried."

I didn't let myself get baited, which was, I assumed, her plan—to bait me and get rid of her guilt for screwing up our quiet evening.

"I took a long walk, sat on a bench, and people-watched. I shut off my phone after we talked. I'm home now, and I'm ready for an evening with Jean and Matthew."

"Are you being sarcastic?"

"No. At first I was pretty pissed. Now I'm fine with it."

"I'm sorry I didn't check with you before I accepted."

I moved closer to her on the bench and put my arm around her shoulder.

"It's really okay. We have the rest of the afternoon. Let's check out the carriage house to be sure it's ready for the furniture."

She smiled for the first time since I returned. "Good idea."

We walked around to the alley and used our key with the X dangling from the chain. The carriage house was clean and neat; we had spent time straightening it up after everyone left the night before.

"We should get in the habit of using this place. It's cozy."

She took my hand and walked me into the bedroom. I set the alarm on my phone in case we decided to sleep some.

I was glad I did. It woke us up.

And, like a scene from a chick flick, we both looked around to try to figure out where we were and why we were naked on a mattress on the floor.

Chapter 24

Jean and Matthew also lived in an Arts and Crafts–style house made from rough-cut stone set off with grapevine grouting. Jean welcomed us into a large living room with a very strong stone fireplace. The dining room was on the other side of the entrance. There were no doors, just large square archways. The rooms were warm with dark oak paneling and Stickley, Morris, and Wright furniture and artifacts, which were past their hundredth year of use; they didn't appear to be replicas. I liked the feel of the place, and I found it interesting that Eric, Jean, and Matthew had the same early twentieth-century aesthetic.

"We're happy you were free tonight. When we discussed how last night ended, we thought getting together, just the four of us, would be a good idea. Matthew and I don't want the fire to be put out just because Alexa had a tantrum. She'll come around soon."

I dropped Jean's hand, which I had been holding ever since she gave me a warm hug at our entrance.

"It's great to be here. I'm looking forward to getting to know the two of you without the complexity of the larger group. You should know I'm not much interested in whether Alexa *comes around*, as you put it. As far as I'm concerned, she's history."

Matthew came out of the kitchen just as I finished speaking.

"Talking about our favorite loose cannon?"

"Yes. But this evening shouldn't be about Alexa or Eric, for that matter, it should be about the four of us."

At this point, Jean motioned for us to sit.

"Of course, Will, I agree. On a more neutral note: What are you guys drinking?"

"White or red is fine with me, Jean?"

I didn't feel like drinking wine. "If a beer is handy, that would be great."

Matthew disappeared for a minute and came back with a big glass of red for Van and a micro-brew for me.

"Thanks, this is good. I see so many of these in the store and I have no clue how to choose."

"Just pick any pack of four and keep notes. It won't take long to figure out what suits your taste. In the end, however, it's just beer."

That felt a little hostile.

"I'll never drink a commercial beer again," I said. I hadn't ruined the evening by being overly sensitive, but we had a good three hours to go. I ventured to move the conversation forward.

"This is a great place; my favorite type of house."

"Why is that?"

I chose to ignore his sharp tone. It wasn't going to be an easy evening.

"These houses seem anchored. Being in them is like having both feet on the ground."

I had always liked these bungalows, which were everywhere in the city except for where we lived. Our neighborhood predated the movement by at least fifty years.

"I agree. This house does make me feel centered. So much so that I've set up my studio upstairs. I've never had a studio in my house before and now that I do, I find it's a perfect place to work."

"Maybe at some point you could show us your studio."

Van shot me a glance, and I knew exactly what she was thinking. *What are you doing? Going into someone's studio whose work you don't know is a recipe for disaster.* I gave her the tiniest of shrugs to let her know that I was aware of the risk.

"Sure. We can take a tour; it's just up these stairs. You have only seen a sketch of my work on my phone. The real work is hard to penetrate. Very few people understand it or like it. You're free to react any way that suits you. I don't care about people's reactions. I need to make it and that's all that counts."

Matthew's studio was spectacular. It was the entire second floor of the house: there were double dormers on each side of the very big room. There was a long table angled in a corner so none of the light from the dormers or the two large skylights could shine on his computers. There was an array of screens and black and silver boxes with red, green, and blue lights. It looked like a mini control room with racks filled with electronics on either side of the table. It was quite a sight.

Angled in the other corner, also free from the glare of the windows and skylights, was a mission library table with four straight-backed matching chairs—two faced the middle of the room and one was on either side of the table. To secure its authenticity, there were two old library table lamps with green glass shades set symmetrically about two feet in from either end of the table. This little corner, which also had a rocking chair and a swivel bookshelf for the current books and a standup shelf for the giant Webster's could have been in the New York Public Library. The table was full of neat piles of clippings from newspapers and magazines. Jean and Matthew were not struggling to put food on the table. Their surroundings were no less high end than ours.

Across from his two desks were four full-sized easels, each with what I judged to be 18 by 48-inch canvases—the four horizontals looked like they were pieces in progress. They seemed to read from left to right. I was good at deciphering patterns, and the lines and colors in Matthew's paintings jumped out at me as a series I could recognize. It felt like I was looking at several electrocardiograms gone haywire and on top of each other. It wasn't easy to put the patterns together to see a whole, but I saw it. Then over-layered on the heart chart were a series of more complicated patterns, each in its own color and thickness. It was not the type of painting that I was usually drawn to, but there was something about the way these four interrelated and their 16-foot scale that had me captured. Matthew could see I was intrigued.

"These are terrific. Not the kind of art I usually connect with, but you've captured me."

"Good. Someday, if we become friends, I'll tell you what it all means."

Between Alexa and Matthew, I was constantly running some form of defense. The simplest comments put me close to declaring war. I was tired of it.

"I'll pass on the meaning, thanks."

Van missed the exchange. She looked at the paintings, which obviously did not excite her, and managed a comment or two. It was time to go back down to dinner.

Jean was in the kitchen. "It's a nice place for my husband, the cerebral artist, don't you think?"

"He certainly has created a space fit for a very big and private brain."

Jean winced.

"I guess he managed to offend you up there. When he's research-ing a painting and beginning to develop its patterns, he gets crazy if anyone says anything about it."

Jean was trying hard to cover for Matthew.

"Then I guess he shouldn't have taken us to his studio. "

Matthew, who had been busy opening wine for dinner, heard the tail end of my comment.

"You asked to see it, Will."

Van sensed that I might not be civil and stepped in.

"Subject change, you guys. Last night we talked about the role of universities in the corruption of our society, and today, coinciden-tally, the papers ran a story about how the big chemical and food companies are buying academics to help them with their lobbying efforts. Today it was sugar. Did you know that a soda with eight tablespoons of sugar in twelve ounces is good for you? At least that's what one research professor has determined. There are lots of issues to occupy our time other than Matthew's art."

"Now children, play nice."

Jean was full of surprises.

"Okay. We'll behave if Matthew will soften a little around the edges," I said. With that settled, Jean motioned us all to sit down for dinner.

The dinner was simple and tasty. I hadn't had beef stew at a din-ner party since graduate school. It fit the feel of the house. I stayed with beer while the others drank a red wine. Our conversation wasn't too serious. We shared stories about growing up and a few from our early careers, as well. And then Matthew pushed his chair back and took us into a new direction.

"I assume you guys know there is nothing random in the apparent chaos of the world."

Matthew said this with a genuine seriousness, even though there was a slight slur in his speech.

"I've been working on chaos theory for twenty years. Chaos is not random. It just works from a different vocabulary. There is a predetermined pattern. We just don't know when it was determined and how the pattern moves and develops, but we will someday, and then the future will be like the past—they'll fold in on each other. Kind of a scary thought."

"No shit, scary," I said with a little too much emphasis on *scary.*

"I'm serious, Will. Whoever gets to crack the code gets to rule the world.

Van couldn't resist.

"Sounds like a job for 007."

Matthew wasn't amused. "Make fun, but some of the best minds on Earth believe we are living in a totally predetermined bubble and that nothing will be free until the bubble is burst by a simple mathematical formula."

Van was in recovery mode.

"I hope you're the one so we can beat the capitalists into submission."

Jean took charge to move the evening along before Van took it further downhill.

"At some point, Matthew will explain how chaos theory is important to what we decide to do in our group, but until then, how about desert, coffee, and cognac in the living room? Matthew, can you help?"

Van and I went across to the living room and took chairs at opposite ends of the large stone fireplace so that we could signal each other if the conversation went in the wrong direction. Neither of us could place Matthew's detour into chaos theory anywhere near what we were all doing. I thought it was probably the wine. Jean and Matthew came out with a very delicious-looking apple pie.

"Pie and politics. That's our motto. We understand that Will is going to do some serious research on our target, but then what?"

I was hoping that Van would take Jean's question. She did.

"Our expectations are pretty low. We'll expose the depth of the corruption in the research labs to see if it will energize the students. We want them to protest the role of the university in the capitalist structure like they did in the sixties and seventies. We don't have the Vietnam War draft, the civil rights movement, the women's movement, or the sexual revolution to fuel the students. So, it won't be easy. We want to see if anything will motivate them other than their identity politics. We need to know if they'll be a force for change."

That helped me figure out what I was doing.

"Do we infiltrate the student body to make sure it all moves in the direction we want it to? I know how to do that."

I was curious to see how Van would respond to Jean.

"That wouldn't be my choice. If we can't get the students to be outraged, then we'll have to do the dirty work ourselves. This is just a warm-up."

Matthew got up and stretched. "I'm with Jean: I think we should infiltrate the student body. I don't think it will spontaneously combust."

I was tired. I wanted to bring the conversation to a close. I got up as well and said, "'Let's make the world spontaneously combust' would be a good motto. We can have it made into a banner to hang over the fireplace."

That got some smiles.

"But now I have to go home and get some sleep. This has been a great evening. It's nice to begin to get to know each other."

"Yes, it has. Remember, I'll pick you up at eleven tomorrow, and we'll get a computer and set your carriage house up with untraceable accounts and give you a secret identity so you can research to your heart's content."

I had forgotten that I had made that plan with Matthew. I had been thinking about a late morning sleep-in and a relaxed day. That was now just a distant dream. We said our goodnights and were off.

Chapter 25

My weekend was full of revolution: researching, dinner with Jean and Matthew, buying a computer, and setting up a new untraceable Internet account. Coming into the office, even with the deal hanging over my head, was a welcome diversion. The comforting routine of a usual Monday morning didn't last for more than an hour.

Jim came into my office and closed the door. That was not a good sign. I got up from behind my desk and we sat at the small conference table in a corner.

"To what do I owe such an honor this Monday morning, Jim?"

"It's off to the city for you. This is the critical week. It will be just you and our senior lawyer for our side. Your job is to finish hammering out the rights and responsibilities of the members of the consortium. Who better to make the compromises that will be needed than you?"

There was a gleam in his eyes as he delivered the assignment. It was out of character. He wasn't a mean person. I must have really hurt his feelings over the last few weeks.

"Is this a sick joke?"

"No. The integrity of the paper is in your hands. I thought you'd like that. It will give you and Van something to talk about when I'm gone."

This was one of the most bizarre conversations I'd ever had with my father-in-law. And we had had some off-the-wall talks since I married Van and moved into a house that was way too big and pretentious for us.

He had set me up. When the paper was totally controlled by stealth outsiders, my complaining to Van would be pointless, since it would have been me who gave away the crown jewels.

"Well done. I'm up for it, *Dad.*"

I never called him Dad. He gave me a knowing look and got up from his chair. He knew our relationship was now in serious disrepair.

"Glad you're on board, *son.* Our lawyers expect you at their offices at five. They've put you in the Mandrake, which is just two blocks from their offices. I know you and Van prefer the boutique hotels, but they're too expensive. Appearance counts, don't you think?"

He said this while standing behind his chair and leaning a little forward. I couldn't tell if the lean was for casualness or for emphasis.

"I'm sure the hotel will be fine. I appreciate your concern. Do I need a secret handshake to be part of the group?"

"No, but you should take your passport. You never know when you might have to get out of the country fast."

I was on the three o'clock shuttle to New York with a plane full of very uptight business travelers and, I guess, that's what I looked like, as well. The trip was too short to focus on my university research or the deal. I just stared into space. I was on autopilot getting my roller bag out of the overhead and heading for the exit.

I figured forty minutes to Midtown, ten minutes to check in, and about five minutes to walk to my lawyer's office should get me there close to five o'clock. I was the client. The show would have to wait for me if I wasn't exactly on time.

The hotel was big for my taste, and the bar had the look of a high-class pick-up spot. I'd want a scotch at the end of the night, and I didn't feel like being accosted by the fancy all-night, sleep-in-your-room, big-city women. I would want to sip my scotch alone with no interruptions and then go to bed alone. I hoped the bartender could waive off unwanted solicitations.

The lawyers had booked a small suite to give me room to work. They had booked it for the week. The living room was a real room; not just an alcove for a couch and a TV, and there was a small hallway that led to the bedroom. There were two bathrooms. It was a corner suite. I had windows facing east and south down Park Avenue. The street noise would be there but not as bad as it might have been if I had been on a lower floor. It really wasn't half as bad as I thought it would be.

I unpacked my clothes and laid out my papers in stacks on the desk in the living room. I felt settled and ready to head to the battlefield. There was nothing in store for me but aggression and losses—all zero-sum issues. It was not the kind of game I liked to play.

The walk to my lawyer's office was long enough to let me know I was in the city. It was too full of smells and people and stimuli to make me comfortable. Washington was much more my speed. And the Middleburg house was probably my ideal pace: quiet with plenty of time to think and listen to the sounds of the natural world. It was counterproductive to be longing for the pastoral. I had to sharpen my edge. Whatever could be salvaged in this deal could only be salvaged by me, and I wouldn't be able to win anything if I were dreaming about horses and cows and big shade trees.

The paper's law firm was first tier with over two thousand lawyers and offices in a half dozen cities in the US, Europe, and Asia. My team was led by one of their senior corporate lawyers, and three other lawyers, arranged by rank, assisted her. It was like a *New Yorker* cartoon—the most junior had the biggest stack of paper in front of her; the next, a senior associate, had a stack half the size of the junior person, and then the young partner had a stack again only half the size of the stack in front of the senior associate. Our leader, of course, had a single page in front of her. It really was a storybook form of command. I couldn't hold back my smile.

"I'm glad to see you're in good spirits, Will. Perhaps better than the last time we were together."

"Probably not. I'm smiling, Christine, because your team is arrayed according to age and paper. It's amusing."

"We have found this staffing pattern works well for our clients."

This was going to be all business, at least while the young lawyers were in the room. "Great. Where do we begin?"

That was what she wanted. The next two hours were spent on the details of the issues and background of the players and the idiosyncrasies of their lawyers. We were scheduled for negotiations from ten to six each day for the next three days. The evenings would be spent in dealing with the events of the day and preparing for the next day. The deadline was to have the deal done by Friday. If Christine and I disagreed on an issue, she was to set up a call with Jim to resolve the issue.

I wasn't too tired to let the process go unchallenged.

"Okay, but if you go over my head more often than I think you should, I'll lobby to have you replaced."

She smiled and sat back in her chair.

"Fair enough. Those are the rules most companies establish. You've seen me in action on this deal. I thought we got along fine."

"We did. I hope we still will."

She got up and put her pad and the paper prepared for her by her team in her brief case.

"It's our first night. I can have dinner brought in, we can all go out to dinner, or you can have the night to yourself. It will be the only night this week that will be yours. I own you for the rest of the week."

"Own me?"

"Yes, for breakfast before the meetings, during the meetings, and for the evening until we feel we're ready for the next day. It's your call for tonight."

"If you don't think it rude, I'd just as soon have the night to myself. I could use the evening to get my head around what we've discussed and to get some rest."

"Good call. I'd love to have a night with my family. We'll meet here tomorrow morning at eight thirty. There will be a light breakfast in the conference room."

She walked me to the elevator.

"Will, this won't be easy. Let's do our best to save as much of the free press as we can."

Chapter 26

I found a seat at a corner of the bar. The place was noisy, but I was too tired to go elsewhere. I was in the mood to sip a good scotch, have a burger, and then watch a movie in my room. I was not looking forward to the week.

As I was finishing my scotch, I noticed the place was emptying, slowly morphing into the atmosphere I preferred. I gave a quick glance at the menu to be sure a burger was what I wanted. The bartender took my order and poured me a draft. I assumed she was an actor bartending to pay the rent. All the bartenders and waiters in the city seemed to be actors or artists working to survive.

I was about to ask her the usual questions—What have you been in? Are you auditioning for anything now?—but a soft hand on my shoulder stopped me. The bartender looked away and I turned to see Alexa.

"Hi Will."

As I was processing my feelings, I noticed the bartender giving a serious look our way. I assume she thought Alexa, who was not a familiar face, was soliciting me and that I should be protected. Newcomers in the trade were not allowed unless properly vetted by management.

"Alexa, what can I get you to drink?" I said her name so the bartender would know this was someone I knew. She came over, took Alexa's order, and the embarrassment of the moment passed.

"Did you just pick this bar out of the ten thousand bars in the city?"

"No. I wanted to have some time alone with you. It wasn't hard to track you down. I asked Eric to ask Van. I arranged meetings here in the city at the last minute to make this happen."

"Is Eric here, too?"

"No, I'm flying solo. We'll see how the night develops."

She was a piece of work. Hell would freeze over before I'd spend the night with her.

"Solo sounds right. I'll buy you dinner, if sitting at the bar is okay with you."

"The bar is perfect."

She looked at the menu and ordered a burger.

"I want to apologize for the other night. I get weird when I think others are playing around the edges of what I care about. I get that way in my lab when some of the researchers take our work lightly. I get that way with Eric, who doesn't really care about issues that are important to me, or any issues at all as far as I can tell. And I was feeling that way when you were all talking about solving the corruption basic to our university structure by seeing if you could inspire a sit-in."

I wasn't pleased that she had shown up, but I had to be civil.

"I think you missed the point. The university target, which was your idea, was to test our ability to motivate young people to seek change. It happened in the sixties and seventies, and the question is, without sex and the other sixties' motivators, can young people be catalyzed to act on issues other than the cancel culture they find safe to rally around? And if not, which I suspect will be the outcome, what new strategies do we have to develop? Should they involve trying to create a movement or should they be more subtle, and rifle shot?"

"I didn't miss it. And, by the way, you won't get anywhere if you put down their identity politics. Caring about those issues defines the generation you're trying to reach. Even if the number of people discriminated against is small compared to the number of people who are poor and hungry and without health insurance, the students are right to try to protect them. It would be a mistake to belittle their commitment to their view of what is right."

She looked at her glass and, seeing that both of our glasses were empty, ordered another beer for us to share.

"I know, but if those in power can keep the college kids focused on issues that don't impact the distribution of wealth to the top, they win. That's the plan of the power elite, and it's something we have to fix."

"A global conspiracy fueled by the press to occupy liberal minds with social issues to keep them from focusing on the distribution of wealth is a sound theory. But back to my point: the problem with your proposed effort to get the students fired up is that it's too little, too late, and too slow. I have no doubt that you can get some students to demonstrate at the bio labs funded by the pharma and chemical companies—so what?

The money will come in through the back door from a no-name foundation; the university will get its overhead, the researchers will keep their jobs, and life as we know it will go on. The CEO will earn another huge bonus for sneaking another one past the FDA. We need to attack the CEOs. That's where it starts."

The conversation was interrupted by our dinner. The burgers were great. We ate them without too much talking. We were starved. This was a perfect dinner in a perfect setting.

"I'm glad I didn't have to track you down in some fancy restaurant."

I rotated my bar stool so that I was directly facing her. We must have looked like lovers with our faces just a few inches apart.

"So, tell me the real reason you've gone through the trouble to find me. I assume it wasn't to apologize, although I appreciate the apology. I assume you know you're on my shit list."

She feigned looking hurt, put her hand on mine, and pretended to beg for forgiveness. I couldn't believe how expressive her eyes were. They said she was sorry, that she would behave in the future, that she loved all of us, that she wanted to get to know us better, that she was 100 percent behind our work, and she would support whatever strategies we developed. That's what I took from looking into her eyes for probably what amounted to two seconds. She still had her hand on mine when she spoke.

"That's not true. I see something in you, some spark that tells me we are going to do great things together. You want me back in the group. You want to get to know me, and you want to fuck me."

She could see she shocked me.

"Is that too real for you? Should I have said you want to become friends and then make love to me?"

She didn't say any of this aggressively. I was still without words.

"Don't look stunned. I knew from our first meeting that we were destined to connect. So, here I am, alone in this big city with no place to stay tonight. You can sleep with me, if you want to, or you can just put me up in your room. I am happy to sleep on the floor."

I was about to say something. She put two soft fingers on my lips to give herself the chance to finish.

"I have big plans, but I can't reveal them until we are bonded. I have a plan that requires help, and my instinct tells me that you're the one to be my partner."

I thought she was playing another one of her games. She would take a picture of us together and send it to Eric and Van with a caption: "Will hitting on defenseless Alexa." But she now had my hand in both of her hands and something about the way she was holding on to me gave me the feeling she was serious.

I wasn't sure how to respond. I extricated my hand to reach for my glass, which was empty. She relaxed her shoulders and signaled the bartender for another beer to share. That was fine with me, except that I needed to pee.

On my way back to the bar, I could see Alexa and the bartender talking.

"I'm back."

"Yes, we can see. This is Anna, our bartender, in case you didn't introduce yourself. She's between auditions. It's hard for actors to pay their bills. I told her that you were on a very generous expense account and that at the end of the night, when she counted her tips, she would find that she has made the rent for the month."

"Sure," was the only correct answer.

"See, Anna, I told you this guy was good for it. And unless he kills the idea, I think we should switch from beer to the Irish coffee you were telling me about. If you are famous for them, we should give them a try."
I nodded my ascent, and Anna was off to make our drinks.

"What have you gotten me into?"

"Not much. She said she was short about a hundred dollars for her rent, which is due tomorrow. I told her you'd add that to her tip. If you don't want to, I'll cover it."

"I'll do it, but for the record, I don't like being forced into things."

"Sorry. Just one more force, okay? Can I stay with you tonight? I'm homeless and this hotel is full."

"You're serious?"

"Yup."

"Okay. You can use the living room. I'm sure the couch is a pull-out."

"Thanks. I'll walk over to the drug store and get a few things. I didn't have time to pack."

This was a very strange Monday: off to the city to negotiate with the dark side to try to salvage the integrity of the free press *and* propositioned by Alexa, who was planning to sleep in my living room. I was glad I had been booked a suite with two bathrooms.

Our Irish coffees arrived in snifters full of whiskey and whipped cream with brown sugar and a liqueur that matched the coffee and the Irish whiskey perfectly. They really were special, and with the first sip, we both knew we were in for two of these wonderful drinks. And I knew I was going to be totally wasted.

"Let's put aside the lovemaking issue for a moment." She said this as if she were a long-term friend with benefits. "At some point, we're going to talk about my plan, which is dangerous and has to be a secret for now. That's why I'm here and why you need to let me back into the group. And you have to agree that when I go to the drug store, you won't call Van and say, 'You won't believe what that crazy weirdo has done: she's here trying to fuck me and fuck with our venture with some secret dangerous plan of hers.' If I put my trust in you, you must return it in kind. I'm dead serious."

The Irish whiskey was doing what the scotch and the beers hadn't quite done. It moved me into very mellow territory.

"I don't keep secrets from Van."

"I'm fine with you telling her I'm here. I just don't want you telling her that I have some secret plan. If you care about her, you need to keep her in the dark. I need your word that whatever we discuss will stay between us. Only I will have the right to bring Van into the tent."

My thoughts were jumping between *this is intriguing* and *who is this nut case?* I decided I would roll with the evening and take stock in the morning when I'd be surrounded by cold, rational lawyers.

"Your secret will be safe with me until I think I'll be safer sharing it. That's as much as I can commit to at this point. I will, of course, tell Van you are here and sleeping in my suite. So, let's finish these drinks, and then you can go to the drug store, and I can do a little work before you come to my room to tell me your secrets, if I'm not too tired to focus."

I always requested hotels make me two keys: one for my pocket and one for my briefcase. I slipped one key to Alexa and wrote the room number on a napkin. Anna saw the transaction and smiled. Paying her rent was worth it. The rush of this make-believe was stimulating.

"I won't be long. Don't be asleep when I get back. We have a lot to talk about."

She leaned over and kissed me on the mouth. Not a long kiss but a solid kiss. This was not good. Even if I couldn't tell Van about Alexa's plan, whatever it might be, I sure as hell was going to tell her about the kiss.

Chapter 27

I was tired and had no enthusiasm for the negotiations. At best, I registered every third word of my lawyer's briefing. We had a few minutes before we had to infiltrate the enemy lines. I poured us each a little more coffee and asked for her best guess as to where the negotiations would end up.

"We won't be able to move the needle very far. Your father-in-law wants the deal pretty much the way it's structured. Take some comfort in the fact that this deal was done before you had anything to do with it."

"I've been told that you're the best, so why can't you help fix this?"

"Forces considerably more powerful than the companies we have been negotiating with control this deal. This is the final piece of a master plan. I've watched it develop for a few years, both from the sidelines and in the trenches. This piece of the puzzle makes me sad."

I knew she wouldn't tell me who was behind it. I didn't even bother to ask. She said it was time to go, and I doubted she would share any more of her thoughts about the deal with me.

She was impressive. Her face changed ever so slightly, which signaled that she had returned to her role as the lawyer who had to wrap up the deal before the end of the week. There were a few business points she had to win and that was that. The editorial control issues had been decided long ago, but we would go through the charade of negotiating them. I was there for show.

The day was awful: tedious, contentious, and totally boring. At one point, I noted for the record that the deal would provide an opportunity for the Federal Trade Commission to come after the papers for fraud. My lawyer called for a break so she could talk with her client, me. We went into a small side conference room.

"What are you doing, Will? You did this the last time we were together. I thought you understood the risk. Keep your feelings to yourself. These people will sell you out without giving it a thought. Got it?"

"Sorry, but if they're so evil, how can you do this day in and day out?"

"That's a long story. Maybe someday I'll show you my life and you can show me yours."

I promised to behave, and we both went back into the conference room: she with a docile client and me with a deeper appreciation for her.

When the negotiating session was over, we walked back to her offices to debrief her team. I hoped that my night with my lawyers would be short. It was. I thanked them for their hard work and my gladiator walked me to the elevator.

"Will, we may get it done tomorrow. Your only hope is that the controllers, as I like to call them, become so heavy-handed the outside world sees what's going on and comes to your rescue."

She reached out her hand for mine and we were done for the night.

Outside in the dark, I took deep gulps of air. Even though it was city air, it helped settle me down. Van's father had sold the soul of our paper and countless other papers, and there was nothing to be done about it. To the outside world, this was just a deal to share printing plants and ink and trucks and people. It will be hailed as a model for other industries to follow in this short-term, profit-driven global economy. The dangers will go unnoticed.

With that thought, I took one more deep breath and walked back to the hotel. I hoped Alexa was still there. If not, then I hoped Anna the bartender would be there. A friendly face would make my dinner more relaxed.

The bar stool I had sat in last night was waiting for me and Alexa, in the same clothes she had worn the day before, sat adjacent at a right angle.

I kissed her on the cheek. She pulled back. She looked into my eyes and leaned over and kissed me on the mouth. I was a little surprised. We were in a public space. Van and I shied away from public displays of affection. Our bartender smiled and came over.

"Nice to see you two are still together."

I was about to protest, but Alexa put her hand on my thigh to signal silence.

"He's a hot one, and if you're interested, you could join us upstairs later."

Our bartender, with a big smile, said, "Maybe. I'll see how tired I am when the bar closes." She gave Alexa a look that I couldn't read and went to the other side of the bar to get drinks for the people sitting there.

Alexa left her hand on my thigh until I put my hand on hers and brought both hands to the surface so Anna could see that we had all four hands on the bar.

Anna asked if we were going eat at the bar, at a table, or in our room. She was trying very hard to contain herself. I wondered if she and Alexa had previously agreed to see which one of them could embarrass me the most.

"We're eating at the bar if that's okay with you, dear," I said, taking both of Alexa's hands in mine.

"That would be fine, as long as we can take our cognac to your room, I mean, our room."

She had me. The bartender raised her eyebrows in mock dismay and brought over two menus. At this point, I wondered whether she had taken our picture and posted it on a half dozen platforms with the caption: *Another lonely businessman in over his head.* Alexa could hardly contain her laughter.

"Are you done? I'm very glad I don't have to have dinner alone or with my lawyers, and I would like to be glad I'm having dinner with you, but you're making me very uncomfortable. I assume that is what you and Anna planned. Is the bar okay for dinner or would you like to go somewhere else?"

"I like it here. It's quiet and easy. Let's eat here and then go up to the room, if you don't mind me bunking in with you another night."

She was an enigma: one part hard, two parts strong, four parts very smart, one part funny, three parts sexy and beautiful, and one part soft and vulnerable. I couldn't really tell what parts were at work anymore. She had charmed me.

"Sure. We can watch a movie."

"We'll see," she said.

And that was the end of our planning. We ordered a repeat of the night before. We stayed in serious conversation about the world and our places in it until past eleven. She didn't show any of the craziness that had me vowing never to let her back into the group. I couldn't tell if it was because Eric wasn't with her, or if it was because she was getting to know me better.

I took her hand in mine and leaned in close to her. "Alexa, you're so interesting and rational here with no hint of the volatility and hostility you've shown whenever we've been with the group. I like this version of you very much. The other you is not my favorite. Why the difference?"

I was attracted to her at some deep level. Van was right. The XDS was going to push boundaries.

She leaned back on her stool.

"Will, I want you to kiss me."

I hesitated, pondering my commitment to Van and my values, and tried to assess whether kissing Alexa was okay. I decided it was a very small breach, which I would share with Van as soon as I got home, and so I kissed her twice, softly.

"That was nice," she said.

It was weird. I hadn't kissed another woman since I met Van. I had a lot of sorting out to do.

"So, which one of you is the real you?"

"This is the real me. The DC persona is for Eric and the others who like to feel the energy of a young, aggressive, beautiful, mixed race, rich PhD who threw rocks at the World Bank. I play into their hands for some reason I can't quite figure out. I'm sure it's not a lofty reason."

I was about say something, I'm not sure what, but she put up her hand so she could finish.

"Don't misunderstand me. I like Eric enough to sleep with him, for now. But I don't think his values align with my own. I'm pretty sure yours and Van's align with mine. Eric has a secret he keeps well hidden. I think it's fundamental to who he projects himself to be to the outside world. If I put on my most conspiratorial hat, I think his secret is something that would make us wish he didn't know our names."

"That's kind of a harsh indictment, but I think I had a glimpse the other day of what you're talking about. I remember telling myself to be careful. I can't remember why. Is that what you mean?"

She leaned closer to me.

"Yes, we both need to watch him. So, you have to let me back into the group."

"I definitely want you back in the group."

She smiled. "Good. Let's seal your re-endorsement with another kiss. A kiss won't compromise your marriage, will it?"

"I don't know. I'll see how Van reacts."

"You're planning to tell her we kissed?"

"We don't have secret lives. I guess kissing me is either okay with Eric or none of his business?"

"I put it in the *none of his business* category. And I'm giving you fair warning: I may want to do more than kiss you tonight."

A kiss was enough of a stretch for me. I couldn't see myself becoming more intimate with her. I felt like I was on the steep downward hill of a roller coaster.

"Don't worry, I'm not ready to go all the way, yet. Mostly, I want to talk about revolution: what it means, how it can be done, and the risks we must take. We need to have the conversation we were too tired to have last night. Let's pay Anna and go up to your room. And remember, you've agreed to keep what we discuss a secret, even from Van. You're still bound."

"Yes, I am."

"There is one possible hitch to my plan," she said with a broad smile.

"What's that?"

"If our fabulously sexy bartender takes me up on my offer, our night will take a different turn. Is that okay with you?"

"Give me a break. Don't keep teasing me."

"I'm not."

Chapter 28

Van and I were in our ritual positions in the living room sipping a fine single malt before dinner. I had come home directly from the airport and changed into jeans and a sweater, and Van came home earlier than usual so that we could reconnect.

"Did you destroy our heritage?"

I leaned toward her, and we clinked glasses.

"I did. That's what your father had planned and had asked me to do. My lawyer told me it was the only course available. She knew the downside to the deal but had no way to fix it. I wish she lived here. We could invite her into the group. She was first class."

"If she was so good and you're so good, why didn't the two of you kill the editorial panel?"

"Because your father told her that she wasn't authorized to help me derail the deal, and editorial control is the key to the deal. She suggested there were well-hidden puppet masters who have created this deal as part of a much larger master plan. Frankly, I think your father might be one of them or, at least, he is obligated to them in some way."

That got her full attention.

"Maybe his dark past is catching up with him."

That was the first time I had ever heard her talk about her father as if he had a dark past.

"What past?"

She wasn't going to answer the question. I decided not to push. "I'm beat. New York has drained me. I hope we have a free weekend. No friends, no family, no concerts; just us."

"We don't. I've set up a meeting for Friday night. Should we ask your new lawyer friend to fly down and join us?"

Her edge was palpable. It was as if she knew I was holding something back.

"I'm not in the mood for your sarcasm, Van. I'm really whipped. And, no, I don't think we should ask her to join us. Instead, I think we should ask Alexa to come back."

"Whoa—where's that coming from?"

"Having her sleep in my suite for two nights has changed my mind about her."

Her response was immediate. "What the fuck."

I told her the story.

"She just showed up and asked to sleep with you?"

She was trying to be cool and modern, but she was pissed.

"No. She asked to sleep in my hotel room. I had a suite: two rooms and two bathrooms. It gave me someone to drink and talk with so that I could keep my sanity, and it gave me a unique opportunity to get to know her."

"Unique opportunity? Is that what you call it? This is like a cheap novel. Husband goes away on a business trip and sleeps with a friend.

Buying someone from an escort service would have been better than sleeping with Alexa."

I stayed calm.

"Yes, that's probably true, but guess what? I didn't sleep with her, as tempting as that might have been, but I did kiss her."

"You what—on the cheek, the mouth, tongues? You really are in deep shit."

"It was no big deal. And, by the way, she's way more rational and thoughtful than she has appeared to us in the group. Her DC persona is one that plays to Eric's need to feel young and radical. She questions how much of his left-wing politics are an act."

"That's disloyal. She definitely can't be trusted."

"She was just being open about her boyfriend. I want to invite her back into the group. She'll be an asset."

Van stayed silent for a while.

"No more kissing and no touching, right."

"Absolutely, no more."

I tipped my glass to her. I had a lot to sort out about Alexa, but one thing was for sure: she and I were now comrades.

"Did you and your new plaything plan a grand strategy for the XDS as your bodies relaxed under the sheets?"

"We were never in the same bed, but we did plan a strategy as we drank beers and ate burgers at the bar."

"Do tell."

I told her that Alexa's plan was for the group to try to mobilize students and young faculty to keep Eric, Matthew, and Jean occupied while the three of us planned and executed a more direct strike at the executive level of our target company.

"So much for honesty and transparency."

"That's one way to look at it."

"Actually, Will, it's the only way to look at it."

"Alexa thinks executing interventions at the highest levels of our target requires a very small group that's tightly bonded and trustworthy. She wants to be careful about revealing her thoughts. She thinks Eric is a spy for some nameless federal agency."

Van sipped the rest of her scotch and motioned for more.

"I'm opposed to a secret inner-circle."

"Okay. No secret threesome. I'll tell her your views when I invite her for tomorrow night."

Van had responded just as Alexa thought she would, so, with her decision not to be part of a secret subgroup, I began my double life.

"Why should you invite her? Just tell Eric to bring her along?"

That gave me an opening to close the subject.

"Not feeling much like a feminist today?"

"You're right. I'll invite her. Now let's make dinner and talk about the paper and, if you're not careful, I'll want to talk more about your kissing experience."

We had a quiet dinner. From an aerial view, we were the typical upper-class foodie couple: eating fish and organic salads and drinking carefully chosen wine.

It wasn't our liveliest dinner. Van didn't question me about Alexa, and she was less interested in the details of the paper deal than I thought she'd be. She was interested in setting an agenda for our meeting with the group and whether it should be pizza and beer or sushi and wine. She seemed quite out of character.

"Pizza and beer would be the easiest, and we should put on the agenda whether the food responsibilities should rotate or whether we should just stock up with peanut butter and crackers instead."

"Good for you, Will. That'll win their hearts and souls: a discussion about pretzels and potato chips. This is not a time for high school dance planning. We'll take care of the food."

I decided not to call her out on her hostile response, since I assumed it was coming from my revelation about spending the evenings with Alexa.

"We can rotate the responsibility. I'll get the pizza."

That satisfied her. She tried to refocus. "So, what should we put on the agenda?"

Something inside me resisted being serious.

"We could take off our clothes and get to know each other better."

"Shit, you did sleep with Alexa."

"That was a joke, Van. Lighten up. The agenda is simple. We've chosen a target company and university. I've done a fair amount of research to show how deeply they are connected. We can discuss how to get out the information in a way that might shake things up."

It was late and the next day was going to be full of debriefing meetings for the key management people. Each group had to be told a slightly different version of the deal. Only Van's father and I knew the whole deal. The conspiracy had started. I was chief implementer.

"Van, if the group decides to blow up buildings, the paper should be a target. Then I can tell the authorities that some mysterious group is after me and that should keep the officials off our trail."

She got up and said, "On that scary note, let's call it a night."

Chapter 29

Eric was the first to arrive. Alexa decided to wait for a call before coming, since a unanimous vote was needed to let her back into the group.

"I told her it wouldn't be necessary now that the two of you were so close. But she said rules were rules and she would play by them. I guess you had a profound effect on her, Will. Two nights in your hotel room and she has become a different person; it's like she's moved from being a rebellious teenager to a woman. You must be a very powerful person."

Eric left no space for me to respond.

"She told me you were in some intense deal negotiations involving your paper. Maybe that should be the subject of our meeting."

He had put a distance between us that was very wide.

"I'm glad that Alexa has moved into womanhood status in your mind. I hope that doesn't disappoint you. I thought she was a woman the first time I laid eyes on her. And she is quite a woman, isn't she?"

I wasn't going to be bullied. And Eric wasn't going to be side-tracked.

"We agree on that. So, as I said, let's put our discussion of your relationship with Alexa aside and discuss the paper and its secret deal. I've heard a little about it from friends but not enough to know exactly what's going on. Why would you set up such an elaborate joint operating agreement, and why would you invite your advertisers into the room? I thought the content world was supposed to be shielded from the money world. You guys seem to have joined up with the darkest part of the dark side. Choosing to get into bed with the drug, chemical, and the health insurance industries seems like a recipe for disaster. Why would you do that?"

The lid on the deal was supposed to be airtight. He didn't get the details from Alexa because the only thing she knew was that I had long days of meetings about a newspaper deal.

"Not much to tell. Joint operating agreements to reduce costs are the wave of the future: the need for efficiency driving business. And newspapers are a business."

I was surprised with how glib I could be.

"Bullshit. I won't rest until I know what's going on."

"Whatever."

"And when I find out what you guys are up to, I'll tell the world."

"Fuck you, Eric."

At that moment, Jean and Matthew came up the stairs. Matthew's voice was loud enough to be heard throughout our little carriage house.

"This is so cool. I feel like I'm in a James Bond movie. I spent the day searching patterns to discuss in our secret meeting house and now we're here."

"And hello to you, too," I said with a remnant of the animosity I was feeling toward Eric. Matthew didn't deserve my edge.

"Sorry, Matthew, I'm feeling a little rattled. Van is late and Eric is being a total asshole, so my humor level is lower than usual."

"I like what you've done with the place. It's so revolutionary," he said.

Jean stepped in before the tension between us could escalate. "Okay, Matt, the joke is played out. We get to bring Alexa back into the fold tonight, we get to set a course of action, and we get to hear all about the newspaper deal that Will has been working on in New York."

I caught a glance from Eric to her that said *not now*. The two of them were connected in some way that was more than casually working in the healthcare area. It would be dangerous to Van and me if they were both working for the government and watching us.

"There's nothing to discuss about a newspaper deal. And, as soon as Van arrives, we can vote Alexa back into the group and get down to business."

On cue, she came up the stairs with two big bags of food. I had agreed to get the pizza, but she had changed her mind at the last minute and decided to get something better. She thought it was too soon to make the group function like a bunch of college kids eating slices out of a box.

"Sorry I'm late. Matthew, will you help me put this stuff in the kitchen and then we can vote on Alexa?"

He took two of the three bags she was carrying and followed her into the kitchen. He closed the door, which was odd.

"Will, do we really need to vote? I'm sure she's sorry for her behavior. Isn't that right, Eric?"

This seemed rehearsed—Jean's second rehearsed speech.

"Will, who has spent two nights with her in New York, wants to play by the rules, his rules, I guess, so far be it from me to interfere."

There was nothing for me to say. I waited for Van and Matthew to emerge from the kitchen. They took more time than I thought was needed to put away the food. And she looked a little flushed when they came out. She stood behind a chair and took charge of the group.

"Our first order of business is to decide whether to invite Alexa back into the fold. She needs a unanimous vote. All in favor raise your hands."

Eric relaxed into his chair and said, "No discussion. Don't we want to dissect her behavior and set out some rules for her to follow?"

"Don't be a troublemaker, Eric."

Van was good at this.

"Hands up for Alexa." All hands went up. "Will, give her a call and get her up here."

Five minutes later, Alexa bounded into the room.

"Did you guys miss me? I want you to know that after spending two glorious nights in the city with Will, drinking beer and eating forty-five-dollar hamburgers at the hotel bar, I'm now fully on board. I promise not to make fun of any of our efforts. I also want to state for the record that I think what we do here might be the catalyst to healing the country."

Matthew burst out laughing.

"You're going to be worse than you were before, aren't you?"

"No, Matt. I meant every word. Will and I spent hours talking about the way a few industry sectors have put a noose around the neck of this country. We have real work to do. I do like poking fun at you guys, but what we're about is important. We might succeed only because we all live in the upper stratosphere of our caste society. We may be safe because no one would suspect that we would jeopardize our protected status. Unless, of course, someone in this group is a rat."

This was going to be a serious meeting.

"Welcome back, Alexa, we're glad to see you. I know Will is especially glad to be able to spend more time with you, but now it's in the glare of the team and not in some dark bar on Park Avenue."

I was surprised by Van's direct attack. I thought she had let the New York stuff pass, since it was mostly innocent.

I saw Alexa square her shoulders, not much, but enough for me to see. I doubted anyone else noticed.

"Van, anything that I'm prepared to do with Will in a dark bar or in his hotel room, I'm prepared to do in front of all of you, especially you. I promised Will that if he didn't blackball me, I'd behave. From now on, I'll be as good as gold. And, speaking of gold, I think the gold has compromised our free press. So why don't you guys tell us what we need to know about the state of the free press?"

"I'm just a reporter. That's a question for Will."

Alexa was right. We couldn't drill down on the main causes of our society's breakdown without seeing how involved in the lies and manipulation the press has been. I launched into my stock answer: *the press is a player in our downfall.* I left out names and dates and events that were confidential and potentially recognizable. The group appreciated my candor even though they knew I was holding back mountains of information.

I paused to give the group a chance to ask questions. Matthew took center stage.

"Will, I've been examining the patterns in the major papers for a few months for a series of paintings. There are two companies at the epicenter—everything seems to move from them: the congress, the treasury, the regulators, and the marketplace. It's too obvious, so I assume you guys have manipulated the news to hide the real puppet masters."

Matthew was good. I would have been content to find the companies at the hub. He assumed crumbs were laid out to lead people to a false hub. He was right.

The group went off on that discussion.

Van was in awe of Matthew's use of pattern theory. This was a good discussion. Everyone was engaged. I took a break from the conversation to arrange the food for our informal supper. It was safer for me not to be in the middle of the conversation and risk more questions about the deal.

I was whisper singing "freedom's just another word for nothing left to lose" when I felt a warm hand on my shoulder.

"Hiding in the kitchen from the conversation, or from me?" Alexa asked.

"From the conversation. You can help get the supper ready for the group, if you'd rather be here than there."

She moved to face me on the other side of the smallish island in the center of the kitchen.

"I'm here because I wanted to look into your deep brown eyes without Van getting all bent out of shape, and because I want to be sure we're on the same page."

"You're spooking me, Alexa."

"You're easy to spook. I want it to be clear that whatever I agree to in that room does not change our deal."

She put her hand on mine. I was under her spell. There would be time enough to put on the brakes if she proposed something crazy.

"Yes, I'm on your team until it involves doing something that I don't want to do."

And with that, we opened the kitchen door and brought food and more drink for the starving revolutionaries.

"What have I missed? Are we going to blow up our target?" I asked.

I could see that Van assumed something went on in the kitchen.

Eric said they were discussing how our target should be made to pay for making children dependent on drugs.

"What did you all decide?"

Van answered me.

"We decided to stay focused on the company's corrupting influence on our chosen university; we'll talk about more drastic action later, Will. If you hadn't spent so much time in the kitchen with your new friend, you could have participated in the discussion."

I was surprised by her anger.

"We agreed that if you shopped for our supper, I would do the preparation. The time had come to eat. Please back off and stop with the Alexa stuff. It's unworthy of you."

We never aired our issues in public. This was going to be difficult to fix.

"We should save this fight for later." Her tone wasn't quite back to neutral.

Matthew came to the rescue.

"It's been a very productive evening. Let's eat and talk about movies and art."

Jean looked surprised. Being the peacemaker must have been a new role for him. He had saved the evening. We ate and drank. We talked and moved into small subgroups that created our own intricate pattern of involvement. At no time did Van talk to me. Not even as we cleaned up. I was getting the silent treatment, which was not in our rulebook. So, after a few attempts to get us into a conversation, I let the silence win.

But when she said that she was going to sleep in the carriage house, I stopped trying to placate her.

"Bullshit you are. If you have something you want to fight about, then let's do it, but silence and slinking off into a guest room isn't part of our deal. Grow up."

It worked.

"Okay. But I don't want to talk."

"Fine, but we'll have to talk about this soon. Especially since there's nothing to talk about, yet."

I couldn't resist the *yet*.

Chapter 30

Van got up to refill her drink. We had spent days in a cold stand-off. I settled back into my corner of the couch in our living room and sipped my single malt.

"They put you in charge. That's totally fucked up."

"No shit. Your father said I had the trust of the five other paper groups, and I was elected on the first ballot. It was probably the tenth ballet after everyone else turned it down. I'm going to turn it down."

She didn't hesitate.

"No way. This is perfect. You'll be where the conspiracies are hatched and can be the eyes and ears of the revolution; you're already the XDS Romeo and now you can be its 007."

She just couldn't let it go.

"Nothing went on between Alexa and me. And, by the way, I saw the way you looked at Matthew after your too-long stay in the kitchen. Should I be concerned?"

"Concerned? You don't own me."

We were on the down escalator.

"I didn't have sex with Alexa in New York, and I don't plan to. If you can't accept that, we should disband the group and I won't ever see her again."

I was clear in my words but not so much in my head. I had been running a fantasy scenario of having an affair with Alexa, which made me smile at the same time it made me very anxious.

She put her glass down on the leather coaster I had put in front of her. She wasn't always careful about where she put down her drinks, so this motion was a signal that she was moving into precise territory.

"Listen, I know you're attracted to her, and to tell the truth, I find Matthew intriguing. His unique mind turns me on. I guess we're even. I don't want to disband the group. Our marriage is strong enough to withstand a storm or two, and maybe even a brief infidelity. I'm not sure about that last thought. A little flirting is probably okay, and I guess maybe natural. More is another story. So, for the record, I'm not willing to commit not to sleep with him, or someone else, for that matter, and it isn't right for me to make that demand of you. But I don't plan to sleep around, and I will be really upset if you decide to sleep with anyone else but me."

I took the two giant steps needed to come to her and I hugged her. She hugged me back. I wanted the conversation about me and Alexa and her and Matthew to be over. I realized I was more ambivalent about the issue than I had thought I would be. For the first time since we met, I entertained the thought of sleeping with another woman. It was extremely unsettling.

"So, you get to represent the domestic and international press in secret meetings on the dark side and yearn for Alexa's touch, and I get to be the head of the group that cracks open Corporate America like it was Humpy Dumpty and maybe I sleep with pattern king. Then we live happily ever after in some faraway place with new identities."

"Are you stoned?"

"No, why?"

"The stuff you're saying is totally off the wall. That's why."

"Lighten up, Will."

I moved back into my corner of the couch, closing this bit of craziness for the evening.

"So, now that you are in charge of the dark side's control of the press, what happens next?"

"For starters, I'm off to meetings in California on the Big Sur this week. Come with me. We can put our feet in the Pacific. Then we can spend the weekend in Napa and fly home on Monday."

She loved the Big Sur. This would be a good way to have some quality time together.

"Don't you need permission to bring a guest?"

"I wouldn't tell them. You'd stay at whichever hotel the group isn't in. We could meet for Irish coffee at that restaurant that overlooks the Pacific to watch the sunset or jump into a hot tub by the sea in what remains of the hippie world. If we have lots of time together that would be great; if not, you could get a lot of work done and we would have the weekend together. I'd really like it if you came."

I kept silent to give her time to decide.

"That's the second nicest offer I've had this week. I can't do it. I am totally jammed for the week and the weekend." ·

"Second nicest offer?"

She smiled. "I was offered a story on the disaster surrounding federal funding of research on hyperactivity and learning. Right up our alley. There's a scandal brewing and they've picked me to cover it. So, work first, revolution second, and love third. Sorry."

"Bad call. When I send you pictures of the Pacific crashing on those rocks, you'll be sorry you're here working on a story that won't get by editorial."

She moved over to sit next to me.

"I know. I'm glad you asked. If I get lonely and all our friends are busy, I'll call a meeting of the group. I assume I have your proxy."

"I'm way more interesting than our friends and the group. And we can start the revolution on the West Coast. We can burn down the resort when it's full of evil corporate execs. We can bolt the door from the outside and let them out only if they agree to principles of fairness and equity. That message would be hard to ignore in the world of CEOs. We'll stamp XDS on the gasoline cans so when people see the logo on the side of buses, they'll know who is cleaning out the oppressors."

She kissed my cheek and let her hand rest on mine.

"You're getting carried away. I like trying to get these creeps to fly right, but I don't want to kill them. Are you channeling Alexa?"

"Nothing to do with Alexa. I'm going to the land of rainbows and free love. My invitation is open-ended. You can decide to join me last minute."

"Thanks, I'm not going to change my mind. I'll spend my revolutionary energy writing our manifesto of fairness and equity. If major companies agree to it, we'll leave them alone. The ones that don't, we'll organize business-to-business boycotts against them to disrupt their supply chain."

Her idea of boycotts to disrupt supply chains had potential. She was moving past the sixties and seventies model and making a toolkit that made sense in a world that measured everything in dollars:

no morality, no ethics, only what makes or loses money in the short term.

"Disrupting the supply chain is a terrific idea. A message from the shipping department that they can't get boxes, or shipping tape, or a truck to come on time might get the attention of greed-based management."

"Thanks. I think it is worth exploring. And what are you going to do in your meetings with the dark side? Are you going there to party or to work?"

I couldn't tell if she was being playful or trying to get information about the meetings. The Inner Square—IS, as the group was called—had a no-agenda rule. I would be briefed when I arrived. I had a secure iPad, and I would get a text with a security code when I was supposed to turn it on and read something. That was all I knew.

"I have no idea what to expect."

She shrugged and left the room. Not her normal end to a conversation.

I went after her, turned her to me, and tried to read her. She was a sphinx. I leaned in to kiss her, but she turned and give me her cheek.

"What's up with you?"

"I don't like you living in a secret world that will do so much damage. I'm afraid we're headed into a black hole. I know I've dragged you into the revolution thing, but now I'm scared. I think we should cash out. Fuck the paper, and fuck the XDS, which is, after all, just a kids' game. It should be just you and me and a new life. That's how I feel right now. I don't feel like kissing you or making love to you, and I don't want you to go off to California. I don't have a good feeling about it."

We were still standing and facing each other.

"Are you in Van or journalist intuition mode?"

"Both. And the feelings are getting stronger. There's something bad about what you, we, are doing. We should have quit the paper as soon as it became clear what my father's deal was all about. I think one or both of us is going to get hurt."

She was freaking me out. I asked her if hurt meant physical or emotional. She slumped into my arms and said both. This was so weird. I thought she might be playing with me. I took her by the shoulders and moved her back a few inches so that I could look into her eyes. There were tears. She wasn't playing a game. I walked us back into the living room and sat us on the couch again.

"You're freaking me out. We agreed I would play along with the dark side, and I'd keep you informed if I didn't think the information would come back to bite you or me in the ass. We've been having some fun with our group. Did something happen that you haven't told me about?"

She dried her few tears with the sleeve of her sweater.

"Nothing has happened. Somehow thinking of you on that rugged coastline with the fog not lifting until midday set off these feelings. I have a premonition that things are going to change. I don't want them to. I don't want us to get hurt. I'm panicked."

She tried to smile. I could see the effort that she was making to keep it all together.

"Well, I don't feel it. Usually when you have a strong premonition, I have some of the same feelings. I know we're playing with fire. I'm the one at risk, so I should be having the same feelings. If they suspect I am a spy, they might throw me into the Pacific and call it a hiking accident. The danger is not registering with me yet."

That relaxed her a little.

"I want you back here in one piece as my lover and best friend. I don't want our relationship infected by the distance that comes from you being stuck in a conspiracy you can't discuss, and I definitely don't want you coming back to me in a box."

I said I had no intention of coming back in a box. We drank the rest of our scotch in silence and went up to bed.

Chapter 31

S ince my flight to California wasn't until late afternoon, I spent part of the day in the office reviewing stories dealing with health issues. I had become the master censor.

The pushback was less than I had expected. A few of the editors told me to fuck off, and I responded with the usual—*do you want to work here or not?*—and they gave in. The smart ones said they would keep a log of my edits and when the time came, they would write a book on the destruction of the free press. I smiled at the two editors who were smart enough to take that approach and told them that I thought it was a great idea if they gave me credit. I admired them for their ability to see what had to be done, and to be honest enough to tell me what they planned to do.

Even though notes and tapes and videos have brought down men and women from very high places, including the White House, I decided I would keep my own records. My strings were being pulled, and the least I could do after my reputation as a journalist was finished and I was in prison was to provide the ammunition to those left standing. That idea helped me through the morning. That, and a surprise visit from Eric, who suggested a walk to Lafayette Park so we could talk without being overheard and see the White House from our bench. He wanted to talk about the newspaper deal. I told him the subject was off limits.

"You know I'll find out the details one way or another, and if it turns out that we should bomb your newspaper, then that's what we'll do."

I told him that bombing our building was fine with me. He laughed and promised to be sure I wasn't in the building when he and Jean set off the car full of explosives that would be sitting on the first level of the building's parking garage. Then we spent a half hour in pleasant conversation.

"This has been a great interlude, Eric, but I need to get back to my office. I have some work to finish up and then a plane to catch." To my surprise, he didn't press for any more details.

I wrapped up a few odds and ends at the office and headed to the airport. I was looking forward to five hours in the air with no interruptions. I traveled in the front of the plane for trips over three hours—a compromise policy from the time when budgets and life were not carved up into little pieces of profit.

The level of secrecy of the IS was a benefit. There was nothing for me to do to prepare for the meetings. The travel time was mine, and I spent it reading and just zoning out. I was going to rent a car at the San Jose airport and drive the two hours to the Big Sur. Our first event was a dinner at the inn—a cluster of cabins in the woods, which was a euphemism for a very fancy hotel on the ocean side of Route 1. The food and wine would be first class. The company would be awful.

My plan to rent a car changed at baggage claim when I saw a man holding up a sign with my initials on it. I thought about walking past him to the car rental counter, but I was sure he would pay a price for not finding me at the airport. I signaled and he came over to help me with my bags. For a second, I panicked, thinking that I would be locked in the back seat of a town car with someone from a pharmaceutical company or a black-ops agency. There was no need to panic, I was alone in the back seat.

I arrived while there was still enough sun to cast beautiful shadows on the classic rugged California-style group of low buildings connected by stone walkways and arches, fountains and waterfalls, and beautiful boulders. The plantings—part high desert, and part California coast—were perfect. The Big Sur was one of the wonders of the world. I hoped I'd have time to walk the gardens and go down to the local retreat to sit in a communal hot tub overlooking the ocean, as well as time to walk on the beach.

The woman at the registration desk was tall, wide-shouldered, and athletic-looking with bright blue eyes and blond hair in a thick braid that trailed down her back. She was wearing a faded denim skirt, Frye boots, and a white western-style shirt with black pearl snaps. To top it off, the bottom of her braid was tied with a red bandana ribbon—a cultural throwback to the sixties. I was definitely in northern California.

"Hi. I'm here to check in."

"Wonderful, I hope your trip was easy. I just need your first name. We haven't been given any last names and we're not allowed to ask."

"Very cloak-and-dagger. I'm Will."

She smiled. "Hi, Will, I'll take you to your room. I'm Cassandra. I'm assigned to you. It's my job to be sure that all your needs are satisfied."

The *all your needs are satisfied* part was weird.

"Thank you. My needs are simple. There is one thing I'd like to ask. May I take a picture of you to send back home? You're the image of California we carry around in our heads on the East Coast and I'd like to show people back in our little town that you're real."

That was way more than it needed to be.

"Of course. You can take my picture, but I'm very plain compared to the rest of the men and women your leaders have brought here to take care of you and your colleagues. They have imported a gorgeous staff to satisfy your every want and desire. But you certainly can take my picture."

She gave me a smile that was warm enough to melt an M&M.

"Thanks."

I took her picture, and then we were off to my room. We walked along a pathway that looped through what seemed like a jungle of overhanging, tunnel-like greenery that opened to a cluster of small buildings, each with two or three doors opening to suites of different sizes and configurations, I assumed.

"Since you're among the first to arrive, I've selected one of the best suites for you. We were told this was a first come first serve room allocation. We weren't provided with the usual pecking order list. You might be getting more or less than you deserve in our capitalist society. This is my favorite suite."

She opened the door to a beautiful living room furnished in a simple western style. There was a fire in the fireplace and a small bubbly fountain in the corner by windows that opened to a view of soft, rolling hills. I had no idea what the other rooms were like, but this one was just right for me. She showed me the oversized bathroom with its copper tub and shower lined in fieldstone, and the bedroom with the same view as the living room, which was a clear view to the hills in the distance with live oaks and manzanita making random patterns on the hills. This was like a photo in a Sierra Club calendar. It was beautiful. I wished Van were here to enjoy it with me.

"This is great."

She smiled and hesitated for a minute, then she said in a soft voice, "Can I ask a favor?"

"Sure."

"I sometimes sit here for twenty minutes or so to get centered so I can go back out and face the world. The basic rule of the Inn is that if I get caught in a guest room without the guest's permission, I'm out on my ass. This booking is different: the rest of the staff, which is a temporary staff, has been brought in from L.A. and have been hired for full-service assignments, so they will be in their assigned guest's room. This is my permanent job and I really need it. So, I can only come in here if you're okay with it, otherwise I'll be fired. I'm not full-service. If you need that, I can arrange for it."

She was solid. I liked her.

"If you decide to meditate in here, it'll be fine with me, whether I am here or not, and I won't have any needs that would compromise you."

She smiled, thanked me, and then she was gone.

I surveyed my new surroundings and unpacked. I settled in to review the background material that would appear on my iPad when I put in the code sent to me by text—my arrival package. As the sun went lower in the sky, the hills with their lonely trees scattered here and there took on a very somber color. The hills were buff colored, and the trees had leaves of a soft olive green. The deeper greens were on the redwoods and tall pines that I could see out of my bathroom windows. But, from my living room window, soft light browns dominated the palate while a sky moving to dusk turned the landscape a grayish blue.

The background materials were a series of newspaper and magazine articles on various healthcare issues. There was no agenda and no list of the people attending the meeting.

I had an hour to relax before what would be the first of a series of bizarre encounters with the dark side. I poured a scotch from the bar that had been set up on a table in the corner of my living room. On a tray were full-sized bottles of scotch, bourbon, gin, vodka, tequila, and rum, as well as macadamia nuts that were in a very tasteful handmade ceramic bowl. I took my drink and my bowl of nuts to the balcony to watch the light continue to change.

Chapter 32

There was no way I could spend enough time under a hot shower to wash off the slime that had accumulated in the four days I spent in meetings and at dinners with the nine other people who made up this committee of the Inner Square. As beautiful as it was on the Big Sur, and as much as I enjoyed my conversations with the open-hearted Cassandra, who did use my room to get herself centered, I was glad to be alone in my hotel in San Francisco. I had promised myself a weekend off, with or without Van. It was her call to stay in DC. I was going to try to get my head cleared and soak up the energy of the city.

Before I could make the break, I had to play back the meetings to Van to be sure someone else knew what was going on just in case I was pushed into the path of a cable car.

"You really should be here. I'm lonely. I'll have to eat by myself and walk the streets at night without a companion, assuming, of course, that I don't call the cowgirl Cassandra, my new friend, to come up here and enjoy the weekend with me."

I could almost see the smile on Van's face.

"Don't put yourself at risk, dear. She'd say no, and she might not be that gentle about it. You were lucky to have had her around for the few days you were there. She sounds like she was a real person in a group of crazies. You know you could've come directly home. You'd be in my arms tonight instead of 3,500 miles away sleeping alone in a hotel bed. It was your choice. I have no sympathy for you. I've been getting an enormous amount of work done and I love my freedom. Stay as long as you like."

I looked out at a very nice eastern view of the Bay Bridge, which would be in lights in a few hours. I had seen that jeweled necklace before, and I was looking forward to seeing it again.

"You're so sweet to tell me to stay as long as I like. If I didn't know better, I'd be jealous. No wife says that to her husband unless she's hoping to extend the time she's spending with her lover. Go ahead, put Matthew on."

"Caught me."

She was laughing. I asked her who was there, still half joking, but not all joking.

"That's for me to know and you to find out."

I hadn't heard that since the fifth grade.

"Where did that come from?"

"My huge memory bank, I guess. Anyway, I assume you called to tell me about the meetings. Is your phone secure?"

"I hope so. If not, I'll be dead."

"Spare the drama. Have the members of the Dark Square all gone their separate ways, or will you see them at the hotel bar?"

"It's the Inner Square, but I like Dark Square better. I have no idea. I left as soon as I could. Some of them might be spending the weekend at the Inn with their assigned escorts. I was probably the only person who turned down the offer of intimate companionship. These people are really disgusting."

"Will, I'm waiting to hear about the meetings."

"Okay. Our first meeting was spent on reviewing the procedures: the rules of confidentiality, the code of conduct, the secret cell phone numbers and email addresses. I assumed some black-ops team leader who was too old to jump from tall buildings designed it. All the sectors were present: drugs, chemicals, insurance, finance, research universities, and to my naive shock, a person from Treasury and a person of similar rank from the EU and a wild card whose affiliation was kept secret. The group was international. The wild card person, who was from Germany, was the group leader, or facilitator, as she preferred to call herself."

"Names?"

"Only first names."

I cracked the seal on a little bottle of Johnny Black, poured it into a glass, and relaxed into the reading chair that was in the corner of my room, turning it to face the window. I could tell my story and look out on the San Francisco skyline all at the same time. I figured the group would assume I shared secrets with Van, so if they decided I was a risk, they would decide she was, too. They wouldn't ask; they would just act. So, I wasn't putting her any further at risk.

"Everything about the group was bizarre. The conversation was beyond any rational person's sense of real. They talked as if they already had the world under their control. The major subject of the meeting was when and how to reveal the cure for cancer they had already developed. There was a brief detour to discuss Alzheimer's disease, but the consensus quickly developed that it would be at least two decades before the economic effects of the aging population would impact the economy. It was cancer and its financial underpinnings that occupied the group."

"I'm not following. They talked about existing cancer cures and medicines?"

"More than that—they have a cure already available for all forms of cancer. There were slides showing the profits by industry, the size of the research commitments in the pipeline, and a very complicated formula to show when there would be crossover from ultra-high profits to normal profits based on the introduction of generics and a host of other factors. They determined there was a seven-year window of significant profits, after which they would be prepared to release their inexpensive cure."

"That sounds crazy."

"Evil. They're all evil. The reason for the presentation was to get buy-in on the timetable from the drug companies and their universities. They had a timeline for the announcements of the various breakthroughs and had prepared talking points for the newspapers to incorporate into their cancer stories over the next seven years. Seven years of more unnecessary deaths."

"You're making this up."

"I'm not. The finance and insurance guys talked about how they would adjust their business model to account for the loss of federal money as cancer receded from the foreground and dementia, diabetes, and Alzheimer's moved to the top of the list. There were more charts and multicolored lines that ascended and descended and crossed over each other. The first-tier countries need to adjust their economies to deal with a cancer-free population. A lot of people and expensive radiation machines will be out of work. They even discussed whether radiation therapy could be repurposed. The woman from Germany suggested research to show how radiation would help stem the tide of Alzheimer's. The university rep said that she would get right on it, assuming blank checks would be on the way. That little aside took no more than five minutes. So, now you know the outcome of the first set of face-to-face meetings of the IS, and my role in it."

"What does that mean?"

"It means that I have to develop a plan for our reporters to write articles over the next seven years that support the timeline and get the other newspapers to do the same."

"No fucking way."

"Don't you wish you were here to hold my head over the toilet bowl?"

"Nope. You wanted to be a revolutionary. Now you have a cause. Stay alive, dear. You're in very dangerous territory. As they say on aircraft carriers—YOYOMF."

She was trying to be funny to avoid accepting the reality of the situation, but I needed a little more sympathy.

"You're in it, too. So, don't be so cavalier. I'm trying to process this stuff. It isn't easy."

"Sorry, it's too weird. I'll be better tomorrow when we talk. By the way, I got a call from Eric yesterday. He wanted to know where you were. I told him you'd be in San Francisco over the weekend. How did he know you were traveling?"

I took too big of a swallow of scotch and started coughing. It took a while to catch my breath. Van stayed silent.

"I'm okay, thanks for asking."

"I thought you were making up the coughing spell to avoid telling me that Eric found out your plans from Alexa."

"Enough. He stopped by for coffee the morning I was leaving so he knew I was going out west. I told you he was snooping around and that you should keep an eye on him. His insistence on figuring out where I was going freaks me out. I can't believe you told him I was here. That was dumb."

I could picture her processing my last comment.

"I've got to get back to my research. That's what I'm doing on a Friday evening while you're enjoying San Francisco. We'll talk tomorrow. Love."

I poured the rest of the scotch from the little bottle and looked out at the deep blue sky. Getting some fresh air would do me good, but I just couldn't get out of my chair. I let my mind wander from the magnificent coastline of the Big Sur to the faces of the hollow people I had just spent four days with to the stretch of the Bay Bridge I could see from my window to a very erotic picture of Cassandra. I was just getting into my fantasy when the phone rang. Not my cell but the phone in my room. That was a jolt. Other than Van, no one knew where I was staying.

"Eric, how did you find me?"

"It wasn't easy. I knew you were in the city, but finding the right hotel took some doing. I have friends in high places. I'm in the lobby. Come on down for a drink and I'll buy you dinner."

"I don't know about dinner. I'll meet you in the bar in ten minutes."

So much for a quiet late afternoon walk. I wasn't in the mood to be with anyone, and I definitely didn't want to be questioned by Eric.

The hotel bar was elegant, paneled in walnut and furnished with comfortable leather chairs and couches in seating arrangements for two, four, six and more—very old-fashioned. I had checked it out before I went up to my room and decided it would be a nice place to spend some time—alone time. Thinking about meeting Eric there shifted the warm feeling I'd had about it. My mood had pretty much soured by the time I got off the elevator but seeing Alexa at the bar changed my mood instantly. They got up to greet me—Eric with a typical man hug and Alexa with a nice light kiss.

"Why did you guys track me down? I know it's not a coincidence. I'm a little surprised."

Alexa sat back in her chair and sipped her drink. This was going to be Eric's show.

"You looked so stressed in DC on Monday, I figured we should follow you and bring you some cheer."

I ordered a club soda.

"That's total bullshit, Eric."

He didn't appear to be rattled in the slightest by my tone.

"It's pretty obvious. Your paper's up to something, and I want to find out what it is. Alexa tried hard to keep me from coming. She didn't want me to meddle in your affairs. It didn't work, so she decided to come, too."

He emphasized *affairs*.

"I have to side with Alexa on this one. I have a private life, a work life, and now a revolutionary life. You are entitled to know about my revolutionary life and that's it."

"Don't be so dramatic, Will. I'm here because I'm speaking at a conference in Palo Alto tomorrow. When you said you were going west, I checked with Van to see if you were going to be in northern California. It's that simple. Alexa likes this part of the world, so she decided to join me, at least for today. You can entertain her tomorrow if that's what you both want. Now let's get out of this bar and pick a place for dinner. I'd love to hear about your secret deal, but this meeting is just for fun."

I didn't believe him but walking around the city and having a great dinner just for fun, as he put it, was fine with me.

"Thanks for offering my company to Will, Eric. But I'm planning to head home tomorrow. I have a pile of work to do. I hope that's okay with you, Will."

I didn't hide my disappointment from her.

"That's fine. I had planned to be alone this weekend. I had invited Van to join me. As you can see, she declined."

I signed the bar bill, and we were off to walk the streets and then to dinner. True to Eric's word, we didn't talk about the deal or anything else serious.

Chapter 33

I was finishing the coffee I had brewed from the little coffeemaker in my room when the hotel phone rang. I wasn't in the mood for another surprise visit from Eric, even though I enjoyed the dinner. I was looking forward to my own Saturday in the city.

"I decided to stay. Can I come up and stay with you?"

I didn't hesitate. "That would be great."

I gave her my room number. I had a nice room with a King, a desk, two reading chairs, and one bathroom. It would be a little more intimate than the suite we shared in New York.

"Did you miss me?"

She had a smile that sucked me right in to her. We hugged. I leaned back just enough to look at her. And she moved her head toward me. We kissed. It was more than a kiss hello.

I took her case and rolled it to the closet and put it on a suitcase holder. She looked around and realized we would be sleeping in the same bed.

"Thanks for agreeing to share your room. Will I like it?"

It was an odd question.

"You'll like it if you like me. Otherwise, you might find it a little cramped."

That brought out another of her broad smiles.

"We'll see. We have the day in front of us. What shall we do? Stay in the city or rent a car and go over the Golden Gate to Sausalito, or into the forest."

"Let's hike in the forest," I said. "Maybe tomorrow, if you stay, we can go to the ocean."

"Suits me. I'll change."

And with that, she opened her case, took out clothes for a walk in the woods, and began to undress. I got up to look out the window to give her privacy, which she didn't seem to need. I turned back while she was still half naked.

Even though there was less than ten years difference between us, this was definitely generational.

"You should change so we can get started; I'm excited to see the redwoods."

I changed in the bathroom while she arranged for a car. Within a half hour, we had crossed the Golden Gate heading for a very old redwood forest.

The day was warm in the sun, but under the forest canopy, it was at least ten degrees cooler: perfect hiking weather. We walked along for an hour, gaining altitude with each step. I was glad I had been going to the gym. I would have been embarrassed if I'd had to stop to rest. The hikes in the Middleburg estate were mostly level. Uphill hiking is different. We came to a resting point, and she said, "Shall we turn back? I may have things planned for later that will require us to be full of energy."

She was one surprise after another. I put her hand to my mouth and kissed it. Not a particularly neutral move, but I was in the open air, I was free, my head was clearing, and I was in the moment. Even so, it was a very old-fashioned gesture. I should have been embarrassed, but for some reason I wasn't.

"Somewhere along the ridge there's an ocean lookout according to the map at the trail head. I vote for another ten to fifteen minutes up to see if we get to the top. If you're up for it?"

She nodded and we walked on in silence. In about ten minutes, we spotted a marker pointing west to a lookout deck. It was worth the effort. We could see the coastline north for what seemed like a million miles and a substantial amount of coast to the south, as well, and if we turned more to the east, we could see the tip of the bridge. We were standing on top of the world and there were no other hikers in site. We were in the sun. Alexa took off her sweater and unbuttoned her shirt to feel the sun on her chest.

"Come and kiss me properly. This should be a highlighted moment in our histories. On this beautiful Saturday, Alexa and Will kissed on a mountaintop and then they returned to their hotel room to plot the destruction of capitalism. This is a good day. A very good day."

I did as I was told and, aside from a short burst of guilt, I was soaring like an eagle. The feel of her skin on my arm—her shirt was open and knotted to expose her stomach and the small of her back—it was like I was touching a woman for the first time all over again. We untangled our bodies at the sound of approaching hikers. She buttoned up her shirt, and we headed back down to our car.

Chapter 34

Waking up with a naked Alexa at my side was very strange. Even though the bed was wide enough for four people, she was snuggled up to me: her front to my back. That was not the way Van and I slept. Van would be on her side of the bed, and I would be on mine. We would come together when we woke up, but we didn't sleep right up against each other.

Alexa and I had agreed, during the dessert we shared the night before, that we would not have sex, and we didn't. We kissed and touched each other, but that was all. As I felt her body against mine, still asleep, I wondered why we had made that agreement. I was on shifting sands. I thought of the line from the Bob Dylan song: "May you have a strong foundation when the winds of changes shift." My foundation was weak, and the winds were picking up. I was sure others had been through this conflict; novels and movies and plays have been written about infidelity since the beginning of time. But this, if it happened, would be happening to me in real life. It had my mind a total jumble.

I played the day back in my head. We'd had a great hike in the woods and then another hour of walking in the city before we went back to my room to clean up and change for dinner.

She picked the restaurant. She loved picking restaurants. I hated that responsibility. If I picked wrong and Van wasn't pleased with the food or the service or the atmosphere, I felt responsible, even if she didn't blame me for the choice. Alexa didn't appear to have that problem. I remember her saying: "If you live to be one hundred, this dinner is only one out of over thirty-five thousand dinners."

She picked well. We had a great dinner. She told me about the scientists she worked with who were developing mind- and body-altering chemicals that were part of a nano-technology initiative. A simple touch of anything with one of the micro cells embedded in it, a skin lotion for example, and it would be as if you had had the substance injected directly into a vein. We learned more of each other's histories. We discussed love and relationships. We talked about our dreams and the way we saw the future: mine with Van and children, which we couldn't put off much longer, and hers as a free agent. The energy of bonding, a beginning instead of a middle, was highly charged, and our conversation moved to the night ahead of us. I wanted our relationship to be intentional, and she was prepared to follow my lead. If I was going to do something that violated my commitment to Van, it couldn't be because I was swept up in the moment. That would not be fair to me, to Alexa, or to Van. If Alexa and I made love, it had to be with our eyes open and with an understanding that it wouldn't be a secret. She never responded when I asked if her relationship with Eric demanded the same intentionality.

Even with the awkward "shall we sleep together" conversation, we were in perfect harmony.

"Alexa, I'm feeling feelings that I'm not supposed to feel."

"Me, too. I feel at ease with you; totally open. I don't think I'd feel this way with someone else. If you're feeling the same way, I am thrilled, but I'm not ready. Is that okay with you?"

I took her hand.

"My body is ready to be with you, and my heart is, too, but my head isn't. Let's make a deal. We won't go all the way."

She couldn't keep from laughing.

"The last time someone said 'we won't go all the way' to me was at my high school prom—third base only. Okay, third base. That's a deal."

She kissed the palm of my hand, a long thoughtful kiss, and put my hand back on the table.

"Now that that's settled, let's walk back to the hotel."

We'd gone out into the San Francisco night air, which had become thick with the fog rolling in from the ocean. After two blocks, we decided it was too cold to walk. We found a cab and settled in for the short ride to the hotel.

There was a bar at the top floor of the hotel. We decided to avoid testing our resolve a little longer by sipping cognac and watching the lights of the city go out as people in their houses and apartments went to sleep.

We didn't need to say much, knowing that soon we would find ourselves together naked in a warm bed. We honored the letter of our commitment, but I doubted that either Van or Eric would have been pleased to know how satisfied we were as we drifted into dreamland.

I don't know how long it took me to play yesterday and last night through my internal projector. It was long enough for Alexa to stir and open her eyes. I was sitting at the edge of the bed looking down at her, and she was all wrapped in a duvet that was an eggshell white with a cocoa trim that pretty much matched her skin.

"Good morning. You match the trim on the duvet."

She propped herself on her elbow, looked at the cocoa brown stitching, and smiled.

"It's a new day and our vow has expired. I want us to make love this morning. Then we'll talk."

With that, she went off to the bathroom. I sat there, admittedly not as confused as I should have been.

Our bodies fit together nicely. Our ability to read and satisfy each other's needs was close to perfect. Thankfully, I had remembered to put out the Do Not Disturb sign the night before.

By the time we were ready to venture into the Sunday world of the city, it was time for lunch. The fog had lifted, and the sun was out. We decided on a picnic in the park. We still had our rental car, so we had our choice between Golden Gate Park or the park at the ocean.

"Let's picnic in Golden Gate Park at the place they used to call Hippie Hill. If we're going to start a revolution, we should pay our respects to the sixties and the place where a lot of the energy began. Then we can drive to the museum, eat ice cream, and look out at the ocean. I'm ready to reveal the essential details of my plan."

She held me spellbound in her gaze as she set our course for the afternoon.

We got directions to Hippie Hill on my navigation site, but it didn't pinpoint the exact spot, so we decided to try to find some-one who might be able to describe the exact location. The people in the gourmet shop where we bought our picnic food had a rough idea of where it was, but they weren't sure if they were thinking of the actual hill or the field where the bands would set up. They directed us to a new age store a few blocks away owned by some old stoner.

The shop was full of crystals, chimes, books, and music to induce calm. There were meditation bells, mats, stools, and little things to call on the good spirits and to scare away the bad. There was an old oak table in the middle of the shop with a few carefully protected first editions of the *Whole Earth Catalogue*. We were in the right place, but the person sitting at the desk and focused on her computer wasn't old enough to have any idea what we were looking for.

Alexa gave it a try.

"Hi, my boyfriend and I want to have a picnic on Hippie Hill. Do you know how we can find it?"

The young woman pointed to the back of the store. Alexa shrugged and led the way. I wondered if we had said the magic words to unlock their fine homegrown weed, mushrooms, and other exotic hallucinogens. Alexa may have been having the same thought.

"Do you have a lot of cash on you? I have about two hundred," she whispered.

"I have plenty. I'm sure we won't need that much."

To get to the back of the store, we had to go through a maze of bookshelves filled with geodes and clear crystals, incense burners, sticks of incense and white sage smudge. We assumed we'd find a long-haired, tattooed, gaunt stereotype of an aged hippie, but instead we found a very large map on the back wall. It was captioned: IT'S THE SIXTIES—FIND YOUR SPOT. The map had more than a dozen spots circled—the Filmore, the Avalon, City Lights Bookstore, the corner of Haight and Ashbury, and not far from that circle was a circle in the park that was labeled Hippie Hill. There was a stack of the maps on a table for sale.

I bought a map and a crystal necklace for Alexa. The crystal was the size of a new silver dollar; it had a hint of jade color and it hung from a black twisted leather chain. It was the first time I had bought something romantic for another woman since I met Van. The week, the weekend, the day were full of firsts.

We checked the Hippie Hill location on our map. It was northeast of where the navigation app had claimed it would be. We were glad for the map.

Chapter 35

Our picnic lunch was a truly mind-blowing experience. We ate sandwiches and drank beer on a beautiful hill that was once the site to hang out and listen to Saturday afternoon pop-up concerts from the Grateful Dead, Country Joe, Big Brother, Steve Miller, the Jefferson Airplane, and others who have since drifted into the purple haze of the last century, while Alexa revealed a conspiracy that was orders of magnitudes worse than the cancer-cure conspiracy I was now a part of.

"That can't be for real."

"It is and we have to stop it."

Here we were, picnicking on the spot where the youth of America thought it could stop a war, stop misogyny, and end racism. And now at the same spot, we were discussing an evil that none of those would-be revolutionaries would have ever imagined.

"I guess the stuff we've been talking about doing in the group is child's play."

She reached out for my hand. "Not really, it's all important, but that's why I got so crazy that night."

"Why didn't you tell the group about it?"

"As far as I can determine, there are only two people who know how the pieces of the project fit together. The rest, working on discreet parts, don't know the whole, and most likely have been told that what they are working on is good for the world. I couldn't risk sharing this information with Eric or Jean. I think one or both may be connected to the group charged with running it or the group that is trying to get under the tent. It's just an instinct, but a very strong one—I have put Eric in the high-risk category, and, for our safety, I've put Jean in that category, too. They go back very far together. I get weird vibes from them. I assume some of the people you were meeting with this week are involved. You need to watch your back. They'll take no prisoners. And since Van decided not to be part of our secret group, she can't know about this unless I decide to tell her. You can't tell her anything about it. Agreed?"

"Agreed."

I needed time to think. I put my finger on her lips to signal a silent period. She leaned over and kissed me. Then I leaned back and watched the clouds moving against the deep blue of the afternoon sky. She followed me down, and I put my arm under her head so that she could rest on my shoulder. I had bunched up my jacket for a pillow. I was in a comfortable enough position to stay that way for a while and I hoped she was, too. The sun was warm on my face and the spot vibrated with good feeling. At least that's what I told myself as I drifted in and out of thought.

After about twenty minutes of just being there together in what really was a restful state, she broke the silence.

"It's time to make a plan. Let's spend some time at the ocean, have dinner, and maybe repeat this morning. Tomorrow, you go back to DC to tell Van about our weekend and to deal with the others. Fairness requires disclosure."

She was right. Once I told Van and she told Eric that we were lovers, if that is what we were, we would have to tell Jean and Matthew.

She hesitated for a second and said, "There will be no room to look back. We're either in it together to the end or we aren't, in which case, we go our separate ways for good."

"Okay." I said in a tone that hid my fears. "It will make a nice story: two members of the upper class—lovers—sit on a bench facing the Pacific planning to save the world without anyone helping or even knowing about it."

She rolled over on top of me and pressed against me so that I was not very far from having an orgasm. And I suspect she wasn't very far from one either. She knew what she was doing and stopped in time. She rolled off and stood. We stuffed our trash in a bag and walked back to the car. We were about thirty blocks from the ocean and the museum, thirty blocks from our no-turning-back moment. I needed more time to consider the leap. I suggested we take a quick tour of the museum and then have coffee in their café. She wasn't fooled.

"That's fine. You should take as much time as you need to decide your future. This is very high risk. Just so you know, I am compelled to act whether you're in or not. So, you're free to make whatever decision makes you comfortable."

The museum was a good call. There were two galleries full of large Diebenkorn paintings that were calming for me. They seem to have had the same effect on her. I could see her body relax into the rooms. After a half hour with the paintings, I suggested coffee. She agreed, and now we were just a few minutes away from walking to the ocean.

We found an isolated bench under a very elegantly windswept tree that looked like a drawing on some seventeenth century screen from Japan. The fog was moving toward us, and if we looked to the north, we could see the top of the Golden Gate. This was a fairytale site suitable for a life-altering decision.

Alexa took my hand and held it between hers.

"So, what's it going to be?"

I surprised myself.

"I'm in; it's time I took a real risk to save the world from tyranny."

I thought she'd either laugh at my "save the world from tyranny" or lean over to seal my commitment with a kiss, but she didn't do either. She just looked straight ahead at the ocean and let tears slide down her soft cheeks.

Finally, she spoke.

"You know we may do things that neither of us, nor probably anyone we know, would ever dream of doing. We could die, we could go to jail, your relationship with Van could be weakened. Think hard on it. This is a very serious commitment you're making."

She was right. And, to protect Van, there could be no sharing of information.

We looked into each other's eyes. It was corny, but that's what we did.

"Let's do this."

We hugged. I still can't quite explain to myself how this all came about. It was way more than Alexa's charisma. It was more than the after-burn of the IS meetings or even the existence of that unholy group. Something inside me had changed. The no-risk switch had been turned off. I had broken my boundaries by not only making love to Alexa, but by agreeing to be part of a secret two-person group that would carry out a dangerous clandestine mission. I had become open in a way that should have frightened me more than it did. I wondered if the new me would be obvious to Van.

The fog was getting closer, and the blue sky was giving way to gray. The temperature dropped and it was time to go.

Alexa stood and brought me up to her and said, "I think I'm falling in love with you."

She put her arms around me.

Anything I would have said at that point would have been foolish. I just held her as tight as I could. We walked back to the car in silence.

She picked another terrific restaurant for dinner. We tried not to talk about revolution, but we were overwhelmed by the project we had committed to stop: a long-term effort controlled by a small group of domestic and foreign government entities whose initials I had never heard of and two large chemical/pharma conglomerates. The key to their project was to destroy as many species of pollinators as possible so the natural food cycle would be interrupted and then could be replaced by bioengineered plant species controlled by the government and the chemical companies; that is, kill the bees, the butterflies, and the bats and a bunch of other pollinators. This was a key part of an old white paper developed by the neocons after the turn of the century when they were in complete control of a weak president to deliver world dominance to the US. The title of the paper was "Control the Food Supply for Dominance." Their hubris was palpable. She wouldn't tell me how she got her hands on a copy of it, which, she said, also described the project she assumed I was working on. She said if I was with the Inner Square, it means

I'm working on one of the cornerstones of this world domination scheme. And her source told her that the new administration wanted the project to move forward at full speed. This didn't surprise her, since the person whom everyone recognized as a mentally ill, power hungry, US-centric bully now occupied the White House.

"Alexa, you know I can't tell you whether I was here for a meeting of the IS."

"That's okay. I know you're the newspaper's rep to the Inner Square, and I respect that you need to honor your oath of secrecy. It's Eric who is trying to out you. It won't be good for him when I find out what he's up to and why. Anyway, I don't need you to breach an oath for me."

We shared more of our personal histories and finished dinner.

The night together was even more wonderful than the morning had been. How I was going to share this with Van was not yet in my consciousness. I was in the moment. After what seemed to be hours of lovemaking, it was time for sleep. I had a mid-afternoon flight to DC. Alexa was going to go to Berkeley to see friends. She planned to return to DC later in the week, which would give me time to figure out my next steps.

Chapter 36

I t was a scene out of a movie. I tiptoed into the bedroom and blew a kiss to my half-asleep wife and made my way to the bathroom.

"You smell so good. You should always shower before coming to bed. You must be exhausted."

She said all of this in a whisper with half-closed eyes.

"I am. It's been a hell of a week. I'll tell you about it in the morning. Can we have a civilized breakfast tomorrow?"

"I have a seven-thirty meeting. We can talk tomorrow night."

"Okay. Love you."

I was glad she would be gone early. I needed the house to myself for a few hours before facing the office. I needed time to figure out how to tell her about my weekend. The consequences were going to be big. But a lie about Alexa and me was the type of a lie that could rot a marriage from the inside. Worse than the infidelity itself, I thought, perhaps naively. I didn't know how I would answer the inevitable question: *What does this mean for us?* My last thoughts before finally drifting off were of Alexa.

I hadn't set my alarm. I liked to wake naturally whenever I could. The morning light usually got me up around eight o'clock. It was more than the sun this morning. It was singing coming from the kitchen.

"Is that you down there?"

The singing stopped.

"Good morning, dear. I decided we'd been away from each other for too long for me to make work a priority. I moved my meeting to the afternoon. I'm yours all morning so rise and shine."

It was time to face the music.

"Be down in a couple of minutes. We have a lot to catch up on."

"Yes, we do."

I tried to stretch out getting dressed, but after about ten minutes, she called up and asked why I was taking so long. I had no choice but to go downstairs.

"Are you planning to go to work in those clothes?"

"No. I wanted to feel like I was on vacation, to extend the weekend you could have spent with me."

My subconscious was working to sabotage me.

"Was that meant to make me feel guilty? It wouldn't be a nice way to start this morning."

"Not consciously."

"Okay, I'll give you a pass this once. I've made us a great breakfast to get our slow Tuesday morning on the road. Here's coffee and juice. The rest will be out in a minute."

She would not ordinarily let me off the hook for saying something mean. And breakfasts were generally my responsibility. Something was up.

"So, my darling black-ops husband. Tell me more about your week?"

I gave her a very detailed report. It was definitely worse than she had thought it was based on what I had described in general terms on the phone.

"Wow. These people are really evil beyond belief."

"Yup, and I'm one of them."

We talked for at least another half hour about the ins and outs of the week. She was blown away.

"So, before we get to my weekend, which was also groundbreaking, how was your week? Is your Pulitzer in hand?"

"Groundbreaking?"

I got up to make more coffee and to put some physical distance between us.

"We'll get to that, but first tell me what went on in your week. You said it was an important week. What happened?"

I came back to the table with a new pot of coffee. Occasionally, she would put sugar in her coffee, and this was one of those times. It was a mindful process: a silver spoon dipped into a beautiful porcelain sugar bowl decorated with black dragons and gold trim. She stirred two half spoons of sugar into her coffee. The whole process took only a minute or so, but it very successfully created suspense and set the stage.

"It was a productive week. I got to the bottom of the story I've been working on. Our target company, and the feds have been paying researchers for the last three decades to create hysteria about boys afflicted with ADHD and similar disorders. The market is huge even though there are well-respected psychiatrists, psychologists, clinicians, and educators interested in child development who believe the research has been bogus. The feds may not be innocent players in this game. And starting about five years ago, the company has been focusing its research grants to show that girls are also subject to the affliction."

What she described was not news to anyone who paid attention. She read my thoughts.

"Don't look so bored. I know this is common knowledge to those who follow it. What's new are the memos I have going back thirty years that lay out the entire plan."

"What do you mean?"

"I got a copy of the original planning documents that give a time-line, a sequence of research projects, a list of the universities to be paid to research, names of post doc candidates to be given initial grants, lists of the newspapers and magazines that have to be pressured into publishing articles and in what order, and get this—suggested ingredients to put into packaged foods targeted to children to enhance the tendency to attention deficit behavior. That may be where the feds come in. I think they have hidden the known dangers of these ingredients. The memo is addressed to the president of the company and to two people who were high up in the government at that time. They all have passed on to the great beyond. The paper was written by a team with the code name Help Children Learn. Every step laid out in that original paper has been taken, and I have emails and memos to prove it. It used to be one in a few hundred or so that needed drugs to focus. Now one out of every three kids in America needs to take a pill or two every day, at least until they're done with college. That's not bad for a marketing strategy."

"That's a Pulitzer; and it could lead to a few criminal prosecutions. You did it."

I was very excited for her.

"We'll see. I'm betting you'll be forced to kill the story by your new IS friends."

"Let's play dumb. You write it and send it up the channels. We'll see what happens. If I'm instructed to kill it, you can send it to Congress. How did you put it all together? I'm the pattern guy. You're the master of intuition, but this is a pattern story."

She turned a little red in her cheeks, blushed. I had very little experience with seeing the phenomena; it wasn't something she did.

"I got Matthew to help. We spent the whole weekend on it. We barely ate or slept."

That explained the blush. She had some serious weekend stories to share, as well. Mine would be softened if hers went first.

"That's interesting. Did you barely eat or sleep in our house or in the carriage house?"

Her look was between *don't push me* and *please help me get this burden off my chest* to *I'm sorry.*

"We lived in the carriage house."

"And I slept with Alexa in San Francisco."

The moment stood still for both of us.

"I'll go first."

She nodded.

I told her that once it was clear she wasn't going to join me, I resolved to dedicate my weekend in San Francisco to deciding what to do with the IS and the XDS and our lives. I was starting from her thought that we should leave DC and set up a new life outside the US. I wanted us to be happy expats with time to write great fiction and useful nonfiction. That resolve and the weekend I had planned was shattered by Eric's call on Friday afternoon.

She interrupted my story. Her voice was soft and a little weak.

"So that's why that son-of-a-bitch was pumping me to find out where you were. I don't trust him. He set her on you for a reason."

"Alexa doesn't trust him either."

She looked pained.

"I'm not ready to hear her name."

I got up to get more coffee and asked if she wanted some more coffee and toast.

"That would be nice." Her voice remained soft.

I came back to the table with fresh toast and coffee.

I told her the whole story: the walk in the redwood forest, the decision not to have sex the first night, the different decision the next morning, and the trip through the 1960s in the park. I didn't tell her about Alexa's secret plan.

"Will, are you going to leave me for that slut?"

I thought she was either going to throw her cup at me or cry.

I wanted to say something funny like, "No, not if you promise to behave," but I thought that might not be productive.

"No, I'm not going to leave you. I love you. And she is no more of a slut than you are or than I am. I assume you slept with Matthew this weekend, or at least came close, right?"

She put her head in her hands for what seemed like ages.

"It wasn't planned. I was reading my research notes out loud. Matthew had a big sketchbook, and he was making lines and dots and using different colors. I had no idea what he was doing. We were hungry. I made us some peanut butter sandwiches. We decided to change our surroundings and we went into the carriage house. We spent the afternoon around the coffee table with my notes and his notes and sketches and, suddenly it all came clear. Matthew rearranged his sketches on the table and the puzzle was solved. We pulled a dozen newspaper clippings that he had keyed on his drawing and there it was. Our faces were close to each other. He turned to me, and we kissed. And, without discussing what we were doing, we were in bed together."

I swallowed my first instinct, which was to attack. I was hurt and angry, even though I was in an identical position and didn't think of myself as having done something irretrievably bad.

"Our experiences were the same. Are you planning to leave me for Matthew?"

"No, of course not, I love you."

"Good, I love you, too."

We stood and hugged. We stayed that way for a long time, each of us in our heads but the collective part of us was trying to deal with this new world we had created.

We were talked out.

"Let's get ready for work. I'd rather spend the rest of the day here with you, but you have the meeting you put off and I missed yesterday. I think we both have lots of stuff to sort out."

"Okay. We'll get through this. One last thing: I got Matthew to hack into the computers of our target. That's how I got the memos—apparently some dummy scanned it into his files titled 'ADHD History.' I wanted you to know that in case the FBI knocks on our door."

"That's a crime."

"I know."

We were quiet for a few minutes. There was nothing more to be said.

"I'm tired, Van. I'm going to rest some before I go to work. You take the car. I'll walk. It will do me good."

My effort at trying to rationalize my behavior as well as Van's had exhausted me. The confusion swirling in my head wasn't helpful. The old double standard was pushing at me. *How could she do this to me?* As though it were okay that I had done it to her. She had done the exact same thing I did. If what I did was okay, then I had to make peace with what she did. I went up to our bedroom, set the alarm for noon, and dozed off.

Chapter 37

The early afternoon passed in a whirlwind of meetings. While the IS was now my reality, I still had a paper to help run. Any glimmer of hope that I would be clearheaded at the end of the day was pure fantasy, and there was no place for me to turn for comfort. Van was busy outlining her new story and Alexa was in Berkeley. I couldn't talk with our friends without having to reveal why Van and I had been so remote over the last two months, and I couldn't share anything about the XDS or the new people in my life. I decided to call Jean under the pretext of talking about our university target just to hear a voice that was familiar. I assumed she didn't know about my relationship with Alexa or what was going on between Van and Matthew.

I was about to pick up the phone when Van's father came in without knocking. The paper had an unwritten open-door rule, which I decided not to follow once the deal conversations began. Our HR department regarded a closed door as a sign of either drinking or of harassing coworkers. I regarded it as a rational requirement when most of my conversations were confidential. No one had called me on it until Van's father opened the door.

"Door closed. Are you drinking or cheating on my daughter?"

That pissed me off and I crossed a line.

"Fuck off, Dad."

He was dumbstruck.

"What?"

"Sorry I lacked appreciation for your joke. It was a really shitty week on the West Coast. You knew it would be, and you know why I need to keep my door closed."

He wasn't sure whether to sit, as he had planned, or to turn and leave. I didn't help. I just let my last comment hang in the air. In the end, he pulled a chair close to my desk.

"I'll need more of an apology than that weak crap, son."

He was raising the stakes.

"If you're here for more detail about the meetings, I don't know whether my oath of confidentiality extends to you. I'll make a call on my secret phone using my secret security code and ask some mysterious person whether I can share the details with you. What you've signed me up for is way beyond evil. And, if I knew you had no idea and no role in its creation, I'd give you a more acceptable apology. But I think you're aware of what you had signed me up for, and you should be asking me and your daughter for forgiveness. What you've done is outrageous."

He didn't say a word. He got up and left my office. He didn't close the door behind him. I had made a tear in the fabric of our relationship that would be the subject of some real soul searching between Van and me.

That would wait for another time, though. Right then, I had to find out whether Van's father could be told anything about the IS. I made a call.

The response was immediate.

"You cannot share anything with anyone who was not at the meeting. A violation of confidentiality will subject you and whomever you share information with to serious harm."

I lost my appetite for anymore work. I packed my briefcase and left for the day. I called Van from the car and left her a message.

"Hi. Fought with your father. Can't stay at work. See you at home."

I hit the beginning of rush-hour traffic. My twenty-minute commute was going to be at least twice that. I settled in for a slow drive and some deep breathing. Finally, I was home. I changed into casual clothes and settled myself on our patio for the hour or two before Van would get home. That was as much as I was prepared to plan. I thought about the response from the IS. I had to take them at their word. I needed to warn Alexa and Van.

I called Alexa and got her voicemail. I left a cryptic message: "The veil of secrecy is thick. A breach could mean the end." I left Van a similar message. They were stupid messages.

That task completed, I settled in to drink my beer and pictured a house painted in a pastel color on a cove in Anguilla. The Anguillans would accept us and not treat us like we were outsiders, and if we needed the services of a big island, St. Martin was just a short boat ride away. I drifted off into a light sleep.

The sunlight was fading when I opened my eyes to see Van coming toward me.

I told her what happened between her dad and me.

"You've done it this time: not only the *fuck off*, which is pretty bad, but the sarcastic Dad with the capital D. You must be way more stressed than I thought you were. Is it me and Matthew, you and Alexa, or the IS?"

She was being considerably more rational and empathetic than I thought she'd be. I shrugged and focused on my beer.

"If you can't keep your shit together, we're going to be in jail or dead." Her tone was serious.

"A little dramatic?" I said, trying to match her tone.

"Maybe not. Jean called me this afternoon. She has some plan she wants to put into motion. She wants to call a meeting for this weekend."

I started to shake my head no.

"I'm ahead of you. I told her you were wiped out by your week on the coast, and you might not be ready for a group meeting. I said we'd decide by Friday, and if we did meet, it would have to be on Sunday. She seemed satisfied. We were sitting a healthy distance apart. She chose the distance, which was fine with me. I still had Alexa on my mind. I knew they would both occupy space in my heart. I wanted the spaces to be separate.

"Van, what do we do when we meet with the group? We don't know if our affairs are out in the open."

"I have no idea. Are they affairs? I don't know. Maybe just a one-time thing. I'm still trying to sort that out on my end."

I had to tell the truth. "I don't think mine is a one-time thing, but I don't know what it is."

The rest of the night and most of our free time for the rest of the week was spent discussing who we were to each other and who we could be to Alexa and Matthew. We moved freely from our affairs were *no big deal* to *they were the biggest of deals* and all of the gradations in-between.

The week went by in a blur. I did my work. I avoided Van's dad and he avoided me. I had a dozen or so secret messages from the IS, none of which required me to do anything out of the ordinary. I got a text from Alexa telling me she got my message and that she would call—no hint about the weekend we had spent together.

Finally, on Friday night, after two weeks of no physical contact, Van made the first move, and we were back together. It was sweet and I was glad. We decided we would not reveal our relationships with Alexa and Matthew to the group, which meant that I wasn't to tell Alexa about Matthew, and Van wasn't supposed to tell him about my relationship with Alexa. It would be up to them to tell their significant others. We would be free to see our new lovers, and we would tell each other when we spent time with them so there would be no secrets between us. We agreed we were not entering into an open marriage; our step outside our vows was limited to these two people and only for a short time. We decided this on Friday night after we made love. We didn't know if they were the right decisions, but they seemed right at the time. We didn't know if we would feel the same way in the morning.

Chapter 38

Van found me in the living room just staring at my phone.

"Did Alexa send you a picture of her radiant body in a wet T-shirt? Is that what you're staring at?"

"No pictures. Just a message about our meeting on Sunday. Why didn't you clear it with me?" My tone wasn't exactly friendly.

"I had to line up everyone else first. I know your schedule."

"What if I'd made plans with someone and hadn't gotten around to telling you?"

She stood there, her stance wide, totally grounded.

"If you had plans, you would've had to cancel them. But you don't. It will be an important meeting. Time for action."

I wanted her to tell me more, but she said the subject was closed until Sunday. She took my hand and led me into our library.

"Tonight, we're going to get stoned, listen to music, eat, drink, and fuck. Then we're going to watch a movie. And then we're going to sleep. In the morning, you're going to make me a fine breakfast, and then I'll have to work."

She was off the wall; she never described our lovemaking as fucking. I overlooked it and went to my desk to get us a pre-roll. I didn't like vaping.

She took too big of a hit and succumbed to the inevitable coughing fit.

"We need our time together. With Alexa on her way back to town and me needing more help from Matthew tomorrow, we'll want to have some good quality time under our belts."

And then she burst out laughing and coughing.

"Under our belts—get it?"

I brought her close to me and reached my hand down to hold her between her legs. She looked up and smiled.

"You got it."

It was going to be that kind of a night.

We drank and smoked and made steaks on the grill. We slipped in and out of laughing and making love in our living room and listening to our favorites. It was a great Saturday night. By the time we stumbled upstairs to go to bed, we were totally exhausted. There was no time for a movie.

Making love to, and being with Van, was a joy. And as far as I could tell, she felt the same way. And then breakfast came and went too soon. At around noon, she declared the rest of the day a workday and the evening a time for revolution.

I thought it was a little abrupt and I told her so.

"I told you last night that we could have the evening and breakfast to ourselves and then I had to get serious. I have work to do, and, as I told you last night, Matthew is going to help me. See you at five thirty."

She kissed me and went out the back door to use the private entrance to our carriage house. I was a little stunned by her not-so-subtle instruction that she should not be disturbed before five thirty.

I had piles of work to do . . . and no motivation to do it.

I spent part of the afternoon reading articles for the IS, and the rest of the afternoon sitting under my favorite tree and reading for pleasure. I was more relaxed than I thought I would be, knowing that Van was in our carriage house with Matthew. I didn't know why I wasn't going crazy with jealousy. Maybe I didn't feel threatened, or maybe it was because I wanted to give myself permission to continue connecting with Alexa. I had read enough to believe this extra-marital stuff worked for some people and not for others. I wondered where Van and I would fall on that spectrum.

At about five o'clock, Van came down to the yard. We hugged and she was off to shower to be ready for our meeting.

Everyone showed up on time. I wasn't sure what to expect: would Alexa greet me with a kiss, a neutral hug, a wave, or just a nod? How was I to greet her? Did Eric know? Did Jean know? It seemed like Van could read my thoughts. She came over and whispered that everything would be okay as long as I acted as if nothing had happened last weekend. She was right. We all gave each our standard greetings and made ourselves comfortable around the coffee table.

The evening was productive. Van, with Mathew's help, had made a sophisticated Power Point to help us reach consensus on the next steps in our plan to expose our target. It was more formal than I thought we were ever going to be. She used charts and graphs and animated slides. I was impressed.

The target was the drug company Van had been investigating for its role in the baby formula lobby, which was the same company that was exploiting ADHD. The profits were extraordinary. The whole thing was so outrageous we threw popcorn at the screen whenever a slide came up that showed the company's logo or the CEO accepting an award from some foundation dedicated to helping children. She was a stately woman in her early fifties. She didn't look like the devil incarnate, but that is what she was. We had the most fun screaming at the commercial Van had pulled off the Internet showing a little boy fidgeting in his chair before he started on the drug and then sitting with his hands folded after just two weeks of taking the medicine. It was kind of like watching a modern version of *Reefer Madness.*

I raised the question of whether Van's work on the international baby formula lobby would create enough of a link for the company or the authorities to find us once we start our efforts to attack the ADHD activities. The others did not share my concern. They thought it less likely the connection would be made since it was so obvious.

Jean suggested we fashion a campaign like the MADD and SADD campaigns by mothers and students against drunk driving to get parents and educators to boycott the company. We all agreed and tasked Matthew with the job of creating an untraceable pathway for a social media campaign.

I thought the meeting was over, but Eric kept pumping Matthew for an explanation of how he would create an untraceable campaign. He wanted a step-by-step tutorial on how it would be accomplished.

Alexa finally shut him down, but not without giving me the subtlest of facial expressions that told me to keep my eye on him.

We took a short break so Van could order our pizza. She called using a burner phone and a credit card issued to our fake identities. We were officially underground.

The last piece of business was to discuss what should be in the manifesto that Jean and Eric and Van were assigned to work on.

We agreed that to avoid being targeted, a CEO had to care about all of a company's constituencies—customers, employees, communities, shareholders, the environment, and the survival of a robust democracy in the United States. They had to live by a set of values that would foster diversity, inclusion, compassion, tolerance, equity, and fairness. They had to run their companies as beacons of decent values worldwide and not as instruments of short-term profit. If they refused to sign on and live up to the manifesto, they would become our target. We would organize business to business boycotts to disrupt the company's supply chain. If it caught on, we would have made a difference.

By the time the pizza arrived, we had agreed on an action plan. We set some deadlines, made some jokes, and put our revolution aside for some good Sunday night camaraderie. I tried not to pay attention to the casual touches Van and Matthew were trading, and I'm sure she tried to do the same for Alexa and me. It didn't work for either of us. A distance was growing between us. Not a big one, but one that we both could feel and didn't want to acknowledge, one that was new to us.

Chapter 39

Y ou seem nervous."

She put her hand on my shoulder. Her touch almost put me at ease, but I still wasn't sure how I let myself get talked into meeting her in a hotel two blocks from my office. The facts, on the surface, were simple enough. She said she had some very important things to tell me and that she would need about two hours. She gave me the room number and asked me to meet her at noon.

"It's not something I've done before, either. It's always the man who books and pays for the room. So, next time it's on you."

Then she moved her hand from my shoulder to my neck and gently pulled me toward her and whispered, "Just kidding. I've never done this before. But this kiss is all I could think of on Sunday night. Our time in California was special. I want to see if it will be the same here."

We were under the covers with no more words to be said. It was more than a thrill to be with her; it was magic, trite as that sounds—

pure magic. When we both were totally satiated, she snuggled her head on my shoulder and said, "This could become a habit."

I was so deep under her spell that I surprised myself with my response, which was to begin again. I had no idea from what well we drew the energy.

Then it was time to discuss the important things she wanted to talk about. And after that, I would go back to the office in a dream-like state, which would last until I had to face Van and tell her about the afternoon.

I didn't know if I should shower. Alexa solved that by bounding out of bed and pulling me into the shower with her. This was a refurbished hotel with a shower big enough for two: glass enclosed and tiled with marble to the ceiling.

She passed me a robe, and we sat in the two small armchairs near the windows that looked out at a small park. Naked under fine cotton, she moved her chair close to mine and took my hand.

"Will, my feelings for you are getting very strong. I hope that's okay."

"Mine, too. And it's very much okay as long as I don't try to figure out what it means or where it's going."

She grew a little pensive.

"It should scare you. You have more at risk than I do. I've already given up on Eric. That's one of the things I want to discuss."

I withdrew my hands from hers and sat back in my chair gently enough to let her know that I needed to process her statement but that I wasn't upset. I waited for her to talk. I was afraid she was going to tell me that she wanted me for her own, and there was no room for Van in the picture.

"Remember, we are bound by the pledge we took in San Francisco. What we share with each other in secret needs to remain between the two of us. Are you still bound?"

"I am, but you know it doesn't apply to our relationship. I'll tell Van about our being together." My voice was strong, but my heart was pounding.

"Of course. That's not what I'm talking about. I've been watching Eric's behavior over the last few weeks. You saw the effort he made to follow you to California. What you haven't seen is his effort to get me to help him. I thought it was a game at first. He knew something big was happening with the paper and he wanted to see if he could find out what was going on. It's more. Quizzing Matthew relentlessly on the techniques of hiding our tracks was the tipping point for me. So, after our meeting on Sunday night, I decided to find out what was going on."

I got up and took a small box of chocolates out of the mini bar.

"He left a lot of tracks on his computer. He's working for someone in the White House—I couldn't tell from the group's initials whether it was part of NSA, or some black-ops group. He has been tasked with getting the names of the members of the IS and its agenda. Apparently, there is a group in the White House that's part of it, and the people Eric works for aren't in the loop. His handlers know you're the newspaper person in the IS."

She continued, "Eric isn't part of the XDS by chance. His group knew about the newspaper deal and that you'd be picked to be their rep. He was tasked to watch you. The formation of the XDS is a significant side benefit. He now gets to spy on you and our revolutionary efforts. And some of the memos I found lead me to believe that Jean may have some role in all of this, but I can't figure out what it is; maybe she's in the group that knows what's going on. Her name comes up with initials beside it that I have never seen."

I opened a sparkling water for us to share.

"What do we do with this information—confront him, watch and wait, or put him on our kill list?"

I meant the kill comment as a joke.

"It might come to that if he becomes a serious threat. Let's wait and watch for now. You should tell Van that you're concerned about Eric. It would be good to have another pair of eyes on him and for us to be a little more careful with Jean. But that's not what I wanted to talk to you about."

The fact that Eric was a plant seemed important. It was hard to think of what could be more so.

"Don't try to guess. I've found out more about the core of the food conspiracy."

"Do you want to talk about it now? I still have a time before I have to get back to the office. I set up meetings this afternoon so no one would think that I just took off to play golf like some of the people in management do with some frequency."

"That management crap is between you and Van. It doesn't work on me. Okay?"

That was the first time she snapped at me since we had connected in New York, which seemed like a lifetime ago.

"I'm sorry. I guess the paper hierarchy has been etched into my thought patterns."

"I'm the one who should apologize. I guess I'm more concerned about how we relate, and your relationship with Van, than I let on. I'm quite traditional, and I'm not sure how to handle the fact that I'm falling in love with a man who is happily married. And what I've been discovering is so big and so venal that when I get ready to talk about it, I lose my composure. I'll try not to do anything like that again."

We both got up and hugged with open robes. It was touch and go whether we would fall back onto the bed or continue talking. Touch won. Our discussion about the food conspiracy would have to wait. We were in a zone that not everyone gets to experience.

Chapter 40

The weather was perfect. We were going to have dinner on our patio.

"I looked for you this afternoon. You didn't tell the receptionist where you were going. That's not like you, Will. A little afternoon delight in a local hotel?"

"Yes, and more."

That answer was not what she expected. She was tending to a big tuna steak on the grill. She turned and knocked the platter for the fish to the flagstone.

"Does your lover do things that I don't?"

"Whoa. I didn't come after you for your little session with Matthew in the carriage house on Sunday afternoon."

"Lunchtime on a weekday in some sleazy hotel is different."

"Why?"

We were both on our knees picking up the pieces of the platter that were big enough to handle. There were a lot of layers in my question: Do you care that we met? Should we meet only in our houses? Do you want to know before or after we meet?

"It is different, and it matters."

"Do you want to talk about rules?"

We finished picking up the big pieces and I went inside to get a dustpan and broom. She didn't answer my question until we had finished cleaning up the mess and I took the tuna off the grill. She was ready to talk when we sat at the table.

"I don't know if I want a lot of rules or just a few. This thing is stretching me. I don't know how you feel about Alexa and about me and Matthew and about us. And I'm not ready for a long conversation about any of it right now. But there is something about leaving work to go to a hotel that really bothers me. Maybe I wouldn't like it any better if you had met in her apartment or in the carriage house in the middle of the day, but for now, I think there has to be a no hotel rule."

I moved my chair back a little from the table.

"So, the carriage house is to be our extra-marital sex house? Are you serious?"

"Yes, I think I am. We'll figure some signal to show it's taken and have all the members agree to the privacy rule."

"That makes no sense."

I got up to pace.

"Why doesn't it make sense? Using your credit card to buy a room in a hotel by the hour or half day or whatever can't be considered discrete."

"I didn't book the room; Alexa did."

"What difference does that make? No more meetings that involve any third parties knowing where you are and who you are with. That has to be a rule."

"Okay."

"And we need to tell each other when we're going to be with our lovers beforehand and not after."

I could live with those rules, but it felt like we were going down a rabbit hole.

"We could stop. Our relationship is way more important than each of us exploring territory that is unknown to us, and that we really don't need to explore."

I hadn't thought about it before I said it. I would have agreed to stop, or at least to try to stop, if that is what she wanted. My body wasn't the least bit ambivalent about being with both of them, but my mind and my heart were a little reluctant to push what we were doing to the limits.

"I don't want to stop. There's something clicking between Matthew and me that I need to stay with, at least for a little while."

I was relieved. She took the responsibility for keeping us on our trip into the unknown.

"Settled. No DC hotels and mailbox flags on the front and back door. If they're up, the house is free, if sideways, it's not free but not private, if it's down, not free and it's private. That should give the group a good laugh."

My suggestion was now the new rule, assuming Alexa would agree to it.

"You said something other than lovemaking was going on in that hotel. What was it?"

I told her that Eric was tasked by some black-ops group to get information on the IS from me.

"What the fuck?"

"I know. I should have seen it."

She put her hand on mine.

"How could you have seen it? You met him at a routine meeting. Maybe she's wrong. You know what? I can't focus on it now. I'm too rattled. I want to zone out with a stupid movie and then go to bed."

That was the best choice for me, too. Given the nature of our truth session, it was getting more difficult to keep the real secret from Van. Watching something dumb on the screen and then a warm bed was just what I needed.

Chapter 41

A few weeks of very hard work at the paper, extra hours on the XDS project, and more hours in secret on the plan that Alexa had chosen for the two of us was all taking its toll. Van could see it in the way I was dragging myself out of bed. She knew of two of the demands but not the third. Finding the time to do everything and the time for Alexa *and* then to have an open heart for Van had placed me at the edge of a very private cliff.

I vetoed two stories and changed the theme of three more, which was a lot of management intervention in a three-week period. I'm sure the staff thought I was on a power trip, which was embarrassing, but that was better than having them suspect I was taking orders from a cabal manipulating the world's financial markets.

Van knew my actions were connected to the IS and that I was in a cold, dark cave. She didn't ask questions and I admired her discipline. I wondered if I would be as disciplined if she were the one carrying out the secret orders of the IS.

At three weeks into my new world, I broke down from exhaustion. Van stayed home with me, and I brought her even deeper into the IS tent. We concluded that if they decided to kill me, they would kill her, as well, under the no-loose-ends doctrine. So, telling her the IS secrets wasn't adding to her risk. My special project with Alexa was still a burden I carried alone.

"I would say you're making this up, but you aren't that creative. It's so weird that my father would put us both in such danger."

Her father had become an enigma. For all I knew, he could have been given the newspaper decades ago so that he could make this deal happen now. These were not short-term thinkers. Some of the conversations in our meetings in California were for plans to be implemented fifteen years out. I didn't share my thoughts about her father's involvement. She had enough to deal with in trying to keep me together. She didn't need to turn on her father, who was speaking to me only on an as-needed basis.

"I'm going to assume my father's motivations were to keep the paper operating by giving up some independence. I will not assume, for now, that he's part of this grand conspiracy."

I could tell that deep down she believed he was fully aware of what was going on and was most likely a part of it, maybe even as an original planner.

"Enough about my father. What can we do to get you back to normal? Maybe rest and some tender care will do the trick. You need to be better by the end of the week. There's a gala on Saturday night at which the CEO of our target company is going to get an award. The paper bought a table and I have tickets. We're going to say hello to this devil in disguise and tell her we're working on an investigative piece on her company. That should get things moving."

"You're the reporter on assignment, I'm not. If I go, I'm drinking and not working. What's the charity?"

"Some children and health foundation. Our table will have our health desk editor and her husband as well as two reporters on the health beat and their spouses or dates or whatever."

"What makes you think you're going to get the chance to talk to her?"

She stroked my head like I was a little boy with a fever.

"I sent her a link to our manifesto and said that I was protecting the source but wanted comments from her on it."

"I sure hope Matthew is as good at this untraceable stuff as he says he is. If not, I assume the FBI will be at our table."

Van let that comment pass.

"She wrote back and said she was looking forward to meeting me and asked if I could bring the high school kids who wrote the manifesto. She would like to give them a lesson in capitalism, she said."

I was too tired to respond. I was fading fast.

"Thanks for making me stay home today. Maybe we can go out for dinner if I feel better after a nap."

"Maybe."

With that, I went upstairs and was asleep in five minutes.

I was stirred out of my sleep by familiar voices. I had slept away the entire afternoon. Alexa and Eric were in the kitchen with Van.

"Welcome back to the land of the living."

They said this in unison and gave me a hug. Alexa kissed me on the mouth. Eric turned away. I wasn't sure what she was doing.

"Okay, you two. This is supposed to be a casual dinner among *friends*. Do you hear the emphasis on the word *friends*?" Van was having fun.

Alexa laughed and said, "In my generation, my beautiful Van, there are friends and then there are friends with benefits. I don't think you had those things in your day. I know Eric didn't. He's old."

At that, Alexa almost fell off the kitchen stool laughing. They were all acting totally wasted. I wasn't sure if I wanted to catch up or stay straight. I decided to stay straight, which turned out to be a wise choice. Alexa was faking it, and I needed to be on top of my game to figure out what she was doing.

Van announced that we were going out to dinner at our favorite tavern. I was hungry and her plan sounded great. I was surprised she would pick a place where we were well known. I assumed she had her reasons to expose the four of us and she would share them with me later. I was too exhausted to try to change the venue.

This had turned out to be a pretty good day for me. I had skipped work, spent a nice morning with Van unloading a good part of my secret burden, had a long afternoon nap, and was going to have one of my favorite dinners in one of my good luck spots with my wife and my lover. As far as I could tell, everyone was in a good mood. Maybe Eric's mood was the softest, but that was understandable. His girlfriend was slipping away, and he was leading the double life of a spy, neither of which made for easygoing happiness.

The tavern was dark and three quarters full. The beer flowed and the burgers were especially good. Van and Eric were still stoned. They leaned into the table when they thought they were going to say something important. It was funny. Alexa acted stoned when she needed to, but she was all eyes and ears. A few of the regulars at the bar came over to say hello, which Van handled with her best manners—a little exaggerated but probably not noticeable by anyone other than the bartender, who kept glancing my way.

By the time our coffees arrived, Van was almost back to herself. She was in the corner diagonally from me and Eric was on her side. Alexa was next to me and had her hand on my thigh the whole night. And when she took it off to eat or take a drink, I put my hand between her legs, and she obligingly slouched enough to do her part in our secret game. I don't think Van or Eric had a clue. This was an evening full of pheromones or whatever it is that makes the air thick with possibilities.

I still hadn't figured out why Van set this up. I hoped it would come clear at some point, and it did.

Van told them about her exchanges with the CEO of our target. We all agreed that her arrogance was beyond belief, and we should go after her. We were getting into it and talking too loudly. The bar was nearly empty. I motioned all of us to whisper. That alone got them to laugh even louder than they had been talking. Our bartender came over with shots of Irish whiskey for us to sip, which I had ordered on my way to the bathroom. I didn't want Eric to lose his buzz.

Van poured a little cold water on our enthusiasm by telling us that to go after someone personally instead of going after companies required a unanimous vote of the group. We agreed and raised our glasses to Jean and Matthew.

Van didn't leave it there. She invited Eric and Alexa to the gala. She said we had two extra tickets and that it would be a good opportunity for them to meet this CEO. The invitation was accepted. I didn't know why Van wanted to invite them. It was high risk. If we wanted to keep the XDS and its members secret, having the four of us together meeting with our target CEO seemed cavalier. Putting that risk aside, I was excited at the prospect of having Alexa sitting next to me at a Washington black-tie gala.

Eric gave me and then Van a warm hug. Alexa kissed us both—real kisses on the mouth, which to my surprise, Van did not resist. And they were off.

Van took my hand as we walked home.

"She has a nice mouth for kissing. I see why you like to make love to her. I know I said no threesomes, but I might make an exception for Alexa."

Van was on the top of the world. I let the threesome issue pass.

"What the fuck are you up to?"

"I thought you'd never ask. I talked with Alexa this afternoon while you were sleeping and told her about the gala. She was very intrigued. She suggested our dinner and the invite at the end. She wants to see what Eric is going to do with the information, and she would like to meet the CEO."

I was a little surprised that Alexa and Van would conspire without including me. That was scary.

"And why did you pick our favorite restaurant? I thought we agreed that our relationship to the members of the XDS was supposed to be kept in the deep dark."

"I thought it was important for the outside world to see us having fun midweek with friends. We didn't act conspiratorial, so I thought maybe this would be good cover. I assume everyone sees us as total workaholics with very few friends. We didn't whisper in the corner; we laughed and got loud. So now the bartender and the waiters are witnesses to the fact that Alexa and Eric are drinking buddies."

I wasn't sure I agreed. She shrugged and told me to trust her.

Chapter 42

This was a typical Washington charity gala. Drinks and a silent auction were in a large room that opened onto the ballroom where tables were set for dinner. The silent auction had the usual items: local whiskeys, foods, dinners catered by chefs from farm-to-table restaurants, and bottles of wine from the cellars of the rich and famous. Van was usually in charge of bidding for us. We stuck to nonperishables. Our rule was to go home with at least one thing we could carry. Van bid the take home price on whiskey from West Virginia.

These galas always had live auctions, which were hideous beyond belief. The charity would hire some professional auctioneer who was usually loud and obnoxious. And while we were trying to have a conversation around a big table for ten, the auctioneer would fill the air with noise to sell a weeklong stay at someone's summer house in Nantucket, or Palm Springs, or Europe, or a weekend getaway in New York. And then the men—usually it was the men, but not exclusively by any means—would puff up and outbid each other for charity. I've done it, so I know the feeling. I should have been less judgmental, but the public display of wealth bothered me. I could see it bothered Alexa, too. Van never paid attention to the live auction so it never bothered her, and as far as I could get into his head, I think Eric wanted to puff up and bid. He didn't.

I had Alexa on my right and an editor I liked on my left. So, to the extent there were interludes of quiet, I had two people to talk with that made the evening tolerable. But even when the auctioneer quieted down, the ballroom was still noisy. There were at least a hundred tables of ten. This was an important charity.

Usually, we slipped out early. This time, we had to stick it out to the bitter end. Van had set up an after-dinner meeting at the hotel bar with our target CEO. We were very low down on the food chain for an important CEO to bother with us. It didn't compute, even if Van, playing reporter, was the daughter of the paper's owner.

As the dinner wound down, Eric left the table to check in with a congressman nearby. And, to my surprise, Van said there were people she had been trying to meet with to get some background for her big story, so she said she would leave Alexa and me to secure a quiet corner of the bar for five and she'd join us when she finished her work.

I was up for some quiet time with Alexa.

"Will, are you getting turned on escorting me to a corner of this elegant bar, watching all of the men and some of the women stare at me with lust in their eyes?"

Her raunchy side was not something I had seen before. We had been very serious about our sex and our feelings. She stopped us in the middle of the room, took my hand, and leaned over to kiss me on both cheeks, pressing her body against mine. This was a level of danger we had agreed to avoid. Then she laughed so that people around us might think her gesture was a joke among friends. We found a corner spot with enough banquet and chairs to sit seven in case Eric or Van or our guest of honor added someone to the mix.

"I want to make love to you right here and now. I could move over and straddle you; maybe no one will notice."

I thought she was serious. I was about to respond. She just laughed and said: "I'm not that much of a free spirit. And I don't want to jeopardize my mission."

I thought we were all on the same mission: to get a sense of the CEO's role in the long-term destruction of the youth of America. Why had she called it *her* mission?

"Do you have your own special mission?"

The waiter came and we ordered bourbons to sip.

"Meeting this CEO might be part of my private mission. I need to see if she is truly evil, which requires more than wanting to be on the cover of *Fortune* as the most powerful female executive. If she has an evil heart and soul, then I have a mission which is mine alone. The time will come when I'll share it with you, but until then, no questions."

She took my hand and kissed my palm and gave me hers to kiss. It was a deal sealed with a kiss.

We had another ten minutes or so to talk about how weird these charity events were and how most people would just as soon send in their money and not have to sit in some hotel ballroom and listen to speeches. Alexa had the same approach we had. Her parents taught her the rules when she was still in high school. She was to pick something useful in the silent auction and then bid the final amount immediately whatever that amount was. And, if she was a guest at the event, especially if it was someone from the board of the charity who had invited her, then she should try to buy something that cost at least double the price of the seat. Those were the rules.

"What did you get, Alexa? We got six bottles of West Virginia blended whiskey."

She smiled. "I got two bottles of fine bourbon. I bought them for the carriage house. You should put yours there, too."

I leaned over and kissed her on the cheek. And, as luck would have it, that's when the rest of the crew walked into the bar, and with them was a very elegant CEO. They seemed to be deep in conversation as they came into view, but they caught my kiss.

"Marianne, let me introduce my husband, Will, and our friend, Alexa. We caught them in a compromising situation, which I'm sure they can explain."

She said this in a light tone that I read as: "What are you doing? You promised to be discreet. You'll pay for this." All that was in the space between the words *can* and *explain*.

Alexa rose to the occasion. I didn't know if she could read any of Van's anger, but I was more than happy to stay silent.

"I'm so happy to meet you. Your speech was quite interesting. And I know we all have a lot to talk about that's not particularly related to Will and my celebratory kiss for getting the best at the silent auction. Will got six bottles of handcrafted blended whiskey and I got two bottles of fine bourbon. We were kind of excited to stock the bar in our clubhouse."

Van turned pale. I did, as well. Before I could say anything to fix what I thought was a major indiscretion on Alexa's part, Marianne fell into the trap.

"I heard about your club. Eric was briefing me yesterday about what goes on here in Washington, and he said a few of you had formed some club to watch over the misdeeds of big bad Corporate America, and that you met in a carriage house in Georgetown."

We were all stunned.

"Eric, I judge by your friends' shocked looks that you've revealed something they would just as soon keep secret."

Alexa moved fast.

"Let's get some drinks and then we can pursue this."

The waiter came on her signal. Marianne ordered bourbon. I assume she did that to make us whiskey-drinkers feel comfortable.

"The club I was referring to is what we have come to call the bar at Van's country house in Middleburg. The last time we were there, we finished off her father's favorite whiskeys. So, I thought this was a fine time to do some good while paying back our debt. Apparently Will did, too. You guys caught us congratulating ourselves for having the same charitable thoughts."

Then she paused and turned to Eric. "I didn't know Marianne was a client of yours, Eric. What clubhouse were you telling her about? I don't know of any Georgetown carriage house club."

By the time we made a few toasts, the need for Eric to answer Alexa's question had passed. Instead, we moved on to questions about ADHD and Marianne's view of the various governmental programs designed to test kids in poor neighborhoods.

It was an interesting conversation. Not surprisingly, she was well informed about education policy and its related drug therapies. She had very strong views about the FDA and the effort of some senators to force a nationwide negotiation of drug prices. And she almost stood on her chair to extol the virtues of her First Amendment rights to advertise her drugs for off-label uses if "we don't go too far into unchartered waters." That's how she said it. She spoke with her arms and hands. Her arms practically rippled with muscles and her hands looked strong. She could have been a T-shirt model. There was no doubt that she was a two-hour-a-day workout fanatic.

Alexa read my mind.

"So, Marianne, down to the really important stuff. Did you get those fabulous arms working out, or does your company make some secret 'look buff' drug that it isn't ready to market?"

She blushed and blew Alexa a kiss across the table. She was close to being just a little drunk, which was very odd for a CEO of a Fortune-100 company.

"It's the gym—a personal trainer for two hours every weekday morning from five thirty to seven thirty—then it's off to work. That's my life. Just sitting here at a bar drinking is not a typical event for me. I'm all work and no play. There are mountains to climb, markets to capture, countries to conquer—that's what gives me pleasure. And since Eric has vouched for all of you, I'm glad to have a moment to relax, even if Van is a reporter on a mission. I assume you will treat me nicely. Yes?"

"Of course, this is all off the record. But I wouldn't want you to feel like the night was purposeless. Perhaps you could tell us what you thought about the manifesto I sent you. I promised my source I would try to get an important CEO's take on the piece, which has a direct connection to companies like yours that make so many products crucial to the well-being of our people."

Van signaled for another round for the table. We were going to settle in for serious conversation. I was surprised Marianne was willing to talk freely. Then the thought crystallized: not only had Eric vouched for us, but she probably knew I was part of the IS. That was it. She thought we were all insiders.

She talked at length about how naive the manifesto was and how it showed no understanding of the global corporate arena. She did acknowledge that some of the principles in the document reflected views of old-time company owners. She said the only CEO's who could survive with the guiding principles laid out in the manifesto would be those who ran their own companies with no outside shareholders. She said any company that was publicly traded had to view things like fairness, equity for workers, protecting the environment, and responsibilities to local communities as dead concepts. Short-term profits ruled: that is what the university endowments, the pension funds, and the hedge funds demanded. She was on a roll, drinking bourbon and holding court. She began to slip into a Texas accent—she had grown up in San Antonio—and it was amusing to hear. On two occasions, Van tried to steer her into a conversation about her ADHD drug, but she didn't bite. Then Eric, to create cover, but not knowing it was too late, laid out the case for making an illness universal and then producing and selling a cure.

Marianne looked at him, knocked back the rest of her bourbon, and said in a thick drawl: "That's what we call capitalism. Now, who wants to join me in the ladies' room? I hate going alone."

Alexa was up in a second.

Chapter 43

I was staring out my office window watching the clouds move at a fast pace from west to east when the phone brought be back to Earth.

Alexa cut to the chase. "Will, can we meet at the carriage house around four o'clock? And if you like, you can ask Van if the three of us can have dinner together. I met with Marianne yesterday. I need to tell you guys about it."

I agreed, hung up, and called Van.

"What's up, dear? I'm swamped."

"I'm going to meet Alexa at our carriage house at four; the flag will be down. Alexa suggested the three of us have dinner together. You up for it?"

After a few seconds of silence, she said, "Okay, new rule: if you're up for Alexa before dinner, then you'd better be up for me after dinner."

She hung up without saying good-bye—a first. If I were making a list of Van's top twenty strange behavior, this conversation would be on it.

Staying focused on work until it was time to meet Alexa was not easy. I had a conference call scheduled for 2:30 with the IS. This would be the first time that we met as a group by phone. I was instructed to find a secure conference room and to use my IS phone. I was also told that I needed to be sure the iPad screen could not be seen through any glass walls in the conference room or through any windows. I assumed the secrecy wasn't necessary, but I followed the instructions.

The call was short. There was a story running in my newspaper and others the next day that had to be stopped. It was my job to kill it. To do that, I needed a document to show my managing editor the story was based on a compromised source, which wasn't true, as far as I knew. Within two minutes, a document was sent to my iPad: a very official-looking letter with the NSA seal that showed the source of the story was a spy from an Asian country with a mission to discredit an American drug company. I printed out the document and took it to the managing editor. He went pale.

"I can't tell you how I got this, but I understand that based on our work, a number of the key papers here and in Europe are going to run this story. You need to kill it here and wherever else you guys have seeded it."

He was an arrogant prick. It was rare that anyone could tell him what to do. I just had, and he had no choice but to carry out my instructions.

I went back to my office and put my head in my hands. No amount of rationalizing could make me feel okay with what I had done. I knew there was a chance that playing their game now might put me in a position to do good later, but it still felt awful. I packed my briefcase and headed for home. I put the mailbox flag in the down position and went into our carriage house. I hoped I had gotten there before Alexa. I needed a few minutes to calm down and to wash the day off my hands and face. When I got up the stairs and opened the door, Alexa was there to greet me.

"Hi, I just got here. I rushed out of the lab and didn't have a chance to clean up. You look about as frazzled as I feel. Let's shower."

At that moment, there was nothing I wanted to do more than to make love with her as if it were the end of the world and we were the only two people left on the planet. And that is what we did until we could see the pink in the western sky. We must have been in bed for almost three hours. My phone vibrated on the bedside table and stirred us from our half sleep.

"I can't come over until you raise that damn flag and I'm hungry."

I looked at my watch.

"I didn't know it was so late. Come over at seven thirty."

"I'm bringing Matthew and Jean with me so be presentable. They may not know about you two."

I rolled over to be squarely on top of Alexa. She opened her legs wide enough to take me in and asked in a whisper if we had enough time. I smiled and we were once again transported to another world.

"We have about fifteen minutes before the three of them come knocking on our door. What was it you wanted to talk about?"

Her face was full. Her lips were a little swollen. I was sure mine looked the same. It would be easy to read us, to know that we had been making love, and there was a significant part of me that didn't care if our secret was out. It was a fact that Alexa and I were lovers, and Van had blessed it. I was feeling somewhat free and crazy.

"How do you want to explain our being here this afternoon. They're going to know we spent the afternoon fucking."

"It was more than that Alexa. We were making love. Let's say we were checking notes on the university efforts."

"I would like to save the love talk for another day. Let me tell you about the lunch I had with our target CEO, before they get here. Remember she wanted company to the bathroom at the end of our drinking session. There are very few black female biochemist PHDs from fancy schools in the marketplace. I would add a lot of points to her score card. That's why she invited me to lunch. She wants me to work for her."

"Was that a surprise?"

"No. I needed to know if she was truly evil or just ambitious. Matthew had her dead on. Her company has plans to make everyone so whacked out about their inability to sit still that there will be no one left who isn't on their drugs. And, get this, they are working on a drug they claim, if taken by women trying to conceive, will lessen, not eliminate, the chances that the baby will have serious ADHD. Their child will have only mild ADD."

"No fucking way."

"It's true. I think she thought she could persuade me to join her executive team by confiding that many on her team and most of her board were not in sync with her plans, but she knew how to silence them and to put her plan into effect. She said the dollars to the company and to her were in the stratosphere. Without her, that company might change its ways. She has to be stopped."

"Holy shit," I said, "we picked the right target."

"Matthew gets the credit. He targeted them. And, when I asked her about the Manifesto and her view of the XDS, she just laughed. She said she initially thought it was written by a bunch of high school kids, but as she thought more about it, she was sure it was written by one of the comedy groups at Yale or Harvard. I guess Eric didn't tell her we were behind the manifesto. He's definitely playing a very complicated game with her."

That was a lot to process in the few minutes I had to wash up and try to look presentable for dinner with the others. If Alexa was right, and the elimination of this CEO would change the course of the company for the better, then maybe we had to act against her. That would be a change in course, since one of the group's principles was to attack entities and not individuals. I wasn't sure where I stood on the issue.

Chapter 44

Van had picked a tapas restaurant near the convention center for our dinner, which required a twenty-minute cab ride. I would have preferred a place within walking distance.

The restaurant was noisy. We changed tables twice to find a spot quiet enough for conversation. Finally, on our third move, they put us at a table off to the side of the big room that served most of the very loud younger group.

Jean and Matthew agreed to order for all of us if we gave them at least two things that we did not want to eat, which was a relief, since I wasn't in the mood to read the four-page menu.

With the food ordered and two big pitchers of beer in front of us, it was time for serious talk. I assumed that our first order of business would be Eric and the red flag he raised at the gala, but Alexa put him off-limits. She told everyone that he was out of town and that she had his proxy if it turned out we needed a vote on anything.

I assumed she had a good reason to put his treason off-limits. A nod from Van told me she was prepared to make the same assumption. Alexa then turned to a description of her meeting with Marianne. She started with a toast to Matthew for uncovering the drug company's game and for highlighting the CEO's role in the fraud on consumers. As modest as he was, Matthew liked the toast.

"Aren't you proud of your husband, Jean? He laid out the case for going after this CEO. That was a tour-de-force. We're raising our glasses to him, but you seem subdued."

My sentence hung in the air as the waiters delivered what seemed to be an endless supply of little dishes along with detailed descriptions of the contents of each one. I could recognize the main ingredients in most of them but that was about it. I decided to eat only the flat bread and some vegetables.

After what seemed like way too much silence, Jean, having had the chance to weigh her thoughts, put her cards on the table.

"I'm very proud of Matthew's analytical skills. I'm not proud of his extramarital skills. He's free to be with you, Van. Those are our unwritten rules, but I don't have to like it. I find you threatening. You're smart and almost age appropriate. I would rather that he would take up with our young friend here. No offense intended, Alexa. The fear of mortality drives men to seek younger partners. That I can understand. That is not what's driving Matthew to want to be with Van. I'm hurt and don't feel much like raising my glass to him."

Matthew reached for her hand, but she moved it away. Van was about to say something.

"There's no need for discussion. Will noticed that I didn't put my all into the toast for Matthew. I've answered him. Let that be an end to it."

There was an awkward silence, which Alexa broke by pointing to a dish that was in front of Jean and asking for it to be passed. And with that, we all focused on eating, passing the plates of food around the table, and filling our glasses.

When Alexa finished eating, she began to talk about our target company and its CEO.

This company was pure evil; from burying research that didn't turn out exactly as hoped for, to running a very sophisticated revolving door for both government and academic scientists. Their plans reached far into the future. I could see that both Matthew and Alexa admired the company's long-term planning prowess

Jean brought us back to Earth.

"So, they're a good symbol for us to use to explain the corruption of the capitalist system. I think we all knew that. What do we do? I'm willing to put up with the sophomoric sex games from the four of you. Yes, Will, I know what you and Alexa are doing, too. I don't care if we do something. What are we going to do?"

Alexa shrugged and then, with no warning, she leaned over and kissed Jean, which for some reason, made us all laugh. Then she said, "Are we good? Good, so, let's get to the real question. Can we attack Marianne, or do we confine our efforts to the company?"

She said this and then poured all of us more beer. Van answered.

"We lose the high ground if we go after an individual."

We spent the rest of the evening debating the issue. The high ground won. We would organize a boycott of the company. We would expose its relationship to our target university, which was awash in the company's money for research. And we would expose the university's protocols for allowing their professors and research staff to earn outside income from the research projects they undertook for this company. We set our course, drank some coffee, and made our way home.

Van didn't have much to say on our ride back. She was glad we had decided not to launch an attack on the CEO. But she knew that once we tied research grants to the university, the professors playing into the hands of the company would become known and subject to attack. That didn't sit right with the lines she had drawn to keep the XDS on the high ground, but she knew that was how it would play out.

We were both in a very deep sleep when the phone woke us at seven thirty.

"Did I wake you?"

"Yes, Jean, you did. What's up? You're on speaker," I said.

"Some weird news. Our target CEO is in the hospital. I got a call from one of my contacts in the field. She got sick last night. They have no idea what's going on with her—she's in a coma. It hasn't hit the news yet. We need to figure out how this should play into the timing of our campaign against the company."

Van was fully awake. "We need to suspend our plans for now, but let's talk later. Will and I will think about it over breakfast and then I'll call you. You should see what Matthew thinks about it."

She hung up.

"Life sure is a roll of the dice. Here today, gone tomorrow."

"Will, this isn't the time for clichés. She might have been running an evil company, but she is a real person who we just spent part of an evening drinking and talking with. She's way too young to be on death's bed. It gives me the chills."

I reached over and brought her to me. We just stayed in bed for a while with her head on my shoulder and my arms around her. There wasn't much to say.

Chapter 45

It was a steamy day in Middleburg. This was our second time in the country with the group; it felt familiar. My relationship with Alexa, and Van's with Matthew, were out in the open.

The pool was the center of our activities. The pool area was off to the side of the house and surrounded by ten-foot-tall hedges. There were two changing rooms, a bathroom with a shower big enough for four, and a little kitchen and bar in what was a good-sized pool house at one end of the pool. Van and I had stocked the little kitchen with food and drinks. Our plan was to hang out at the pool during the day and then have dinner inside. The walks in the woods were a little more adventuresome with the early summer growth making the pathway less open and full of poison ivy.

Neither Van nor I was going to venture far from the pool and the shade of one of the big trees that kept us just a little bit cool in the hot Virginia sun. It had been a very full month for both of us. I had had two meetings of the IS in out-of-the-way cities, and Van had

been on the third part of her four-part series on the issues that had
been occupying her for the last few months. They were very good
articles. She really had a chance to win her Pulitzer with them. She
had exposed our target company and the role that Marianne had
played in creating the ADHD crises. She even managed to walk the
fine line between blame and empathy for Marianne, who had finally
recovered from the mysterious illness that had kept her in the hospital for two weeks and had forced her to resign. With Marianne
gone, the company took various public steps to pull back on their
efforts to push the sickness and their drugs onto the unsuspecting
world. It could be viewed as a win for the XDS, even though, as far
as I knew, we didn't really fire a shot. And, to my surprise, I hadn't
been asked to pull or reshape the articles. Maybe the IS saw this
as a well-timed distraction that would keep the attention off their
cancer goals. Our manifesto and Internet presence had gained some
traction over the past three months. It targeted a handful of companies for employing tactics very similar to the ones developed by
Marianne's company. They had used grants to research universities
to support the product claims they knew were false, they buried
research that didn't fit their story, and they paid no attention to the
harm they caused. Their accountants computed the costs of product liability suits and then weighed them against profits and senior
management picked profits.

This weekend was for us to unwind and regroup. The rule was
that we were not to talk business until Van called a formal meeting
to order. And Van and I agreed we could each spend part of the day
with our lovers, but when dinner was done, we were to save the last
dance for each other. I liked that arrangement and obviously Van
did, too, since she was the one who proposed it.

"Will, can we get some time alone?" Alexa asked.

Alexa, Van, Jean, and I were in the pool. Matthew was sitting under a tree in the garden and Eric was reading in the shade near the pool.

"Whenever you like."

"Now would be good. The sun is getting too strong for me. My skin may be darker than yours, but it can still burn."

I signaled to Van that Alexa and I were going in for a little while. She moved closer to Jean and waved good-bye to us.

There were six bedrooms in the house and a guest apartment over the four-car garage with two more bedrooms. I took us to one of the bedrooms in the guest apartment.

By the time we were in the covered walkway that led to the garage and guest apartment, we were nearly running. I was a kid in a candy store. I don't know if she felt the same, but in short order, we were totally full and happy.

"That was more than great. I don't know what I'll do when this affair ends."

"Why would you say that?"

"You know this can't last forever. You and Van are happily married. I'm not a homewrecker. I can help evil corporate types fall into a coma or maybe even take their last breath, but I'm not going to get between you and Van, even if she has a lover."

We had never talked about how Marianne got sick. She got up from the bed and sat in one of the wicker chairs in front of the windows. A slight breeze moved the white lacy curtains a little. It was a scene from an early 1950s movie. All we needed to complete the picture were a couple of longneck bottles of beer, a wife-beater T-shirt for me, and a full, white slip for Alexa. Instead, we were both naked and not the slightest bit uncomfortable with our bodies.

"I guess you haven't noticed that of the seven companies we have targeted for boycotts over the last two months, three CEOs got sick with a mysterious disease and have had to step down from their jobs. None have died."

I had noticed, but I was trying to block those thoughts from my consciousness.

"Nasty coincidence. Maybe we released a curse from the middle-ages—*a plague on their houses*—or something like that. Maybe we can blame it on Matthew's chaos theory. The universe is a loop with everything predetermined and with justice as the driving force."

She smiled.

"We could blame it on a curse or on some chaos theory, but you know that would be only half true. The curse part is true, but it's not coming down from heaven; it's by my hand that these people have taken sick. Remember, I'm a serious biochemist researching nano-technologies. I have helped these CEOs into their state of disarray. Frankly, I haven't meant for any of them to die and, up until now, none of them has. But if one does, so be it."

I was shocked.

"That's harsh. Does anyone suspect you?"

She came and snuggled on my lap. "I think Matthew has figured it out, and I think he is going to want to talk about it today. Do I confess or play dumb?"

My reaction was instantaneous.

"Play dumb. We blame it on a curse, and if Matthew doesn't buy it, I'll throw in the chaos stuff. We can't get sidetracked by a confrontation in the group. I've been digging into this for two months. The puppet masters of the IS are less than a decade away from controlling a substantial amount of the food production worldwide. It's the old English colonial spirit the US has adopted to rule the world.

They've built twenty facilities around the globe to produce seeds and pollinating sprays. They bought a small aircraft manufacturer with factories in South Africa and India, which will supply the crop spraying planes. If we don't stop them, the world will be fucked. We can't risk you being targeted for these CEO illnesses. We have to laugh off Matthew's pattern theory on this one."

"I'm fine with blaming it on a curse," she said and we got back under the covers.

Chapter 46

Look who has decided to join us—our hippie sex kitten and her badass rock star."

That was the first time Van referred to me in public as a rock star—it was a private joke. In college, instead of taking real science courses, I took a class for dummies called rocks and stars. We studied geology and simple astronomy, so she had nicknamed me her rock star.

Alexa was on the ball. "I hope we're not late for the meeting. My bong got clogged."

Van laughed and that lightened the mood for everyone. She was ready to start. We didn't look like revolutionaries. We sat around a big round table on the back patio and drank chilled sparkling wine and ate the fine cheese we had brought from the city.

After a few simple business issues and a summary of what we'd done over the last few weeks, including a report on the traffic to our website, Van opened the meeting to the group.

Just as Alexa had suspected, Matthew laid out his pattern theory on the sicknesses of our targeted CEOs. He said that having studied sickness in CEOs whose companies have come under fire over the last fifty years, the events of the last two months were aberrational. CEOs under pressure have been known to get sick, but not like this, and not with the same form of mysterious illness. In his view, either the CEOs were meeting in secret and infecting each other, there was a crazy out there who was targeting the CEOs named on our website with some unknown virus, or one of us was poisoning them. Or, of course, there could be another company or a foreign government attacking them to get a competitive advantage in the marketplace.

Eric jumped on the last possibility and asked Matthew if he could easily determine if another company or government has benefited by the turmoil created by these sicknesses.

I said that I thought it was a curse. We identified evil people and God sent an angel to exact revenge. "Remember, the Old Testament God is a very vengeful God."

They all gave me strange looks.

"I'm serious. I think it's the hand of God. It makes me feel that our work is not in vain. God is on our side. Or maybe it's the work of chaos theory. Matthew knows how that works—feels random but isn't—totally preordained."

That put Matthew over the edge.

"Enough bullshit, Will. This is serious. As soon as someone figures out the connection between these sicknesses and our website, the effort made to crack through our security net will be extraordinary. If I can find the pattern between our targeted companies and these serious illnesses, you can be sure law enforcement can, as well. I assume they already have, and it's just a matter of time before we are hauled off for questioning. We need to shut down for now."

Contemplating a visit from the FBI was not pleasant. I agreed that our Internet presence should go silent.

Eric thought Matthew was running scared, that there was no way that law enforcement would be on to us and that we should just keep going. Everyone else spoke in favor of shutting down the site for now, but Eric became more strident in his views. I asked whether shutting down the site would make it impossible to trace. Matthew said that once we took it down, we would be safe, unless we had already been traced.

Five of us wanted to put the website behind a thick firewall and kept dormant, but Eric would not let go of the subject. He wanted Matthew to develop a specific plan for securing the site, to share it with us and to keep it online. Pushing the issue further was going to get us nowhere, and since we were operating under a consensus rule, we adjourned the meeting until after breakfast the next morning. If we couldn't get a unanimous plan at breakfast, we would decide by majority rule, which was a new procedure. We were all talked out. It was time to focus on dinner.

The dinner was another of Van's specials. I open three bottles of wine and set the table. It sounded like a good time was being had on the patio and no one came into the kitchen to interrupt us.

"What did you make of Eric's performance? Your lover sure thought it was strange."

"I thought we had agreed not to be jealous or at least not to show it, Van. I don't appreciate the *your lover* comment."

"Just having a little fun."

I didn't believe her, but this wasn't the time or place to have a serious conversation about our relationship.

"Right. What I made of Eric's insistence that we continue business as usual without some safeguards is that he's trying to lead us into a trap."

"That's what I think, too. So, sometime during the evening, when you discreetly have your hand on Alexa's sex, ask her what she thinks."

"Shit, Van, why do you keep upping the ante?"

She shrugged.

"Bring the soup out and call our guests to the table."

When we were settled, Eric said an appropriate grace, half mocking and half real. The real part was fine with me. It made Alexa a little uncomfortable. She was sitting to my right and had my hand in her left hand and Matthew's in her right. She squeezed my hand when he said, "through God's grace may we be granted many fine dinners together." I couldn't tell if she was signaling that I should pay attention or whether she was just in the mood to squeeze my hand.

We had a great evening. Good conversation about plays and movies and books and little stories from each of us about the worlds we had grown up in. I opened another bottle of wine; it was a four-bottle dinner for six. By the time the chocolate cake was in front of everyone, the talk was loud and slurred, and some of it was incomprehensible to me. I couldn't tell whether people were beginning to talk nonsense or whether I had stopped processing. I liked the group and I liked holding Alexa's warm and strong hand under the table. It was just the amount of contact I needed to make me feel good.

The group moved into the kitchen. While Matthew and I cleaned up, the rest of them passed around pints of ice cream.

It took almost an hour to put the kitchen back into its original condition. Now it was ready for breakfast, and we were all ready for bed. Hugs and kisses around and then to our rooms.

"Great dinner. You're really good at it."

Van was sitting on the edge of the bed staring off into the distance. She looked totally wasted.

"Thanks. It's nice to have such an appreciative group. Even though you're fucking that young thing and I'm fucking the technology king, the group works well together."

"What?"

"I don't know. Don't mind me. I'm drunk and dead tired. I just think that given what we're doing, it's interesting that we can all get along. I mean, Jean has accepted my relationship with Matthew, and Eric, hard as he is to read, seems to tolerate his young Alexa having fun with you. I don't get it, but it works to my advantage for now, so I'm okay with it. And, speaking of your young thing, what did she say about Eric?"

"She has a name. Stop being mean, okay? Anyway, she thought Eric wanted to put the group in danger. I wanted to get her alone to ask her more, but you said I could only be with her before dinner."

She laughed.

"Enough about your little cup of cocoa. Let's go to bed."

"What the fuck, Vanessa! That's racist. You owe yourself and me an apology, and you definitely need to apologize to her."

She shrugged.

"I'm serious. People say that racism is just under the surface of all of us and you just proved it. I don't really care if you're drunk. It's a real disappointment you would think of her in racial terms. She is a beautiful, unbelievably smart and accomplished woman who happens to find me irresistible and that does not permit you to call her names."

She rolled on her side and got under the covers. There was nothing more for me to say. In my mind, that was more than a micro-insult; it was pretty far up the scale. Obviously, she wasn't comfortable with our semi-open marriage experiment. Maybe we should call our love affairs to a halt. That would not be easy. Alexa had a hold over me.

I got out of my clothes and took a long shower, which made me feel a little better and ready for sleep. When I got into bed, Van turned to put her head on my shoulder. I found that I didn't want her to be so close. Her comment had put me off. I wanted to drift into sleep on my own. I didn't want to be connected to her, which was a first.

Chapter 47

The logistics of the early morning worked in my favor. Van and I were in the kitchen getting ready to make breakfast for the group when Alexa joined us in a very short denim skirt and a blue and white striped man's shirt opened to her waste. She was a beautiful site. I thought so, and so did Van. Van went over to her, put her arms around her waist, and gave her a very solid hug and a kiss. Not a short, good-morning kiss, but a real kiss. It was a very odd scene.

"Alexa, I have a confession to make. I thought I wasn't over-the-top jealous of the relationship you have with Will, and I never thought there was racism sitting under the surface of my skin, but last night before I went to bed I was angry, and I called you Will's little cup of cocoa. I kid you not. I have no idea where that came from, but I know it wasn't a good place and I want to say that I'm sorry, very sorry."

Alexa was silent for a minute and then leaned into Van and gave her a hug.

"You're sweet to apologize. I am a cup of cocoa, and a very delicious one at that."

And the next thing I knew, we were in a group hug. And the surprises continued.

Alexa leaned over and kissed us both. Before this whole thing could go any further, if that was what was going to happen, we heard someone on the stairs and scrambled back to respectable positions.

It was Jean. We all busied ourselves with breakfast. By the time bacon was sizzling in a big black skillet and pancakes were getting the right shade of golden brown in another, Matthew had found his way into the kitchen. I offered mimosas but there were no takers. I had already decided that coffee would be my drink of choice and the others had, as well.

"Eric's missing. Shall we let him sleep or get him down here while the platters are still full?"

Van was playing host. It was Alexa's call.

"Let him sleep. Maybe it will mellow him. He's been totally off the wall; full of questions and very argumentative. And he tossed and turned all night. Maybe it's his age."

Matthew made a comment about age-discrimination, and we all had to raise our coffee cups to him and to his age and tell him that he seemed young and virile. And, with that toast, Van got up and went to his side and kissed Matthew. Jean turned away. Van was becoming more of a loose cannon every day.

Alexa could sense the building tension.

"Van, you have a devil sitting on your shoulder that's making you very provocative. Let's not ruin the morning. I'm going to get Eric. We still have to decide whether to go into hiding, and it would be nice if we could convince Eric and be unanimous in our decision."

Alexa's speech worked. Jean now put Van squarely in the category of Sunday hungover, off-the-wall behavior and seemed to be fine with it. Once she was sure that the four of us would be okay alone, Alexa bounded off to get Eric.

I got up and poured us all coffee. Our cozy mood was shattered by a shout from the second floor.

"Eric is sick! Help!"

We rushed up to their room. Alexa was sitting on the side of the bed with his head in her lap. His breathing was shallow.

The rest of the day was spent in the logistics of getting Eric settled into a hospital in DC. The next few days were spent in the details and the swirl of tending to Eric, who was in and out of a comalike state. It was a teaching hospital with extraordinary resources, but no one could come up with a credible diagnosis.

Weeks, which seem like a lifetime, had passed and Eric didn't get better. The group took turns watching over him at the hospital. Other than the XDS, his only relation was a sister who lived in France. Since Alexa had spent most of her time in Eric's house, she decided to pack some clothes and stay with Van and me so she wouldn't be alone. She was rattled by his failure to get better. She told me he would recover just as Marianne and the two other CEOs she had poisoned did.

But he didn't.

Apparently, he had been one intense stress away from a major heart attack and was on a list for a transplant, which Alexa had not known. He didn't make it. And even though Alexa and Van and I knew he was tasked by some no-name agency to watch me and get details on the IS, none of us had wished him dead. We took it hard. Alexa accepted Van's offer to stay with us until she felt ready to be on her own.

It was not going to be easy for me to have my wife and my lover under the same roof. My feelings for them, while different for each, were very strong; it was a forest of feelings. On more than one occasion, I suggested to Van that it might be a good idea to help Alexa get on with returning to her own place. Van would have none of it. She wanted Alexa close to her, close to us. Alexa stayed.

We took down the XDS presence online and put our activities on hold to give us time to deal with Eric's death and to beef up our defenses against intrusion. We saw Jean and Matthew for dinner a few times but didn't find we had the energy to talk revolution. Eric was the first person in our circle of friends to have died. It was unsettling. We retreated into ourselves.

After two months of quiet, Alexa asked if we could meet at the carriage house. I was more than ready to spend some alone time with her. On my way out, I stopped by Van's desk and told her I was going home to meet Alexa. Van seemed fine with it. I went to the carriage house early to be sure it was in order and was surprised to find the refrigerator had fresh food in it, which meant that Van had been there recently with Matthew and forgot that we had agreed to let each other know when we were going to be with our respective lovers. I would call her on it later.

I waited for Alexa and tried to quiet my mind. She came in through the back entrance.

"I need to be held."

She wanted to be together under a pile of blankets. She didn't want or need more. We watched the shadows of late afternoon and early evening make their progress on the wall of the bedroom and then blend into nothingness. We closed our eyes and held each other. It was what we needed deep down to reconnect to a world that seemed discordant.

"This was a perfect reboot. Eric's death has knocked me off balance. I never would have done it if I knew his heart was so weak. I just wanted to put him out of commission for a while to protect us from the trap he had set—a trap that would have landed us in jail or worse. I hope I'll be ready to re-engage soon, but for now, I need to work on the enormous guilt that is making me feel so isolated and sad."

I just nodded. There was nothing to say. We remained still under the blankets for a while longer. Finally, she broke the silence.

"I need to talk revolution."

"Shouldn't we wait until Van gets home?"

"No, this is just for the two of us."

She said this in a whisper and put her hand on my chest and moved her head to be more comfortable in the hollow of my shoulder.

"It's time for irreversible action."

"What do you mean?"

"It's time to zero in on our target. Their plan is very tightly protected. Only two people know the full scope of the plan, and they are both part of your IS group. The others working on parts of the plan don't know how what they're working on fits with other pieces. If we chop off the dual heads of the snake, the plan should fall; that's our only chance. Once these monsters bring others into the plan, it will be too late for us to stop it. We have no time to waste."

She could sense my hesitation.

"I need to go over all of my research, which will take a little while. If any of the facts are incorrect, we'll be committing violence for no reason. If I'm right, then I'm compelled to act, but I'm not sure you'll want to be part of it. There will be no recovering from comas for these two. They must die before they share the plan with others. You wanted to make a difference my dearest Will; well, here's a plan we can execute that will save the world from tyranny, at least for a while. Really. But you then live with a mortal sin, as the saying goes. So, you still have time to walk away. There will be no hard feelings."

I couldn't talk it over with Van or anyone else. I had to decide for myself. I was on a dark and lonely road.

I leaned over and kissed her. It was time to go to the main house and see what Van wanted to do for dinner.

Van was in her after-work clothes and had already decided we would go to our local tavern for dinner. We traveled as a threesome, and Alexa was treated as a regular. There was nothing out of the ordinary about our dinner except for the growing openness between my wife and my lover. Van asked Alexa, not me, if we had made love that afternoon. And Alexa casually told her that we just stretched out in bed together. She said she was still coming back to life and wasn't interested in making love to me or anyone else yet.

"When you feel totally awake in that part of you, let's talk. Then we can tell Will what's expected of him."

I had no idea if they were playing with me or seriously deciding to set a course for the three of us. I had no idea if I was interested in being a part of whatever they were planning.

"Listening to the two of you makes me feel like a player in a French movie out of the sixties. Nothing ever happens in those movies, except those sexually liberated character really weren't liberated, and one of them dies, goes crazy, runs away, or is hopelessly broken-hearted in the end. For the record, I don't want to be in one of those movies."

They laughed.

"My dearest Will, we've evolved since then. Don't you agree, my darling Alexa"?

"Bullshit. We haven't evolved one bit. Our little triangle will be what it will be. In the meantime, we have work to do, and we can't do it if you keep making fun of me."

"Van, our boy toy seems to be getting serious. What shall we do?"

"Order more beer and humor him. That's what I suggest."

And that is what they did. We filled our glasses and leaned over the table so that we could hear each other's whispers.

We agreed to get back into action. We would call a meeting of the group and circle back to the companies who had had to deal with their CEOs' mysterious illnesses. The XDS would send copies of its manifesto to each board member and to the key pension fund and university endowment trustees that had large holdings in each of the targets. We would include other companies so the authorities would not focus on our primary targets. We could give each target one more chance to reject its short-term strategies and incentive compensation schemes, which led to the destruction of decent corporate values. Any company that didn't sign on to our manifesto would become the target of new attacks. We decided we would use Marianne's company as an example of one that has changed its behavior and has profited from its commitment to a new value structure. Our assumption was that if we could get at least one more victory, others would fall in line.

The thinking was naïve, but then, all revolutionaries are naïve; otherwise, they would stay home and read books.

Van agreed to set it all in motion. Alexa would work with Jean and Matthew to refine our approach.

We were happy.

Chapter 48

My life was complex. I kept work in a tight box and focused on the dynamic of my home life, which was now officially a family of three. I loved them in different ways, which I couldn't quite articulate, but which made perfect sense to me. They both seem to love me, so going home to them was a treat.

Van still enforced the rule that I could make love to Alexa only in our carriage house, and she played by the same rules with Matthew, although her meetings with Matthew were becoming less frequent. And since the little word play at the tavern, we had not toyed with making love together, although Alexa did bring up the subject with me more than once. My response—which was that whatever the women wanted, the man would follow—raised a generational issue that surprised me. Alexa was not pleased with my passivity or what she felt was a sexist point of view. Van, however, would have thought that my response was the proper response. Alexa wanted me to have a position and to stand up for it. So, I said I would rather continue on a one-on-one basis. I don't think she was happy with my position. I told her it was fine with me if she and Van became lovers. She was really pissed that I thought I had the right to give her permission to do something she had every right to do without my permission. It took days to get us back to a good place.

We spent a few more weeks in what she would have described as a limbo state, and I would have described it as a perfect state of non-work bliss. And then things began to change.

We had a very difficult XDS meeting where we tried to get Jean to tell us which government agency she was working for and whether we should be concerned for our safety. We said we would honor her secret, but we needed to decide whether the XDS should be abandoned. She was furious.

"I am not Eric. I have not been sent to spy on you. Whatever I do for the government—if I do anything for the government, and I'm not saying I do—does not disqualify me from wanting to save this democracy from the rot that comes from the neo-capitalists inside and outside the government. You three may be cozy in your new family arrangement, or maybe I should say you four, but that doesn't give you the right to question my loyalty. Fuck you all. I'm going home. If you want me back, you'd better find the right words to apologize."

And with that, she left. Matthew gave us assurances that our secrets were safe with Jean and then he followed her out.

The three of us were left to clean up. I felt drained and sunk into a chair. I caught Van and Alexa whispering in the kitchen. It didn't take long for their plan to unfold. They had reached an agreement that the three of us were going to make love together but not in our house. Our house was reserved for husband and wife. But here, in our secret space, the three of us would be free to explore. That was the deal they made.

The first time we were together was a little awkward. My teachers were very able and patient. And, if I were to face reality, I would have to assume my first time with them was not their first time together. I didn't know if that was true, but I assumed it was. I never asked and they never volunteered the information.

From then on we frequently spent nights together. It was new enough to occupy the parts of my mind that might have been put to better use trying to figure a way out of the IS horror show.

It had become a constant source of daytime misery. Every day I got orders to manipulate and kill stories. My reputation at the paper was on a steep downward trajectory. Fortunately, no one had yet been able to tie my actions to a specific industry. In fact, I had trouble connecting the dots back to what I had learned at the IS meetings where they laid out one or another of their grand plans. It would only be a matter of time before someone figured out I was not on a power trip but that there was a strategy to my actions.

The physical and emotional overload the two women were causing me could not have been anticipated. I liked having a wife I loved *and* a lover I loved. I'm not sure how much I liked having them blend together, though. And then I had to add Matthew into the mix and my sense of guilt that Jean was left out, even though she was enveloped in her own veil of secrecy, gnawed at me. She never complained, but I can't believe that it was easy on her to be the odd person out. I was totally exhausted on so many levels.

I nearly lost it when I received the call to attend an IS meeting scheduled for the weekend on the Eastern Shore. The event was to start with a late dinner on Friday night, which meant I would be driving in heavy traffic over the Chesapeake Bay Bridge. Van and

Alexa seemed glad that I was going to be away. I think they wanted some quality time together, which didn't please me. I wanted to keep each of them in separate places in my heart; I didn't want to picture them together without me.

It was Thursday, so we made a deal that I would spend the early part of Thursday night with Alexa, then the rest of the evening with Van, and then the three of us would have breakfast on Friday morning before I went off to work and then the meetings. They thought that would be a great way to send me off into the lion's den.

They were right.

The carriage house was sun-filled in the late afternoon. I had some time alone to just sit and gather my thoughts. I was not looking forward to a meeting of the IS. The men in the group were stereotypically creepy: short black hair, tight faces, and lean bodies. I wouldn't go out of my way to have a drink with any of them. The women were similarly tight.

Just thinking about them began to put me into a foul mood, a mood that dissipated the minute Alexa came up the stairs. She was radiant. She was like the sun pushing out a heavy rain cloud and bringing with it only blue sky. She saw my face change; I felt myself light up. She bounded to me and threw her arms around me.

We stayed in that exciting space, almost as if it were our first time, for a very long time—way more than an hour. As I was stretching to make myself comfortable for us to spend another hour or so in bed before going to the main house to join Van, Alexa got up and dressed and wanted me to do the same. She said we had serious stuff to discuss. She went into the living room and waited for me to join her.

"Will, this weekend is our time to act."

I thought she was playing some game.

"This is no game. Two of the people you're meeting with are the co-heads of the snake. It's time to derail their plan."

She was dead serious.

We reviewed our research, and the bottom line was clear. Two men—the head of a large international company, and a man who reported to the President—were the only ones who knew the whole plan to give the US dominance over the world's food supply. This was modern warfare that would put our country at the top of the pyramid for centuries to come. The press and the pundits all talked about cyberwar, but this was where the real war was going to begin. The British, Germans, and French knew only a part of the plan. They had been given a scenario that centered on worldwide patents to keep their treasuries full. They didn't know they would be two rungs down from the top. They didn't know the real plan and its impact. Our operating assumption was that it would be difficult and risky for anyone to whom those two reported, if there was anyone else involved, to get it restarted.

There was nothing to be gained by trying to convince Alexa the time wasn't right. Our course had been set months before. She gave me two little packets of poison, or whatever it was to be called, and said it was up to me and the situation to figure out how to get to the targets. She said the stuff was not a known compound and could not be traced. She had invented it and destroyed her records. She gave me an antidote, which I was to rub on my hands before handling the poison. All I needed to do was put some of the poison on my protected hands and touch the skin of my targets; the nanotechnology would take it from there. It would then take between four and ten days to take effect. There would be no mess over the weekend, and they would die at different times since she had modified the time-release sequence in each dose.

"Will, no one knows about this but you and me. And no one ever will. Once we have put an end to this conspiracy, our work will be done. It will take a long time before anyone resurrects this plan. And if they do, we can come out of retirement."

I was tasked with killing two people—an incomprehensible idea.

"Alexa, it's not too late. Let's not do this. Let's bring Van into the loop and have her write it up? She can blow the lid off their plot and maybe even bring down some people in very high places and we won't have to kill anyone."

She put her hand on my shoulder.

"Will, in this environment, her articles would be considered classic liberal conspiracy paranoia—just another cry from the Deep State that hates the folks in charge. No legitimate newspapers or other news outlets would touch this story, and in any event, the IS would have the stories and the reporters, including you and Van, killed."

She was right. The administration had been stepping up its disinformation campaign and its attack on the media. Scientists and politicians all over the globe were beginning to buy into the reality that our bees and butterflies and pollinating species were doomed because of global warming and natural diseases. None of them would ever entertain the thought that a chemical company and the US government, with the unsuspecting aid of many others, were killing the pollinators intentionally.

"How certain are we that getting rid of these two will end the plan? The whole enterprise is way too big and well organized not to be staffed with able-bodied people who will step into their shoes."

"I'm not certain. I've repeated my research a dozen times. It always comes out the same. The groups working on different parts of the plan have no idea that their tasks fit into this master scheme. Each element is a clean stand-alone. None of my research has found anyone else involved at the 'know everything' level. If that were to change, there would be too many in the know for us to have any real impact. That's why we need to act now. And this is where Van comes into the picture. This weekend, I'm going to tell her what's going on. After these guys are dead, she'll write a story about one of them, who we'll call the leader of the pack, maybe the White House guy, not sure which one. You'll be asked to kill the story and you won't. And the story will be out."

I needed a drink after that brilliant pronouncement.

"Great plan. We won't live out the week."

Alexa got up and walked around the living room.

"That depends on whether the IS wants to go dormant and resurface later or whether it wants to draw attention to itself. We'll do all the classic things. Write up dossiers and have different people prepared to turn over documents to the authorities here and in a few other countries to be safe. And you'll tell them they should go into hiding and leave us alone or the world will know their complete agenda, including the cancer agenda. That's an evil they won't want out in the open. Maybe none of it will work and we'll have to run away, and maybe they'll kill us. It's a risk we have to take."

I wasn't sure that we weren't on some crazy power trip.

"I have to think about this. Let's go home."

Chapter 49

I was way out of my league. I had signed up to poke a finger in the eye of the establishment. I had challenged Van's comments about blowing up buildings, I have been risk-averse all my life, and now I was going to be an assassin.

My mind was short-circuiting. Van must have assumed that Alexa and I had a falling out, so she was respectful of my privacy and didn't ask me any questions. Instead, she just took me in her arms and said in a whisper. "Sorry to intrude, my dear, but it's my turn."

I don't think I was at my best. I know that Van didn't think so either. I couldn't tell her I was distracted by the task that lay before me. I was going to kill two people. That was an insane thought.

"You're going to owe me big when you get back from your meetings."

"Sorry. If I do get back, I'll make it up to you."

She propped herself up on her elbows. "What does that mean? What's going on? You're hiding something from me, and Alexa is, too, isn't she?"

I turned on my side to get closer to her. "If Alexa is hiding something from you, I'm sure you can get it out of her this weekend. I really need to try to sleep. I promise that after the weekend I will be a new man. Promise."

That worked. She kissed me and rolled over to her side of the bed. I did the same. She slept and I was sleepless.

I was a zombie by the time I got to work late Friday morning, and after a useless lunch meeting, I set out for the IS meeting. The roads were already backing up. This less than two-hour drive was going to be closer to three hours. I tried listening to the radio, but the classical music station played only waltzes and other "upbeat driving music" at rush hour—awful stuff. I tried to listen to a book, but I couldn't focus, so I drove in silence. My head whirled at the thought of what I was going to do. Unless, of course, I chickened out, which, as I got closer to my destination, became a more distinct possibility.

Our meetings were in a quaint inn in one of the small towns on the Eastern Shore of Maryland. The arrangements were not that different from the ones at the Big Sur. Each of us had a suite assigned at random based on time of check-in, and we each had our own hospitality person. Mine was a runway model–type with short hair and very long legs. Unlike the very sweet Cassandra, Becky was prepared to be full service. I'm sure she expected there would be a very large bundle of hundred-dollar bills as a thank-you for her kindnesses at the end of the weekend. When I told her that I wouldn't need her for what I knew she was hired for, she smiled and asked if I would prefer a different shape or size or gender. I said no, but if she could arrange someone to give me a legitimate massage before dinner, I would be grateful.

Her body relaxed.

"I'm a massage therapist. I would be happy to work on you as soon as you're ready. I'll come back in a half hour."

Now I was alone in what was a very nice, rather old-fashioned suite. The bedroom was open to the sitting room. It had a four-poster bed with a canopy made of the same pattern that covered one of the armchairs and the drapes. There were two good-sized Persian rugs on the floor, making the bedroom area and the living room feel separate. The room with its Victorian feel did not offend my aesthetic. I liked its charm. I unpacked and poured myself a very small scotch. I hadn't decided whether I would execute the plan this evening or at the meetings tomorrow. I pushed that thought to the back of my mind and just day-dreamed until Becky knocked on my door. I was more than ready for a massage.

She had me in a relaxed state within minutes. By the time she had completed her work, my body was completely at ease and my mind was almost at peace. I would execute the plan this evening. I thanked her and asked if she could return tomorrow after my meetings. She nodded yes, of course.

"Thanks for giving me the opportunity to serve you. If you would like me to sleep with you tonight, it would be fine. I can come to your room whenever you'd like."

I was about to say no thanks as politely as I could, and then it occurred to me that she might have no place to stay. The IS assumed I would want her for the night.

"Do you have a place to sleep, or is your assignment to be with me?"

She hesitated. "Well, to be honest, they have not booked rooms for any of us. It's assumed that each of you would be pleased with our hospitality, and we would stay with you. So, I don't have a place to stay, and I won't get my full pay if we don't spend the night together."

These guys were first class assholes.

"Okay. Meet me back here after my dinner is over. You can sleep on the couch."

She thanked me and left.

For some reason, the thought that these evil monsters would buy me a woman and then make her pay hinge on my acceptance of her favors made me crazy. If there had been any doubt left in me about my mission, that doubt was gone; the IS represented the worst mankind had to offer.

I dressed for dinner and coated my hands in the antidote cream. Then I put the two packets of poison in my pocket and set out to meet the group. I figured two handshakes and I would be done. I also decided that I would feign a stomach flu in the morning and skip the meetings so I could avoid ever again seeing the men I had infected. Around lunchtime, I would declare myself well enough to drive but not well enough to meet, and I would go. Becky would be my messenger.

Cocktails were in a library on the main floor of the house. There were ten of us: three women and the rest white men in their forties and fifties. I was the youngest. Eight of us had been at the Big Sur, two were new. I was the last to arrive. The two new members were not introduced to me; not even by their first names, which was odd. My targets were each surrounded by attentive group members. I wanted to yell out, "Snakes! Off with their heads!" and charge them with a machete, but that wasn't the plan. I had to maneuver into each group, put poison from one of the bags on my hand and then be sure to shake only the hand of my target, and then excuse myself to get to the bar and prepare myself for the next assassination. I only got to one of them before dinner.

We sat at a long rectangular table. There were no assigned seats. I tried to find a seat next to my second victim, but they were filled. Just thinking that word—*victim*—was beyond any reality I had ever dreamed. So, I spent the dinner between two of the worst members in the whole IS; they were world-class narcissists—one from London and the other from Chicago. I would suffer through dinner and think about what I had done and the one more death I had to deal.

When we all gathered back in the library for after-dinner drinks, I found my chance. My target was standing alone reading the titles on a very elegantly rebound set of the Harvard Classics. I went over to the bookshelf and pulled out a volume at random and handed it to him. I had covered the leather with the substance from my second envelope. Alexa said it didn't need to be flesh on flesh, as long as the person touched the surface spread with poison within two minutes of my putting it on the surface. After two minutes, its potency would become too weak to hurt anyone. He took the book, looked at it, and handed it back to me with a shaking of his head. He wasn't interested. I smiled and put it back on the shelf, excused myself, and went to the bar.

And that was that.

I sipped some cognac and moved into a corner of the room that had a small library table filled with magazines. I picked up a random nature magazine, flipped through some of the pages as if I were enjoying the pictures of birds and flowers. After a few minutes, I put it back on the table, nodded to the other members of the IS, and left to go back to my room.

Chapter 50

It was done. I drove home on autopilot. My mind was a whirl of guilt, although no one was dead or sick yet. Maybe the poison wouldn't work, and I would be free of the assassin's burden. Or, maybe it would work, and I would have saved the world. Or, maybe it would work, and they would find out about it and come and kill me and Van and all the others in the XDS. I was in a state of total confusion by the time I got home and was greeted by Van and Alexa.

Van took me in her arms and held me for a long time. She knew what I had done.

"I'm so proud of you, dealing with this monster responsibility on you own. I'm sorry I didn't join you when you asked me to be part of your secret revolution. I thought it wasn't right to keep secrets from the larger group. I was wrong. Now I share the burden with you and Alexa. Upsetting corporations that are driven by greed and corruption, which I think our XDS has done a good job with, is one thing, but stopping a worldwide scheme to control food production is a totally different order of magnitude."

"It had to be done," I said to try to convince myself.

The two of them walked with me into the backyard. The patio had already been set up with beer in an ice chest and some cheese and bread. They had prepared for my homecoming.

"Yes, it did have to be done. If I could have been in the room with these two, I would have done it. I never would have put you in that position," Alexa said with a shaky voice and tears in her eyes. She was very upset that I had to carry the responsibility alone. She wanted to protect me from the guilt, which, of course, was not possible.

The three of us spent the rest of the afternoon trying to reassure each other that what we had done had to be done, and that we were the only ones who could have carried out the plan. In addition to trying to deal with our guilt, we also spent time mapping a survival strategy.

Our only hope was to expose the IS, which was not without risk. But if the two targets died, we had to take the risk. We hoped that the more public we became in a small but powerful circle, the less likely we would be killed. That was our assumption and the task we set for ourselves. We would implement this task once our targets were dead.

Chapter 51

Both targets died within the two weeks that Alexa had predicted. We then prepared a detailed file describing the pollinator project and discretely gave it to key members of Congress. A secret holy war broke loose that was not covered by the press. The focus was on an elite group in one of the no-name agencies controlled by the White House. Behind closed doors, they shut down the project. Only after weeks of hearings did it leak out that the name of the operation had been Project Hummingbird.

The death of the two members of the IS, weeks apart, was too random for the public to connect the dots. A week after the second death I got a handwritten note from Jean saying *Well Done* and nothing more. If she knew, I had to assumed others in high places knew. My only hope for survival was that the project was being carried out by a rogue group that the rest of the people at the top were opposed to and that Jean was in a group with the good guys.

It seemed like we were in the clear. Alexa had been living with us, or more accurately, we were living together in a new type of family arrangement for almost a year now, and my guilt was receding. Our non-XDS friends realized there was something unique about us, and they were accepting and discreet. Matthew and Van were no longer lovers. His paintings were gaining traction, and Jean became the head of a new federal program established to deal with mental health issues. Our lives were settling into an almost normal routine. The five of us met once a month to keep our corporate projects going and to just hang out as friends.

Our Internet presence was now an important part of the political dialogue and was subject to countless efforts by hackers to pull us out into the open. I wasn't convinced Matthew could stay ahead of the growing effort by the corporate community to expose us. So, when I was informed by the IS that it was reconstituting and that I should attend a meeting in New York City to discuss a website that could disrupt some of the efforts of its members, I knew we had to shut down our site.

Van and Alexa did not want me to go to the meeting. Alexa was the most concerned, which surprised me. She had always been the risk-taker. She said in a supplicating tone, "Will, this doesn't feel right. That group has been dormant for almost a year. Why now and why the effort to go after our site? I'm sure they've known about it for a long time. Don't go. Let Van's father pick up the pieces. Let him pick a new newspaper rep."

Van was sitting next to her on the couch. They were sitting close to each other and holding hands, which wasn't an odd scene. They often sat with each other.

"I agree with Alexa. I think they're leading you into a trap."

"What's with the two of you? They've gone into the woodwork for enough time to let Hummingbird become a distant memory. They have a big agenda, and their game plan involves the cooperation of the media, and that has been me. I would set off a red flag if I declined to show. I'll go and force them to pick someone else to do their bidding. Let's just see what happens."

It was Alexa's turn again.

"Will, we mean it—you can't go. In fact, we can't stay here either. We need to disappear."

"The two of you are being very weird."

"We're not. We have new identities: passports, credit cards, and all the documents we need, and a big pile of money sitting in accounts in various domestic and foreign banks."

Now I was beginning to take them seriously.

"What do you know that I don't?"

"It's your place to tell him," Alexa told Van, pulling Van's hand into her lap.

"There are two things you don't know, dear. One is that you're going to be a father. Alexa is pregnant."

I thought she was kidding; she wasn't. That meant our family structure was set in stone, which was what I wanted. Before I had a chance to respond to the news, which I was really very excited about, she went on.

"The second thing is that Matthew has been playing his pattern game with the papers and magazines and the users of our site over the last three months. Something isn't right. He was charting various trends and then suddenly one line of the users dropped to zero. Two days later, you got called to the meeting. If you go, you die. It's that simple. And, probably more telling, Matthew said that Jean began acting very weird on the same day the line of users dropped off the site. She said she didn't feel well and has been in a depressed state since then. She likes you and she knows what you did. We know she is connected in some way to the IS. Her behavior, at least to me, says you're in trouble. She's tipping their hand, probably intentionally. She is assuming Matthew will pick up on her behavior and that we will also figure it out."

"That's crazy. I'm more spooked about becoming a father than by the IS. What if I don't know how to be a good father?"

They laughed. I went over to hug them. I was happy. We sat in a comfortable silence for a while. When I felt ready, I said, "Let's say you're right. Do you really think we could hide from them?"

Van got up and paced for a minute. She had a plan.

"Yes. I think we can make a deal with them. I've prepared an email for you to send. It says your wife has already written an article about them and their long-term plans, which includes the cancer cure manipulation, with credible back up. It sits on several hard drives throughout this country and three other countries. Key editors and a few carefully chosen nonprofits have access to the material. The recipients have instructions that if anything happens to any of the three of us, or our children, then the lid will be taken off the sealed box and this time it won't be in some secret senate hearings; it will be public. As public as it can get. In exchange for our freedom, the XDS will cease all activity. You don't go to New York. You send the email and then we all go to our new home in the mountains."

They wrapped their arms around me.

Our fate was sealed. I was glad. I was ready to become someone new. Three of us with a fourth on the way and a mountain home. It felt like we'd be part of some luxury witness protection program, except it would be our program. We would leave our friends and families behind. We would be strangers in a strange land. It was going to be hard, and it was going to be exciting: a new beginning, an opportunity to take a new path.

If the plan worked, we would have a new life.

If it didn't, we would be dead. And that would be the end of it.

CPSIA information can be obtained
at www.ICGtesting.com
Printed in the USA
BVHW041911210522
637444BV00001B/1/J

9 780999 311325